TOLD
UNDER THE
STARS and STRIPES

STORIES OF
ALL OF AMERICA'S CHILDREN

TOLD
UNDER THE
STARS and STRIPES

Stories selected by the Literature Committee of the
Association for Childhood Education International

Illustrated by Nedda Walker

THE MACMILLAN COMPANY · NEW YORK

CONTENTS

MAMINKA'S CHILDREN

*The little Bohemian girl is grown up now. She still has
her bright-striped skirt, her little black jacket, her apron,
and her pretty red shawl. . . .*

*And she still has her three children. But they are no
longer pretend-ones. They are real, real, REAL! Their
names are Nanka, Marianka, and Honzichek. They call
their mother Maminka.*

LONG, LONG AGO—and yet not so long, either—there was a little Bohemian girl. She wore a bright-striped skirt, a little black jacket, a black embroidered apron, and, over her head, a pretty red shawl. She lived in the Old Country. She lived with her father, in a little house in the forest.

Her father was busy, much of the time, making beautiful things out of wood, to sell, so that he could buy potatoes. And when he bought potatoes, the little girl peeled them and cut them into chunks, put the chunks in the kettle—and they had brambory soup for supper!

They were very happy, the little girl and her father, living alone together. But sometimes the house was very still and quiet when the father was busy with his work. That little girl might have been quite lonely at those times.

But she wasn't, because she had three little children—two girls and a boy. They were only pretend-children. Her father couldn't see them, and neither could she. But they were there just the same. She used to talk to them, and laugh, and have all sorts of fun. She loved them very much.

But there came a time when her father could sell no more of the beautiful things that he made out of wood. So there were no more potatoes for the good brambory soup. That was when the little girl was nine years old.

"I'm afraid," said her father one day, "that we shall have to go away from the Old Country. We shall have to go to a new country, and try our luck there. But we'll be happy, my little mushroom"—that's what he called her—"I'll always have you, and you'll always have me, and we'll both have plenty of brambory soup!"

"But what about my three little children?" she asked. "I don't want to leave *them* behind!"

"Your three little children? Why! That's easy!" chuckled her father. "Three's just the right number to fit into your heart!"

Then her father took his sharp knife, his long pipe, his red striped coffee cup, and several other things, and said, "Come, my little mushroom!" And she took the soup kettle, and followed him, with her three little children safe in her heart.

And what her father said was true. They were just as happy in the New Country as they had been in the Old. And there were plenty of potatoes for the good brambory soup.

The little Bohemian girl is grown up now. She still has her bright-striped skirt, her little black jacket, her apron, and her pretty red shawl. But they are wrapped in paper and put away, for they no longer fit her.

And she still has her three children. But they are no longer pretend-ones. They are real, *real*, REAL! Their names are Nanka, Marianka, and Honzichek. They call their mother Maminka. Their grandfather they call Old Grampa.

They live on a little farm. Aunt Matylda lives with them.

Old Horse, Old Cow, the red hen, the white hen, and the great green rooster live on the little farm, too. So does Bidushka, Marianka's big speckled hen. And so does Katcha, Honzichek's big goose, whose voice sounds like an accordion.

Right now, Aunt Pantsy and Uncle Edy are staying on the little farm, too. They have come to stay over Christmas.

"Maminka!" shouted Nanka, running down the stairs to the kitchen. "Four more days till Christmas!"

"Yes, my little mouse, I know," said Maminka. "Na, run along!"

"Aunt Pantsy!" shouted Nanka, running up the stairs again. "Four more days till—"

"Christmas!" said Aunt Pantsy, giving Nanka a hug. "Run along, my good girl!"

"Old Grampa!" shouted Nanka, running down the stairs again. She opened the door to his room. "Four more days—Yi! Is that your secret, Old Grampa?"

Old Grampa motioned her to come in, and to shut the door behind her. Nanka tiptoed round Old Grampa's bed to where he sat by the window, whittling with his sharp knife.

Whittle-whittle-whittle! went Old Grampa's sharp knife.

On Old Grampa's table stood a tiny stable, with a roof of straw.

"What is here?" asked Nanka.

And Old Grampa answered, "Betlem." Then he held out two tiny persons for her to see.

She took one in each hand, carefully.

One was a man with a bald head and a beard. He had a long robe on. He was bending over.

"What's his name?" asked Nanka.

"Josef," answered Old Grampa.

The other tiny person was a woman, with a halo on her head. She was kneeling and reaching out her hands.

"What's her name?" asked Nanka.

"Maria," answered Old Grampa.

Nanka put Josef and Maria, very carefully, inside the stable. Then she rested her chin on the edge of the table, and looked and looked and looked, because she loved the tiny Josef and the Maria that Old Grampa had made out of wood.

Next morning there were only three more days till Christmas.

"Old Grampa!" shouted Nanka, knocking at his door. "Three more days!" Then she opened the door and slipped inside.

There was no sound in Old Grampa's room but the whittle-whittle-whittle! of his sharp knife. He sat by the window, making three more tiny persons out of wood. When they were finished, he held them out for Nanka to see.

They were kings, with fancy crowns on and long robes and cloaks on. Two had long beards, and one held a little round box. The long-bearded two were bending over, like Josef. The one with the box was kneeling, like Maria.

"Who are these?" asked Nanka.

"Kraly," answered Old Grampa.

Nanka put the Kraly, very carefully, beside the stable, where Josef and Maria were. Then she rested her chin on the edge of the table, and looked and looked

and looked, because she loved the tiny Kraly that Old
Grampa had made out of wood.

Next morning there were only two more days till
Christmas.

"Old Grampa!" shouted Nanka, knocking at his
door. "Two more days!" And she opened the door and
slipped inside.

Old Grampa had already finished two more tiny persons, and he was whittling a third with his sharp knife.

The two were angels with wings on. One of them,
the smaller, was carrying flowers. The other was carrying fruit.

"What's her name?" asked Nanka, touching, very
carefully, the wings of the one who was carrying fruit.

"Marianka," answered Old Grampa.

"What's *her* name?" asked Nanka, quickly pointing
to the tinier wings of the one who was carrying flowers.

"Nanka," said Old Grampa, quietly.

"Yi!" said Nanka, not so quietly.

Then Old Grampa finished the other tiny person. It
was a little boy, with a big hat on. He was kneeling, like
Maria, and carrying fruit, like Marianka.

"Honzichek!" guessed Nanka right away.

And Old Grampa nodded his head.

Nanka put the three, very carefully, beside the stable,
where Josef and Maria and the Kraly were. Then she
rested her chin on the edge of the table, and looked and
looked and looked, because she loved the tiny Nanka,
the Marianka, and the Honzichek that Old Grampa had
made out of wood.

Next morning was the morning of Christmas Eve.

"Old Grampa!" shouted Nanka, opening his door. "Christmas Eve!" She ran to the table where the stable stood.

And there, at last, by Maria lay the tiniest Baby that Nanka had ever seen, on some hay, with a tiny wooden feather bed to cover Him.

"Jezishek," Old Grampa explained.

Maria was reaching out her hands to the tiny Jezishek. Josef was bending over Him. The Kraly were bowing and kneeling. And Nanka, Marianka, and Honzichek were bringing flowers and fruit to Him.

"You beautiful little Jezishek!" whispered Nanka.

Then she rested her chin on the edge of the table, and smiled and smiled and smiled. She loved the little Jezishek best of all.

Old Grampa nodded his head, and wrinkled up his face, as he put his sharp knife away. He loved the little Jezishek, too!

On Christmas Eve there was a party. Old Grampa came, and Aunt Pantsy and Uncle Edy and Aunt Matylda. The red hen, the white hen, and the great green rooster came, and Marianka's big speckled hen, Bidushka —and Honzichek's big old goose, Katcha. Even Aunt Matylda's little mouse came to the party in its little wooden house. Last of all came Mr. Kuna, the express man.

"Ho!" laughed Mr. Kuna as he took off his coat. "Ho!" he laughed as he looked round at everybody. He looked at all the chickens, the big goose wearing the jacket that Aunt Matylda had knitted to keep her warm,

and the little mouse in its house. He looked at Uncle
Edy's zither, and at Honzichek's huge old accordion,
and at Maminka's beautiful Christmas bread laid out on
the kitchen table. He smelled the good coffee bubbling
on the stove. "Ho! Ho! Ho! Ho!" laughed jolly Mr.
Kuna, rubbing his hands together.

He had never been invited to a party like this in all
his life before!

When the party was over, Katcha and the chickens
went out to the barn again and to the chicken house. And
Maminka took some Christmas bread to Old Horse and
Old Cow, just as she said she would do.

But everybody wanted Mr. Kuna to stay for a quiet
little supper round the kitchen table. Maminka made
brambory soup for supper—good brambory soup, with
noodles and mushrooms. And she filled cup after cup full
of Old Cow's sweet milk.

Maminka set the kitchen table in a lovely way. In
the middle stood a little tree, with long, red apple peel-
ings looped over its branches and a candle on the top of
it. The candle was lighted! Under the tree were the
Maria and Josef, the Kraly, the angels, the little boy,
and the tiny Jezishek—all the beautiful things that old
Grampa had made out of wood. But now they were more
beautiful than ever, for Uncle Edy had painted them in
red and blue and brown and gold. And the light from the
lighted candle shone down through the branches of the
little tree, making those colors bright.

After supper there were apples to eat. Mr. Kuna
chose a big red shiny one.

"There must be a perfect star inside this apple," said Mr. Kuna.

"A star, Mr. Kuna?" asked Nanka, Marianka, and Honzichek, very much surprised. "A star in an apple?"

"Why, bless you!" said Mr. Kuna. "Didn't you know that? There's a star in every apple!"

"When I was a little girl in the Old Country," said Maminka, "we used to cut an apple open every Christmas Eve. We always hoped that we would find a perfect star, for that meant health and happiness during all the coming year."

"Yes," said Mr. Kuna, "when I was a little boy in the Old Country, we used to do the same. Let's do it now! Let's cut this apple!" And he handed the big shiny apple to Old Grampa.

Everyone leaned close while Old Grampa took out his sharp knife. They all held their breath while he cut the apple quickly, crossways through the core, then opened it very, very slowly.

There it was! A perfect star!

"Oh! Oh!" said Marianka.

And everyone looked very happy.

"Our star!" said Maminka, smiling. "Our Christmas star! Every single one of us will be healthy and happy. Yes, every single one!"

Marianka looked at the Christmas star. She looked at her mother and her grandfather, at her brother and her little sister, and at the others, gathered so close together. She looked at the tiny Jezishek, under the tree, and at all the beautiful things around Him. And then

Marianka whispered, "Maminka—you know what? I feel like saying my prayers, right here by the kitchen table!"

"I think we all feel that way, my sweet raisin," said Maminka, bowing her head. Nanka, Marianka, and Honzichek bowed their heads, too. And Mr. Kuna bowed his. And Old Grampa, Aunt Pantsy, Uncle Edy, and Aunt Matylda all bowed their heads while Maminka said a little prayer.

"Our Father," said Maminka, "We pray that the Jezishek may be born in our hearts tonight, as He was born in Betlem long ago."

For a few minutes everyone was very still. Then they were all smiling and talking again.

Mr. Kuna put on his coat, thanked them for a lovely time, and went out into the snow, to drive home in his express wagon.

Nanka, Marianka, and Honzichek got undressed.

Aunt Pantsy folded the feather bed over them.

Maminka blew out the candle at the top of the little tree, and said good night.

And soon they were sound asleep.

While Marianka was asleep in the big soft feather bed, she dreamed a dream.

The little star which they had found in the apple grew, in Marianka's dream, to a great star. It was a great perfect star. And it was shining on the roof of the barn. Up where the little weather vane usually stood, it was shining. It made the night as bright as morning.

Marianka dreamed that she woke up, and saw it. She dreamed that she woke Nanka up, too, and Honzichek.

"Wake up, Nanka! Honzichek!" said Marianka, in her dream. "The Christmas star is shining! It's shining on our barn!"

Nanka and Honzichek woke up—but only in Marianka's dream. And all together, they got up and tiptoed across the kitchen. Out into the snow they tiptoed, in their bare feet. But the snow didn't feel cold at all. It felt only soft, like feathers. They ran across the soft snow to the barn. And Honzichek pulled at the high old door. It creaked on its hinges, as usual.

Then they heard a little cry inside. It was a sweet little cry. It sounded like a baby, waking.

And somebody whispered, "Who is there?"

Honzichek pulled the door open, and they all peeked in. Marianka dreamed that they saw Old Horse and Old Cow standing there together. Old Horse was breathing big sweet breaths. And Old Cow was mooing, very softly. Katcha was sitting down in the hay. The red hen and Bidushka, the white hen and the great green rooster were sitting in a row, on a board. And a little sparrow was perched on the edge of Old Cow's manger.

In the hay, by the manger, a woman was kneeling. She looked very much like Maminka. But her name was Maria.

A man was bending over Maria—he looked like Old Grampa. But his name was Josef. And there, in Old Cow's manger, the dear Baby Jezishek lay!

"May we come in?" asked the children, in Marianka's dream.

And, in her dream, the Mother Maria nodded. Of course they could come!

So they tiptoed through the hay, and knelt down beside the manger.

And, just before the end of Marianka's dream, the dear Baby Jezishek looked up at them—and smiled!

By Elizabeth Orton Jones

PRIMROSE DAY

"When I lived in England," Merry *began, "on my birth-day every year Mummy took me to the country to pick primroses. . . . We would find a lovely place in the woods and eat our lunch. . . . After lunch I made prim-rose chains. I always made one for Mummy and one for me. Mummy and I always called my birthday Merry Primrose Day, 'cause my name is Primrose."*

WHEN MERRY REACHED Rose Valley she thought it was a beautiful place. She had never lived in the country. But her mother had taken her on picnics in the country. She had always gone to the country on her birthday to pick primroses. They called it "Merry's Primrose Day."

Merry loved Aunt Helen's house and especially the little bedroom that Aunt Helen had fixed for her. She was so surprised to find that the curtains at the windows were just like the curtains in her own room at home. They were white with bright red strawberries sprinkled all over them.

"Why, Aunt Helen," said Merry, "these curtains are just like the curtains in my room at home."

"Well now, what do you think of that!" said Aunt Helen. Aunt Helen and Uncle Bill looked at each other and laughed.

"Mother did it on purpose," said Jerry, "so you would feel at home."

"Oh, Jerry," laughed his mother, "you shouldn't have told. That was supposed to be a secret."

"Well, you did," said Jerry. "I heard you say so to Daddy."

"It's a pretty room," said Merry. "I'm going to like living here."

"I am sure you will," said Aunt Helen. "Tomorrow you will start to school. I am going to drive you and Jerry over to school in the morning. After that you will go in the bus with Jerry."

"Will I be in the same room with Jerry?" asked Merry.

"I suppose so," said Aunt Helen. "Jerry is in the second grade."

"Second grade?" said Merry. "What is grade?"

"It means second year," said Aunt Helen. "You call it second form in England, don't you?"

"Oh, yes!" said Merry. "I was in second form in England."

The following morning Mrs. Hobson drove Merry and Jerry to school. The Principal said that she would try Merry in the second grade.

Jerry took Merry into his room. He walked up to his teacher, Miss Miller.

"Good morning, Jerry," said Miss Miller.

"Good morning, Miss Miller," said Jerry. "This is my cousin, Merry Ramsay. She is from England, you know."

"Good morning, Merry," said Miss Miller, shaking hands with Merry. "Jerry has been telling us that you were coming for a visit. We will be glad to have you in our class."

The boys and girls in the room were all chattering like magpies. Miss Miller clapped her hands. The chatter ceased. "Boys and girls," said Miss Miller, "this is Merry Ramsay from England. Will you say 'Good morning' to Merry?"

"Good morning, Merry," the children said.

"Good morning," said Merry.

Miss Miller showed Merry to a seat right behind Jerry's.

Soon the bell rang for school to begin. The children sang a song that Merry knew. Then they had a reading lesson. Merry read very well. After the reading lesson the children wrote words on a piece of paper. Merry got them all right. She was beginning to feel that school in America wasn't very different from school in England.

After Miss Miller marked all of the children's papers, she said, "Now, boys and girls, we are going to do some examples on the blackboard."

"Examples!" thought Merry. "What are examples?"

Miss Miller looked at Merry. "I am going to ask our little girl from England to come up to the blackboard," she said.

Merry walked up to the blackboard. She wondered what she was going to do.

"Now," said Miss Miller, "will you write the example, 'ten take away six.' "

Merry picked up a piece of chalk and began to write out the words, "Ten take—"

All of the children began to laugh.

"No, no, Merry," said Miss Miller. "I want you to write the example."

Merry looked puzzled. "I don't know what you mean by 'example,' " she said.

"Golly," said Bobby Brown, "she's dumb!"

"Bobby," said Miss Miller, "that is very rude. It is very rude to laugh too."

Merry bit her lip. She didn't like being laughed at.

"Never mind, Merry," said Miss Miller. "Jerry will write it on the board. Then you will see what I mean."

Jerry went to the front of the room and wrote a big number ten. Underneath it he put a take away sign and the figure six. Then he drew a line under the six and made the figure four.

"Oh!" said Merry. "I didn't know that you wanted me to write a sum."

"Oh, Merry," said Miss Miller, "I am so sorry. I

didn't know that you called them 'sums' in England. You see we call them 'examples.'"

"I see," said Merry.

Then Miss Miller told her to write the example eight take away three on the board. This time Merry knew just what to do.

At recess time Jerry and Merry went out to play.

Bobby Brown came running up to Merry. "Hello, English!" he cried. "How are your sums?"

Merry's cheeks began to feel hot.

Just then Tommy and Freddy Clark rushed up. They were twins and they were always into mischief. They began to call, "Oh, Merry sums! Oh, Merry sums! How are your sums today?"

Merry felt hot tears in her eyes.

"You leave her alone," said Jerry.

The boys ran off shouting, "Merry, Merry sums! Merry, Merry sums!"

When Merry got home from school, she didn't feel very happy. When Aunt Helen asked her how she liked school, she said, "Oh, all right. Only I didn't know that they called 'sums' 'examples.'"

That night, after Aunt Helen had tucked her into bed and closed the door, Merry cried. She felt strange and lonely. She wished she could be with Molly. Molly talked the way she did. Merry buried her face in the pillow and cried until she fell asleep.

The next morning while Merry dressed for school, she was thinking. She wished she didn't have to go to school. It was so awful to be different from the other children. It was terrible to be laughed at.

After breakfast Aunt Helen said, "This morning you are going on the bus to school."

At half-past eight Jerry and Merry were at the corner, waiting for the bus.

Soon the yellow bus arrived. Jerry and Merry climbed in.

"Hi, Jerry!" the children shouted.

"Hello, English!" cried Bobby.

Merry didn't mind so much being called "English." She was proud to be English. She just hoped he wouldn't say anything about sums. She would remember today to call them examples.

Merry sat down beside Nancy Barnes. Merry liked Nancy. She was a very quiet little girl.

Just before they reached the school a big truck passed the bus. "My!" cried Merry. "What a big lorry!"

"Big what?" said Bobby.

"Big lorry," said Merry.

"That's not a lorry," cried Bobby; "that's a truck."

The children in the bus laughed when Bobby cried out, "She calls a truck a lorry." But Nancy didn't laugh.

Merry felt her cheeks grow hot again. She had made another mistake. At recess time the boys shouted, "Hi, Lorry! Hi, Lorry!" They called her "Lorry" all day.

As the days went by Merry grew more and more unhappy. She was always using words that made the children laugh. Merry would bite her lip to keep back the tears. Aunt Helen said that she mustn't mind. She said that the children didn't mean to be unkind. "They just don't know any better," said Aunt Helen.

One day Miss Miller told the children that she

wanted each one to think of the happiest day he could remember. Then she asked several of the children to tell the others the story of their happiest day.

Merry was so anxious to tell about her happiest day that she forgot how the boys had laughed at her. She raised her hand.

"Merry has a story to tell us," said Miss Miller.

Merry walked to the front of the room. She faced the class.

"When I lived in England," she began, "on my birthday every year Mummy took me to the country to pick primroses. We would go on the tram to the railway station."

"On the what?" asked Bobby.

"On the tram," said Merry.

"Bobby, it is rude to interrupt," said Miss Miller. "Merry means that she went on a street-car."

Merry saw a grin spread over Bobby's face. "Oh, dear!" thought Merry. "Now they will laugh at me because I called it a tram."

She went on with the story. "At the railway station," she said, "we got on a train that went down to Devon. Mummy always took a tea-basket so that we could have lunch and tea out of doors. All the way there were primroses growing beside the railway tracks. It looked like a yellow carpet. When we got off the train, Mummy and I would walk a long way. We gathered the primroses from the hedgerows and put them in a basket. Then we would find a lovely place in the woods and eat our lunch. But the most fun was after lunch. After lunch I made primrose chains. I always made one for Mummy and one for me. Mummy and I always called my birthday Merry Primrose Day, 'cause my name is Primrose."

Nancy raised her hand.

"Nancy wants to ask a question," said Miss Miller. "What is it, Nancy?"

"What is a primrose chain?" asked Nancy.

"Oh, they are pretty," said Merry. "You make a little slit in the stem of one primrose and then you pull the stem of another primrose through the slit. You can make a long chain."

"Now, finish your story, Merry," said Miss Miller.

"Well, there isn't very much more," said Merry. "After tea we took the train back to London and showed our primrose chains to Daddy."

"That was a very nice story," said Miss Miller.

"It won't be long before my birthday," said Merry. "Only this year Aunt Helen will take me to gather primroses."

"I am afraid you will not be able to gather primroses this year," said Miss Miller. "You see, Merry, primroses don't grow in the fields and woods of America."

Merry looked puzzled. "You mean that there are no primroses in America?" said Merry.

"There are a few," said Miss Miller, "but they grow in gardens."

"You mean that you can't go out in the woods and gather them?" asked Merry.

"That's right," said Miss Miller. "You can't go out and gather primroses in America."

Merry sat down at her desk. She couldn't believe that there wouldn't be any primroses on her birthday. Why, as long as she could remember she had always gathered primroses on her birthday. It would be like Christmas without a stocking or a Christmas tree.

On the way home in the bus Merry was so busy feeling sorry about the primroses that she hardly heard Bobby call out, "Hello, English, are you going on a tram?"

When Merry reached home, she rushed into the house and right up the stairs. She threw herself on her bed and cried.

In a few minutes Aunt Helen came into the room. She sat down on Merry's bed. "Merry dear," she said, "what is the matter?"

"There aren't any primroses," sobbed Merry. "I can't pick primroses on my birthday."

"Never mind, darling," said Aunt Helen. "There will be other flowers to pick. I'll take you to pick violets."

"But it won't be the same," cried Merry. "Oh, I wish I were back in England where there are primroses. I wish I were home where people talk the way I do. Nobody laughs at me in England."

Aunt Helen patted Merry's shoulder. "Merry," she said, "there is someone downstairs to see you."

Merry went right on crying.

"It is someone you are very fond of," said Aunt Helen.

Merry turned over and looked at Aunt Helen. "Who is it?" she asked.

"Come and wash your face," said Aunt Helen; "then come downstairs."

Merry got up. She washed her face and brushed her

hair. Then she went downstairs. She could hear voices in the library. They were grown-ups. Merry wondered who they were.

When she reached the foot of the stairs, Molly came running out of the library. "Hello, Merry!" she shouted. "Hello! I've come to live in Rose Valley too!"

Merry was so glad to be with Molly again. Mr. and Mrs. Price had moved from the city to Rose Valley. They had taken a house about a half mile from the Hobsons.

When Molly started to school, she was placed in the same room with Merry. Both of the little girls were delighted. With two little English girls in the class the other children soon grew used to the way they spoke. Even Bobby Brown stopped making fun of them.

When Merry told Molly that there were no primroses in America, Molly thought it was very strange. "My birthday won't be a Primrose Day this year," said Merry. "It won't seem like a birthday at all."

Merry's birthday was on the twelfth of April. It fell on a Saturday. The night before, when Aunt Helen tucked her into bed she said, "Merry, tomorrow you and I are going on a picnic."

"All by ourselves?" said Merry.

"Yes, all by ourselves. Just as you did with Mummy," said Aunt Helen.

"Will we take a tea-basket?" asked Merry.

"Yes," replied Aunt Helen, "we'll take a tea-basket. Only we call it a picnic basket."

"And will we stay for lunch and tea?" asked Merry.

"Just for lunch," said Aunt Helen. "We are not going

as far away as you used to go with Mummy. We'll come home in time for tea."

"Do you think there will be any flowers to pick?" asked Merry.

"I think so," replied Aunt Helen.

"Maybe there will be violets," said Merry; "but I do wish there were primroses."

"Well, go to sleep," said Aunt Helen, as she kissed Merry good night. "Maybe you will dream that you are picking primroses."

The next morning Merry was up bright and early. It was a beautiful spring day. Merry looked out of the window. There was a big fat robin on the lawn. The apple trees in the garden were covered with pale pink blossoms.

When Uncle Bill came down to breakfast, he said, "Happy birthday, Merry."

"Thank you," said Merry. "Daddy always said 'Merry Primrose' on my birthday. Daddy said, 'If you say "Merry Christmas" on Christmas, you should say "Merry Primrose" on my birthday.'"

"I think your daddy is right," said Uncle Bill. "So, Merry Primrose to you."

Just then Aunt Helen came downstairs. She had a birthday letter from Merry's daddy and one from her mummy. There was a photograph of Daddy in one and one of Mummy in the other. Mummy said that she had asked Aunt Helen to buy her a bottle of perfume for Merry's Primrose Day. Daddy said that he had asked Aunt Helen to buy her a new hair-ribbon. He said it must be plaid because he was a Scotchman. Merry laughed because Daddy said he hoped that Aunt Helen had taken Greggie with her to buy the ribbon. He said that Greggie was a good Scot. He would be able to pick out a good plaid ribbon.

The bottle of perfume and the plaid ribbon were on the breakfast table at Merry's place. There was a plaid belt to match the ribbon, from Greggie. Uncle Bill had bought her some plaid socks and Aunt Helen gave her a little jewelry box.

When Jerry came down to breakfast, he said, "I have a present for you, Merry. I'll have to give it to you this afternoon. It isn't finished yet. I have to work on it this morning."

"Don't you want to go on the picnic with Aunt Helen and me?" asked Merry.

"No," said Jerry, "I have a lot of work to do."

Merry saw Aunt Helen wink at Jerry. Jerry looked as though he were keeping a secret.

"Something's up, Merry!" said Uncle Bill. "I can tell. Something's up!"

Everybody laughed. Aunt Helen said, "You had better go or you will miss your train."

Uncle Bill looked at his watch. He jumped up. He ran around the table and kissed Aunt Helen and the children. "So long, Merry Primrose!" he called. "See you later!"

By eleven o'clock the picnic basket was packed. Aunt Helen put it in the back of the car. She and Merry sat on the front seat.

"Is it very far?" asked Merry.

"No," replied Aunt Helen, "it isn't very far. We are

going to a place that belongs to a friend of Uncle Bill's. He owns two hundred and seventy-five acres of land."

"What does he do with so much land?" asked Merry.

"Some of it is farm land," said Aunt Helen. "Part of it has been made into gardens. But we are going to the woods."

"Are his woods nicer than the woods back of our house?" asked Merry.

"Oh, my, yes!" said Aunt Helen. "When we get there you will see why."

Aunt Helen turned the car in at a gate with white posts. The curved drive went up a hill. At the top of the hill there was a big stone house.

"Does Uncle Bill's friend live in that house?" asked Merry.

"Yes," answered Aunt Helen, "but he is away."

They drove past the house and around past some greenhouses. At last they stopped in front of a little cottage.

"Why, this looks like an English cottage!" said Merry.

"Yes, it does," said Aunt Helen, "and English people live in the cottage. This is where Brooks, the gardener, lives."

Just as the car stopped a man came out of the cottage. Merry thought he looked like the postman who used to bring the mail to Heartford Square.

"Good morning, Mrs. Hobson," he said. "I thought I heard the car."

"Good morning, Brooks," said Mrs. Hobson. "This is Merry Ramsay."

"Well, I'm glad to know you, Merry," said Brooks. "I hear you are going to the woods for a picnic."

"How do you do," said Merry.

"I'll show you the way," said Brooks.

Brooks led the way. They went past a rock garden and across the green lawn. Merry could see the trees of the woods ahead. As they entered the woods Merry stood still. She gave a little gasp. She could hardly believe her eyes. There under the trees were yellow primroses. They weren't like a carpet, as in England, but as far as she could see there were little clumps of primroses.

"Why, Aunt Helen," she gasped, "they're primroses!"

"Yes, dear one," said Aunt Helen, "primroses."

"But I thought they didn't grow in America," said Merry.

"They don't grow wild," said Brooks; "but I got these plants from England and I planted them here in the woods. I've nursed them along and every year they come up again. They take a deal of care and nursing though."

"Oh," said Merry, "I don't suppose you ever pick them."

"Oh, yes," said Brooks, "you can pick them. Pick all you want."

Merry was so happy her face shone like the sun. She knelt down and began to pick the primroses. Brooks went off to attend to his work and Aunt Helen sat down under a tree. She took out her knitting.

Merry went from one clump to another, picking primroses. When she had gathered a large bunch, she said, "I don't think I'll pick any more. I should leave some because they make the woods look so pretty."

"Yes," said Aunt Helen. "I think you have gathered enough. Suppose we eat our lunch now?"

Merry sat down beside Aunt Helen while she unpacked the basket. "Now I can make a primrose chain," said Merry.

Between bites of her sandwiches, Merry fastened the primroses together. "I don't think there are enough to make two chains," she said. "It takes an awful lot of primroses to make a chain."

"Well, just make one chain for yourself," said Aunt Helen.

"Oh, no!" said Merry. "I want to make one for you too."

Merry puckered up her brow and looked at the flowers. "I know," she said; "I'll make bracelets. Bracelets won't take so many flowers. Would you like to have a bracelet, Aunt Helen?"

"Yes, indeed," replied Aunt Helen. "I think a bracelet would be lovely."

Merry worked busily at her bracelets. It was slow work. When she finished, she had some flowers left. "Oh, Aunt Helen!" she cried. "I'm going to have enough to make a bracelet for Molly too."

By the time Merry finished her third bracelet it was two o'clock.

"Now we must go," said Aunt Helen.

Merry fastened one of the bracelets on Aunt Helen's arm. Then Aunt Helen fastened one on Merry's arm. "Aren't they beautiful?" said Merry.

"Indeed they are," replied Aunt Helen.

At the cottage she showed them to Brooks. "They are very pretty indeed," he said.

"It has been just like home," said Merry. "Thank you for letting me pick your primroses."

"Ah!" said Brooks. "It's good to have a little English lass picking primroses. It's as you say, 'just like home.'"

On the way back Aunt Helen said, "Now we will pick up Molly and take her home with us for tea."

When they reached the Prices', Molly came running out.

"Look, Molly!" cried Merry. "I've brought you a primrose bracelet."

"Oh, isn't it pretty!" said Molly, as Merry fastened it on her arm. "Thank you," she said. "I thought there weren't any primroses in America."

Molly climbed into the car. As they drove home Merry told her about the English gardener and the primroses. While she talked Merry noticed that Molly had a little package in her hand. She wondered what was in the package but she was too polite to ask. When they reached Aunt Helen's, Molly and Merry jumped out and ran into the house.

Merry called, "Oh, Jerry! Jerry, where are you?"

"Maybe he's in the library," said Molly.

The two little girls ran into the library. Suddenly the room was full of boys and girls. They jumped out from behind doors and from behind every chair. They all shouted, "Merry Primrose! Merry Primrose!"

There were Nancy and Bobby Brown and the twins, Tommy and Freddy. There was a little girl whose name was Susie and another named Patsy. They were all from school.

Merry was so surprised she couldn't stand up. She sat right down on the floor. All of the children had packages for her. They came and put them in her lap. When Bobby gave her his package, he said, "Say, Merry, I'm awfully sorry I made fun of you, 'cause I like you a lot."

"I like you too," said Merry; "only I didn't at first. I guess I like everybody now."

Merry was delighted with her presents. Now she knew what had been in the package that Molly had held in her hand in the car. It was a little silver thimble.

Jerry had made a sewing-box for her. He was very proud of it. That very morning he had painted it bright red. He carried it very carefully because he wasn't certain that it was dry. Merry thought it was a lovely sewing-box.

She had never had so many presents before. There was a string of beads from Nancy and a whole dozen new pencils from Freddy. Tommy gave her a box of paints. Susie had brought her a box of notepaper. When she opened the last package, it was a pincushion with a doll sticking right out of the center. It was a present from Patsy.

After Merry had thanked everyone for her presents, the children played games.

At five o'clock Mrs. Hobson took them out into the dining room. At Merry's place there was a beautiful birthday cake with yellow candles. It had white icing and little yellow flowers that looked like primroses.

Across the top there were yellow letters that said "Merry Primrose." Even the ice cream was yellow and white. It was vanilla and orange ice.

Merry had never had such a lovely party. She forgot all about the unhappy days that she had known.

That night, before she went to bed, she wrote a letter to her mummy and daddy. She thanked them for her presents and told them all about her surprise Primrose Day.

By Carolyn Haywood

LITTLE VON-DOS-SMAI

Von-Dos-Smai sits and listens
     and sits and thinks
     and then he says, "More. More.
     Tell me more. I want to know more.
     I want to know. I want to know."

That is why they call him
     Little Pima Von-Dos-Smai
     because Von-Dos-Smai in Pima means
     I-Want-To-Know.

Von-Dos-Smai is a Pima Indian.
His mother is a Pima Indian.
His father is a Pima Indian.

Von-Dos-Smai is fat and round.
Von-Dos-Smai is jolly and brown.
Von-Dos-Smai is a fat, little brown
        little Pima Indian boy.

Von-Dos-Smai has big black eyes.
Von-Dos-Smai has straight black hair.
Von-Dos-Smai is a little fat, little brown,
            little Pima Indian boy.

His mother is a Pima.
His father is a Pima.
He is a Pima Indian Boy.

They have an arrow weed house,
        very little,
        and an arrow weed shade
        by the house door.

Their house is called a ki.
Their shade is called a vatho.
It is their home.
They live there.

They have a clean sand yard
        and a nightingale
        in a willow cage.

They live in the desert,
        in the hot desert country
        near the dry Salt river.

The hot desert country
    near the dry Salt river
    is a big sand country
    where the cactus grows,
    where the mesquite grows,
    where the flame bush
    and the smoke tree grows.

The hot desert country
    is a purple colored country.
Far away are purple mountains.
Near by is a purple heat haze.
The sky is purple-blue
    and the clouds are purple-gray.

This is the home of the Pima People
    who are called the River People,
    who are called the Basket People.
This is the home of little Von-Dos-Smai.
He lives here.

Von-Dos-Smai, when he is standing,
    is almost big enough for school,
    but he is not standing very often,
He is a SITTING-AND-THINKING boy.

He likes to sit . . . he likes to think.
He likes to do them both at the same time,
    sitting and thinking, sitting and thinking.

The trouble is he has to know
    a lot of things to think about.

The trouble is he has to know
    a lot of things to think about.
    a lot of things to think about.

So he is always saying
    to his mother and father,
"What about these things I see?
I want to know about them.
I want to know. I want to know."

Then they sit beside him,
    his mother and father.
They tell him all the things
    that they have seen
    and heard
    and done
    and learned about.
They tell him all the things they know.

Von-Dos-Smai sits and listens
    and sits and thinks
    and then he says, "More. More.
Tell me more. I want to know more.
I want to know. I want to know."

That is why they call him
    Little Pima Von-Dos-Smai
    because Von-Dos-Smai in Pima means
    I-Want-To-Know.

Little Pima Von-Dos-Smai!
Little Pima Wants-To-Know!

One morning very early
    before the desert sun was up
    Little Wants-To-Know lay
    on his grass mat bed
    thinking things
    to want to know about.

He looked over at the ki
    where his mother was cooking breakfast.
He looked at the arrow weed
    that was woven through
    the saguaro cactus ribs
    to make the ki walls.

He called to his father,
    "We have a good ki.
It has wonderful walls.
It has strong, tight walls.
I want to know about them.
I want to know about the arrow weed
    that makes the walls of my ki.
I want to know about the cactus ribs
    that hold the arrow weed walls.
I want to know about them.
I want to know."

His father came out to the vatho
    to eat his breakfast.
He told his little boy,
    he said, "We River People
    have a story

about the old man cactus
and the palo verde tree.
Once long ago in the beginning,
a Pima boy and a Pima girl
ran away from their grandmother.
Why they ran is not told us,
but they did not want their grandmother
to find them, ever,
so a desert witch turned the girl
into a palo verde tree
to make the desert green.
A desert witch turned the boy
into a saguaro cactus
so he could live forever."

Von-Dos-Smai listened and then he said,
"More. More. I want to know more
about the giant cactus."

His father told him,
"When the saguaro cactus
is as old as you are now
it is as high as your hand.
Every year after that
it grows an inch
and sometimes two inches.
You can guess how very old
the highest cactus is."

Father told him, "The cactus
never has a flower
until it is as old as a grandfather.

Then its flower is white and beautiful.
In mid-summer it turns to purple fruit."

Pima father smiled at his little Pima boy.
    He liked to tell him things,
    that is,
    most of the time
    he liked to tell him things.
He said, "When the purple fruit is ripe
     the people gather it and eat it.
It is the New Year's time for the River people
    when the purple cactus fruit is ripe."

Von-Dos-Smai clapped his hands.
"I know. I know," he told his father.
"I know because the people pick it
    when the August moon is new.
With our long poles we gather it
    when the summer moon is high."

Little Pima boy pushed out his lips.
"I can almost taste it now,
    that good, sweet purple cactus fruit."

Father ate his breakfast,
    then he went to work.
He went to pick the cotton
    in the white man's cotton fields.

Little Pima boy watched his father
    walk along the sandy desert trail.

When his mother went with his father
    Little Wants-To-Know went with them.
He went with them to the cotton field.
He watched them pick the cotton,
    the fluffy balls of cotton.
He watched them fill their cotton sacks.
    their heavy, canvas cotton sacks.
He knew about cotton picking.
When he grew big he would be a cotton picker, too,
    in the white man's cotton fields near by.

Little Pima boy watched his father
    walk along the sandy desert trail
    to the white man's cotton field.
Then he went to sit beside his mother
    in the lacy shade of the palo verde tree.

His mother was splitting willow stems
    with her strong white teeth.
She was splitting them into narrow strips
    to weave into a basket.

Pima mother and Pima boy heard a cactus wren
    singing its desert song
    for the bright blue morning.

Von-Dos-Smai whispered to his mother,
    "What a nice little bird.
    What a dear little fellow.
I want to know about this cactus wren.
I want to know. I want to know."

He said, "I want to know about the cactus wren,
    this fluffy feathered cactus wren
    with the black striped eyes
    and the black striped tail.

"I want to know all about this cactus wren,
    this speckled, dotted cactus wren,
    who has an awful, awful voice,
    but sings a pretty song."

His mother smiled at him.
She liked to tell him things,
    that is,
    almost all day long
    she liked to tell him things.

She told him all she knew. She said,
    "Did you know this, little Pima?
Father Wren builds many houses
    near his wife's round nest
    so that each of his children
    can have a house of his own
    when he is strong enough
    to fly away."

"Did you know this, little Pima?
Cactus Wren builds her nest in the cactus ribs.
Old man Cactus likes her, I think,
    for he never pricks her
    with his thorny spines."

Pima mother laughed. She said,
"Before you ask me, I will tell you
    it's the very same way with the hoot owl, too,
    and the red headed woodpecker.
They never get pricked with the cactus thorns."

A road runner glided by the palo verde tree.
It sailed through the air, not flying, just gliding.
It frightened Little Wants-To-Know.
He could not say a word.
He could just point with a fat brown finger.
He could just look with his big black eyes.

His mother looked up. "I told you about
    the road runner bird. Remember?
I told you about him yesterday.
He can glide through the air.
He can run fast as a horse.
He uses his tail for a brake."

"I know. I know," Pima boy cried.
"Let me tell you. Let me tell you.
Road runner bird kills RATTLESNAKES!"

The day grew hot, so hot, sō hot
    even the shadows crept away to hide.
Mother's fingers working the willow stem
    grew slower and slower.

Mother's answers to her little boy's questions
    grew shorter and shorter.

Little Wants-To-Know was just the same.
He kept on sitting and thinking
    and sitting and talking
    and sitting and saying,
"I want to know."

"I want to know why the mourning dove
    sings a song like a sad bell ringing.
I want to know why the humming bird
    can fly so fast and be so little."

"That's the way they are," his mother said.

Mother took her towel kerchief off
    to let her thick black hair
    shine in the sun.
She bent her head low
    over her work
    getting willow ready
    to weave into a basket.

The little hill of willow splits
    grew higher and higher
    in the lazy shadow
    of the palo verde tree.
The round desert sun
    dropped lower and lower
    below the purple mountains
    beneath the purple sky.

Mother put the willow splits
    in a flour sack bundle.

She tied her white towel kerchief
    over her thick black hair.
She shook the sand
    from her bright blue skirt.

She said, "Come along, Little Wants-To-Know.
Our ki is calling us to come."

Von-Dos-Smai got up slow, so slow.
He walked along beside his mother
So slow, so slow.
Everything he did was slow,
    that is everything
    but sitting-and-thinking
    and thinking-and-talking.

He did not look where he was walking.
    He did not look where he was stepping.
    He got a cactus thorn in his fat, brown toe.

Little brown Pima got a cactus thorn
    in his fat, brown toe
    but he did not cry
    even though it hurt.
He just went limping along
    so slow, so slow,
    and thinking about things
    that he wanted to know.

When they got back to their ki,
    mother took the thorn out.

She wrapped the toe up.
She gave a sweet cake
    made of brown mesquite bean pods
    to her little boy to eat.

Little brown Pima
    sat in his mother's vatho
    sitting and thinking
    and taking slow bites.

Before very long he was talking again.
"Why does the tamerisk tree cry at night
When there is no rain and there is no dew
    and the sand around it is wet every morning,
    it must be crying, what do you think?
Why does the tamerisk tree cry in the night?"

Before his mother could answer that
    his father came walking along the sand trail.
His father came home from the cotton field
    where he had been picking cotton all day.

Father called his Pima call,
    his low, long, lazy Pima call.
Father called his Pima call.
He was home from the cotton field.

Father said, "I am hot and tired."
Father said, "I am hot and thirsty."
Father said, "I am thirsty,
      I want a drink of water."

Mother got water from the olla
    hanging in the vatho.
Mother poured water into the gourd dipper.
Father drank it. It was cool.

Father said, "I am hot and tired."
Father said, "I am hot and hungry."
Father said, "I am hungry,
    I want to eat my supper."

Mother put the supper
    on the table in the vatho.
Mother and father and little brown boy
    ate their good supper.
For awhile all was still.

Then the little boy said
    between bites of cheese
    and bites of bread
    and bites of roasted rabbit
    stuffed with salt bush greens,
"I want to know a lot of things.
I want to know about everything."

"I want to know the reason why
    bees like the mesquite tree
    better than any other kind."

Mother kept on eating.
She did not answer.
She did not look at her little boy.

Father said in a very tired voice,
"Mesquite flowers are sweet.
Bees need sweet food to make their honey."

Mother washed the supper dishes.
She put out the cooking fire.

The world grew darkly purple
    and the heat haze lifted.

Little Pima boy sat by his father
    watching night come over the sand wash,
    watching night come through the dry river.

Mother finished her work.
She sat down by the vatho.
Father and little boy
    sat by the vatho.
The nightingale sang
    in his willow cage.

Father and Mother and little boy Pima
    sat by their arrow weed ki
    in the still, lonesome desert
    where the giant saguaro
    reaches toward the far sky.

An almost cool wind blew the hot day away
    and the stars came out to tell the Pima People
    it was time for bed.

Down on the grass mat where he was lying
 a sleepy boy mumbled,
 "I want to know
 why blue birds are blue
 and coyotes are gray."

Father said, "We have a story about that,
 a story about that,
 about that."
 But he said it so slowly,
 so very, very slowly
 that when he had finished
 saying it,
 Little Von-Dos-Smai was asleep.

The moon looked down.
The stars looked down
 on a tired sleeping father,
 on a tired sleeping mother
 and a little Pima boy
 who all the day had said,
 "Von-Dos-Smai, I want to know.
Von-Dos-Smai, I want to know."

By Ann Nolan Clark

A *PIÑATA* FOR PEPITA

First of all, there wasn't another grandchild named Pepita. It wasn't that she looked different from other grandchildren, except perhaps her eyes were very black and her hair as black as shiny coal. But the thing that made Pepita different was that she could speak English like everyone else in town, and she could speak Spanish, which no one else could speak. . . .

Everything went along very well with Pepita . . . until one day when Grandma Ward asked what she wanted for Christmas. "A piñata," Pepita answered promptly.

IT WAS THE morning of Christmas Eve. In the tiny town of Willowville, which is so small that it isn't even a dot on the map, everyone was up early. For days now, the Christmas tree had stood straight and tall in the center of the town. The tinsel and bright balls sparkled in the sunshine, and by night the many lights twinkled like fireflies.

Although Willowville was such a tiny town, it was one of the best possible places to spend Christmas. The reason was that everyone tried to make everyone else happy—which is a very good way to celebrate Christmas. And instead of having Christmas by themselves, all of the people had it together down around the great tree in the center of the town. So it belonged to everyone, and no one was left out.

But although the tree was finer than usual this year, and the decorations more gay, people were not really happy in Willowville on the morning of Christmas Eve. It was all because of Grandma Ward's granddaughter, five-year-old Pepita. When she came to stay with her grandmother a few weeks earlier, everyone agreed that she must have a very happy Christmas. Of course, grandchildren weren't unusual in Willowville at Christmastime. But this was an unusual grandchild.

First of all, there wasn't another grandchild named Pepita. It wasn't that she looked different from other grandchildren, except perhaps her eyes were very black and her hair as black as shiny coal. But the thing that made Pepita different was that she could speak English like everyone else in town, and she could speak Spanish, which no one else could speak. Her mother, whom everyone remembered as Emily Ward, had taught her English. But her father, who was Mexican, had taught her to speak Spanish. And because she had always lived in Mexico, she had never had a Christmas in Willowville.

Pepita liked to talk, and people liked to talk to her. Sometimes she spoke English, and sometimes she spoke Spanish. Mostly people could guess what she meant, and that made them feel as though they could speak Spanish, too. When anyone said "Good morning," Pepita sometimes said "Good morning," but just as often she said *"Buenos dias,"* which is Spanish for the same thing. When she went into Mr. Green's grocery store and held out her hand with a penny in it and said, "I would like some *dulces,"* Grocer Green knew that she wanted candy. When she thanked him, she might say *"Gracias,"* or she might say "Thank you."

Everything went along very well, with Pepita speaking first one language, then another, until one day when Grandma Ward asked what she wanted for Christmas. "A *piñata,"* Pepita answered promptly.

"Is that a doll?" asked her grandmother.

"No, it's just a *piñata,"* said Pepita.

"How big is it?" asked Grandmother.

"Very big," said Pepita, "but it could be little, too." And her grandmother was indeed confused.

Soon everyone in Willowville began trying to find out what a *piñata* was.

"What color is a *piñata."* asked Mrs. Dean the next time she saw Pepita. *"Muchos* colors," said Pepita. And although Mrs. Dean knew she meant many colors, it didn't help her to know what a *piñata* was.

"Is a *piñata* candy?" asked Grocer Green the next time Pepita went to his store.

"Some of it is," said Pepita.

"What is the rest of it?" he asked.

"Surprises," said Pepita. And Grocer Green was as puzzled as the others.

Then Miss Perkins, the librarian, who knew more words than anyone in Willowville, suddenly had an idea. "I think she means a pineapple," she said. "I am sure that's what it is. *Piñata* sounds like pineapple!" And everyone was happy until they found a book and showed Pepita a picture of a pineapple. She looked at it carefully while everyone waited. Then she said, "Does it have nuts inside, too?" And they were right back where they had started.

When Pepita went to the Christmas party at school, the children asked her about the *piñata*. "Could we play with it, too?" asked Dorothy.

"Yes, you can have all of the dolls in it," promised Pepita generously. And to Freddy she promised all of the automobiles and trucks. "There might be animals, too," she said. And then they all tried to think what could be big or little, with part of it good to eat, have many colors, and have nuts and dolls and animals and automobiles and trucks. And wherever people stopped to talk in Willowville, they asked the same thing— "Have they found a *piñata* for Pepita?" And the answer was always "No."

That was why people were not as happy as usual, for they didn't want Pepita to be disappointed on her Christmas in Willowville.

But shortly after lunch, a very surprising thing happened. The fast train that usually sped through the tiny town with only a hoarse whistle of warning slowed down and actually stopped. Everyone looked to see who would get off. But no one did. Instead, out of the baggage car the brakeman handed down an enormous box, and on it was Pepita's name. Old Mr. Pipps, the station agent, hustled over to Grandma Ward's with the box, and everyone on the street followed him.

When Grandma Ward opened the box, there was a big, bright green and blue parrot. It was made of clay, and was many times larger and ever so much heavier than a real one.

"What is it?" asked Grandma Ward.

"It's a *piñata,*" said Pepita, dancing around the box. "What do you do with it?" everyone asked together.

"You break it," answered Pepita.

They shook their heads, and thought that surely she was wrong about that.

But everyone in Willowville was very excited, and when they stopped to talk, they said, "Did you hear? Pepita has a *piñata.*"

And when Grandma Ward took a better look at the *piñata,* she found a note tucked under the wing of the parrot. It was from Pepita's mother and daddy in Mexico, and they told Grandma Ward just what to do about a *piñata.* And that night, when everyone was through with supper, they hurried over to Grandma Ward's house. There was the *piñata* hanging from a wire strung across the dining room. All the furniture was moved back, and they stood around in a circle.

Grandma Ward tied a scarf around Pepita's eyes, and told her to point to someone. It was a little like playing "Pin the tail on the donkey."

Pepita pointed straight ahead and right at Grocer Green. Grandma Ward took the blind from Pepita's eyes and tied it around Grocer Green's eyes. Then she handed him a long stick and told him to see if he could hit the *piñata*. He drew back the stick as though he were going to bat a ball. He struck first to one side and then the other, and straight ahead. He struck so fast and so hard that the others had to dodge quickly to keep out of his way. He almost hit the window and did hit the wall with a thud, but never once came near the *piñata*.

Miss Perkins tried next. Grandma Ward was ready to tie the blind around her eyes when Miss Perkins remembered that she had on her best pair of spectacles. She took them off and then had the blind tied on. Just then Mr. Pipps started to cross the room and Miss Perkins hit him right on the back, but not very hard. Then, because she was afraid of hitting someone else, she hardly tried at all, and, of course, she didn't hit the *piñata*. Mr. Pipps and Mrs. Dean didn't have any better luck, and neither did any of the others.

Finally it was Dorothy's turn to try to hit the *piñata*. She stood near it and didn't move, even when the stick went swishing through the air without striking anything. She waited a minute, took a firm hold on the stick with both hands, then struck out as hard as she could. There was the sound of tearing paper and breaking pottery, and a shower of many things falling from the *piñata*. Peanuts and candy hit Mr. Pipps' bald head and bounced off. A tiny bright red automobile struck Freddie's shoulder. Soon everyone, young and old, was scrambling to pick up the candy and nuts and toys that fell from the *piñata*. Such laughing and shouting and pushing, until the nuts and toys and every last piece of candy had been picked up. Dorothy snatched the blind from her eyes in time to catch two little dolls.

And when they pulled back the chairs and the sofa and sat down, they looked at Grandma Ward, and all burst into shouts of laughter. For there, perched high in the knot of hair on top of her head was a tiny toy monkey with very bright eyes. She took it out carefully and gave it to Pepita.

After they had eaten all of the good things from the *piñata* and the big chocolate cake which Grandma Ward brought out, they got ready to go home. To some of them Pepita said *"Buenos noches,"* and to some she said "Good night," but it all means the same thing.

And that night Pepita was happy, and Willowville was happy, because there had been a *piñata* for Pepita.

By Delia Goetz

THE MARKET

Lydia is a little Pennsylvania Dutch girl. Her people are Amish. They wear the same kind of clothes that their great-grandparents wore and never think of changing styles.

The Amish people are very industrious and believe that children should learn to work while they are young. Lydia's mother says, "Teach children how to work while they are small, then when they get big they like to work."

EARLY ON SATURDAY morning, Mother come up very quietly to wake Lydia. She took hold of her shoulder very gently and, putting her finger to her lips, said, "Shh! When you come down make shut the door so Nancy sleeps!"

The rain had stopped. The sun wasn't up yet, of course, for this was market day, and that begins early. Then baking must be done for Sunday and all the chores attended to, and the things for the market put in the wagon.

It was very cold again, and Lydia didn't feel much like getting up, especially when she remembered about leaving her hooked mat out in the rain. She had finished it and left it on the seat in the grape arbor when she was called to gather the eggs, yesterday afternoon. In the night she had heard it raining, and knew that her hooked mat on which she had worked so long, would be wet.

"Oh," she thought, "if only I weren't such a scatter-brain like Pop calls me sometimes."

Even though she didn't want to get up, she wouldn't think of not obeying.

Mom had breakfast well on the way, and the kitchen was full of the smell of good things. Malinda was putting a clean white cloth over a basket. The basket was filled with rolls of fresh butter and crocks of smear-case. The end of the table was loaded with things to go in the back of the wagon.

Pop came in and hung his hat on the peg. "Well, Lyddy," he said, and whisked her up off the floor.

Lydia couldn't bear to tell him that she couldn't go

after all, because she had been so "shusselie," and had left her mat out in the rain. Before she could think what to tell him, Pop said, "I guess your mat makes dry, think, Mom? When we come home, I go by the arbor to see if Malinda makes the chicken house door fast. The lantern makes a light on your mat, Lyddy; it lies out on the bench still. So, I thinks, 'That Lyddy, she's a shussle!' But I bring in the mat and make dry by the stove."

"Oh, Pop!" Lydia wriggled down and ran to the stove room, where she found the mat all safe. When she brought it to the light her heart sank! Sure enough, the pink had run into the lighter pink in the middle of the roses so that they looked smudgy. Now she could never sell it, even if Pop did take her to market; Mom and Malinda came to look too.

Mom said, "Yes, well," and went back to the stove to her cooking.

Malinda said, "You know, I like it so. It looks more soft that way!"

Pop just stood a minute, looking at the mat and then at poor Lydia, who was feeling pretty sorry just then. When would she ever get to Lancaster, and how could she ever buy Mom's present now?

"Nice it looks, Lyddy, and makes good and warm by your bed, ain't? The edge iss not so straight anyways. But you *finish,* so!" Pop's eyes twinkled at Lydia.

"You mean I can *go?*"

"Sure! But make quick! Look, by the clock I should be gone already." They all sat down and ate breakfast.

Mother didn't go to market because she had too

many other things to do, and Malinda had to stay home and help too.

Lydia scurried up the stairs and changed her apron and put on her bonnet and shawl. She was so excited she almost forgot to be sorry about the mat.

By the time she came down the things were packed in the wagon and Pop was ready to start. It was daylight, and the sun was just beginning to show over the blue hills. Just as old Bess started out of the yard Mom called out the door, "Stop by Hertzler's mill, don't forget!"

Lydia sat close to Father on the seat of the Germantown wagon. It was chilly riding through the mists that lay in the low places, but oh, it was fun to be going to Lancaster! And perhaps she could make another mat— quickly this time—and sell it to buy Mom's present.

They went the long way round to reach the highway so they could stop at Lavinia's for her apple butter. Pop always helped Lavinia take her things to market.

Henner didn't have much to say, and Lydia was thinking of all the things she would see in Lancaster, so there was no sound but the clop-clop of Bessie's feet as they rode along and the early morning sounds of the country.

By the time Henner and Lydia had reached Lancaster there were many wagons and carriages and cars on the road, and many greetings were exchanged. They had to find a place for the market wagon and get the things onto the counters in the stall.

The big Lancaster market has rows and rows of stalls, or little booths with counters, where the farmers bring all kinds of things to sell. Henner engages his for half a day every two weeks on Saturday.

Lydia arranged the chickens in neat rows. They were all cleaned and ready to cook. Then she put the little pots of cheese and pots of butter in rows. Mother had sent a few jars of homemade pickles and jellies, too, and Lydia arranged the jars of Lavinia's apple butter. She had some parsley that she tucked in here and there. It all looked so delicious!

People began to come in to buy, and everybody had a smile for Lydia.

Pop let Lydia do most of the selling. She was having a wonderful time! Pop wrapped up the packages, but he let Lydia take the money and helped her make change. She was so busy that she hardly had time to say anything to Anna Stauffer, who was in the next stall. Anna was busy too. She had lebkuchen and fastnachts to sell.

Lydia began to get hungry. She had been so excited she hadn't eaten enough breakfast. Pop said, "Not much left to sell—I stay by the apple butter awhile. You go by Jacob Zook's store and get you something. I'll come along. Here! This is for a smart helper."

He handed Lydia twenty-five cents! She said, "Ooh!"

That was more money than Lydia had ever had before! Now she could buy a present for Mom.

Lydia started out in the direction Pop had told her to go. She went gaily up one aisle of the market past stalls of fruits and vegetables, and down another, past stalls piled high with cheeses. She passed stalls filled with dressed turkeys and chickens and ducks, and counters loaded with good homemade things like her mother makes.

There were so many women with market baskets on their arms that Lydia could hardly manage to get through to the door. She came out on the street, but it didn't look just as she expected it would! She had gone out the back door instead of the front!

Lydia looked up and down the street—it really was just an alley—then decided she was going the right way, so she hurried to the corner, where she saw many people passing. She was sure this must be the street where Jacob Zook's lunch place was. Father had told her it was just out the door and around the corner.

There were many fascinating things in the shop windows, and Lydia stopped to look in *every* one.

One window was filled with toys such as Lydia never had seen. Another window was in a hardware store, and was filled with tools of all kinds. She had no use for saws and hammers and files and knives, but they were arranged in such an interesting way that she had to stop and look at them. One window had a display of food. Not home-made food—*"boughten"* food!

The food made her hungry again, and she began to look around for Jacob Zook's store. It was *no*where to be seen! Lydia turned and turned, she looked and *looked,* but at every turn she became more confused.

She walked along a little farther, but no sign could she see that said, "Jacob Zook, Quick Lunch." What is more, she couldn't see the market anywhere, and not a soul she had ever seen before.

Lydia's chin began to quiver. She didn't want to cry, but she felt *very* much alone. The people went hurrying by as if they knew just where they were going. They didn't even see a lonely little girl in a blue dress and a black bonnet.

Suddenly she heard, "Ya, vell, *so here* you are, already!"

She looked up, and *there* was Pop! Never had she been so glad to see him. Never had he looked so big and strong. Lydia took hold of his hand and held on tight. Pop led her around a corner, and *there* was Jacob Zook's. It had been right there all the time!

"Now, up you go!" Pop lifted Lydia up onto the high stool. Lydia sighed with delight. She was really going to have a "store" dinner. And at the end, ice cream, maybe!

Jacob said, "Ach, your Lyddy, Henner, ain't? She gets a big girl, now!"

Henner joked with Jacob, and they talked about the weather, about the crops, about everything.

Lydia finished eating and wished they could go to look in the stores, or maybe "shuss" through some bargains. Perhaps she could find a present for Mom.

Henner finished and paid for his dinner and Lydia's. Lydia looked up as her father took her hand and they left Jacob Zook's. "Could I maybe buy a present for Mom?"

"Ya, a piece of goods gives a nice present for Mom, ain't? Let's go by Himmelreich's."

Lydia skipped along by Pop's side. Now she was happy.

They picked out a piece of the very finest lawn for Mom to use for her caps, and Lyddy's twenty-five cents helped to pay for it. Then they went back to the market-place, got into the wagon and started home.

By Marguerite de Angeli

ARAMINTA AND THE GOAT

Now Araminta knew all about the country this time.
."I know where water comes from," she said. "I know
where my food comes from. I know how mules behave.
I know where to find playthings. I know what pigs like
to eat. BUT," puzzled Araminta, "I wonder how Santa
Claus comes in the country."

THE NEXT TIME Araminta went to visit Gran'ma in
the country, it was Christmas Eve. When she got off the
train at Tuskegee, rain was pouring down. Araminta
was glad she had her raincoat and her rain hat and her
umbrella with her.

Gran'pa was standing on the station platform waiting
for her, and just beyond was Maude hitched to the

wagon. Gran'pa had on his raincoat too, and big rubber boots. The wagon had an umbrella. It was big and covered the seat where Araminta and Gran'pa sat.

But poor Maude didn't have a raincoat and she didn't have big rubber boots and she didn't have an umbrella. So she trotted fast to get home out of the wet.

The rain stopped and the sun came out before they got to Gran'ma's.

"Well," said Gran'pa, "we won't need this umbrella any more." And he let it down and put it under the seat. But Araminta kept her raincoat and her rain hat on, because they were brand new and she wanted to show them to Gran'ma.

They were glad that Maude didn't seem to know the sun was shining, for she kept right on trotting and didn't stop for anything. Else they never *would* have gotten to Gran'ma's so quickly.

Now Araminta knew all about what happens in the country this time.

"I know where water comes from," she said. "I know where my food comes from. I know how mules behave. I know where to find playthings. I know what pigs like to eat. BUT," puzzled Araminta, "I wonder how Santa Claus comes in the country."

"You'll find out tomorrow morning," said Gran'ma. "He's coming tonight."

Araminta didn't see how she could possibly wait until morning. But she had it to do. Santa Claus never comes until Christmas, so there was nothing she could do about *that*.

She ran into the living room to look for the Christmas

tree. There it was, standing in the corner next to the fire-place—a little green pine tree.

"It doesn't have any trimmings," Araminta told Gran'ma, shaking her head. "A pine tree in the old woods looks very nice just plain green, but a Christmas tree is supposed to have trimmings."

"Well, so it is," said Gran'ma and Gran'pa. "We hadn't thought of that."

There wasn't a store, as you remember, where they could buy any trimming. And you may be sure there weren't any gold tinsel or red balls growing in the ground.

"We *have* to have trimmings or Santa Claus won't think we're expecting him," said Araminta.

"But I don't believe we can get any now," said Gran'pa, rubbing his nose.

"We'll just find some," said Gran'ma, "and fool you."

So they both began to look. Gran'ma looked inside the house to see what she could find. Araminta looked outside to see what she could find.

Under the pine tree that grew in the front of the house, Araminta found some pine cones. Under the mag-nolia tree that grew at the back of the house, Araminta found some seed-pods. Then she looked under the back porch, and you'll never guess what she saw there. Cans of paint! There was red paint that Gran'pa had used to paint the roof last summer. There was yellow paint that Gran'ma had used to paint the front porch chairs. There was silver paint that they both had used to paint the kitchen stove. So then Araminta knew where the trim-ming for the Christmas tree was coming from.

But before she started to paint the pine cones and magnolia pods, she peeped into the house to see if Gran'ma had found anything.

"Of all things," said Araminta, "what kind of trimming is *that?*" For Gran'ma was cooking something on the stove. Araminta could hear it. Only instead of hearing: "Bubble, bubble," or "Siss, siss" or "Spatter, spatter," she heard: "Pop, pop, pop."

"Pop corn," announced Gran'ma, "to string for the tree."

They hadn't quite finished tying the red and yellow and silver pine cones on the tree; they hadn't quite finished draping the pop corn strings; they hadn't QUITE finished hanging the yellow and silver and red magnolia pods, when they heard Gran'pa coming.

"Surprise!" yelled Araminta, as she closed the door tight so he couldn't get in.

"Let me in," called Gran'pa. "I don't believe you have any trimming for that tree."

"Believe what you want to believe," said Gran'ma. "But you don't see this tree until Christmas morning."

Suddenly, Araminta and her gran'ma couldn't see the tree very well themselves. They looked out the window and sure enough it was getting dark.

Araminta knew what that meant. It meant that it was time for her supper and then it was time to go to bed; and then it was time to go to sleep. And then it would be time to wake up. And THEN—SANTA CLAUS!

So that's what she did. She ate her supper. She went to bed. She went to sleep. And then—

"Of all things," said Araminta, "it's morning." So

she jumped out of bed and she patted in her bare feet to the living room. There was the tree decorated with beautiful red and yellow and silver cones. There it was decorated with beautiful white pop corn chains. But under the tree there was nothing at all for Araminta. Nothing at all. She thought maybe Santa Claus had played a joke on her, so she looked under the chairs; she looked under the table; she even looked under the rug. But there was nothing for Araminta.

"Well," said Araminta, very sadly, "I guess Santa Claus doesn't know how to come to the country."

But Gran'ma was standing in the doorway, and she said: "Listen!" Araminta listened and she heard a funny noise. It went like this: "Maa-a-a, Maa-a-a."

"Of all things," said Araminta, "what kind of a noise is *that?*"

"Look!" said Gran'ma. Araminta ran to the window and looked out. Now I *know* you can't guess what she saw. A goat! A little white and black goat!

Araminta could hardly wait to get her bedroom slippers on before she ran out to the back porch to see.

"I found her in the shed with Maude," said Gran'pa. "I can't imagine how she got there."

"Of all things," said Araminta, as she rubbed her cheek against the goat's nose. "What a funny place to leave my Christmas gift!"

"BUT," puzzled Araminta, "I wonder how Santa Claus *does* come in the country?"

And she never did find out, either.

When Araminta took Goat for a walk she tied a string around his neck and led him along beside her. He was just a baby goat so he didn't know how to butt. But he *did* know how to kick up his heels. And that's just what he did.

"Stop that kicking up your heels," said Araminta. "You'll get all worn out."

Araminta didn't want Goat to get all worn out, because they were going to take a walk. They were going to walk to the very end of the cotton field—far, far away from the back yard and the magnolia tree and Gran'ma. They were going to visit a boy named John George Jerome Anthony.

Goat walked along beside Araminta and when he forgot what he had been told, he'd kick up his heels. He couldn't remember very well, either. He kicked up his heels so much that Araminta had to walk with one hand holding the string, and the other hand holding Goat down behind.

"That's better," said Araminta. "Now you'll remember what I told you about kicking."

And soon they were at the end of the cotton field.

"Tony! Tony!" called Araminta. For that, as you remember, was what she called John George Jerome Anthony when she was in a hurry.

"Hey," called Tony. "Look what Santa Claus brought me!"

"Look what Santa Claus brought me!" said Araminta.

"Maa-a-a-a," said Araminta's Christmas gift.

"Meow, Meow," said Jerome Anthony's Christmas gift. For Santa Claus had brought Jerome Anthony a kitten—a little white and yellow kitten.

"Bring your goat and climb over the fence," invited Jerome Anthony.

"Goat can kick up his heels," said Araminta, shaking her head. "But he doesn't know how to butt, and he certainly doesn't know how to climb fences."

"Oh, I hadn't thought of that," said Jerome Anthony. "But Cat and I can climb a fence."

And before you could wiggle your nose, there was Cat rubbing against Goat's leg. For that's the way cats say "Howdy."

Goat reached down and brushed Cat very gently with his whiskers. For that's the way goats say "Howdy."

"Now we know each other," said Araminta, "what would be a good thing to do?"

"If we just walk along," said Jerome Anthony, "maybe my Cat will think of something to do."

"If we just walk along," said Araminta, "maybe my Goat will think of something to do."

So they just walked along.

Cat began running in and out between the cotton stalks. That seemed fun, so they all began running in and out between the cotton stalks.

But every time they started to run, Goat bumped into the stalks and got his shiny white and black sides dirty.

"This will never do," said Araminta. So they all stopped running in and out between the cotton stalks.

Goat began kicking up his heels. That seemed fun, so they all began kicking up their heels.

But every time they kicked up their heels, Cat turned somersaults and got her shiny white and yellow back dirty.

"This will never do," said Jerome Anthony. So they all stopped kicking up their heels.

In a jiffy, there they were at the other end of the cotton field. And there was the back yard and the magnolia tree and Gran'ma.

"I'm all worn out," said Araminta, as she sat down on the back steps.

"I'm tired, myself," said Jerome Anthony, as he sat beside her.

But Cat and Goat weren't all worn out.

Cat sniffed in the grass and Goat sniffed in the grass.

Cat found a little black bug and patted it with her paw. Goat found a little green bug and brushed it very gently with his whiskers.

Cat found a board leaning against Maude's shed, and climbed up. Goat saw the board leaning against Maude's shed and *he* climbed up!

When Jerome Anthony and Araminta were through resting, they looked and what did they see on top of Maude's shed but a white and yellow kitten and a white and black goat!

"This will never do," said Jerome Anthony. "Get down from there, Cat."

So Cat gave a little jump and there she was on the grass beside Jerome Anthony. Cats never get hurt when they jump.

"This will never do," said Araminta. "Get down from there, Goat."

Goat walked very carefully to the edge of the roof and looked over. But he stood still. Goats *do* get hurt when they jump.

"Get down from there, Goat!" called Araminta again.

Goat wiggled his ears, but he stood still.

"Get down from there, Goat!" called Jerome Anthony this time.

Goat lifted his stumpy tail, but he stood still.

"How ever can we get that goat down?" asked Araminta.

"We'll just have to go up and bring him down," said Jerome Anthony.

There didn't seem to be any other way. Goats don't always do what you tell them to do.

So Jerome Anthony, who was an excellent climber, went up the board and on to the roof of the shed. Araminta, who was just a so-so climber, went half-way up the board. Then Jerome Anthony took hold of the back of Goat and PUSHED—

And Araminta took hold of the front of Goat and PULLED—

And suddenly—

There was Araminta on the ground. There was Goat on top of Araminta. There was Jerome Anthony on top of Goat!

"Whew!" said Araminta, getting up. "I'm all worn out."

"Whew!" said Jerome Anthony, brushing his knees. "I'm tired myself."

But Cat kept running in the grass. And Goat kept kicking up his heels.

By Eva Knox Evans

BENJIE'S HAT

Benjie was a little Quaker boy, and his home was in North Carolina, where a great many other Quakers lived, though they did not call themselves Quakers, but Friends. *Which is a very warm and beautiful word, when you stop to think about it.*

SOMETIMES IT TAKES a boy years and years of steady growing to become big enough and tall enough to match the name that his parents gave him.

That is how it was with Benjie. For although he had been busily growing for eight years, the name of Benjamin Bartholomew Barnett was still much too large for him. So he was called Benjie, except in very serious moments.

Benjie was a little Quaker boy, and his home was in North Carolina, where a great many other Quakers lived, though they did not call themselves Quakers, but *Friends*. Which is a very warm and beautiful word, when you stop to think about it.

In all his eight years, Benjie had never been anywhere except over into the next county to visit his grandmother, Judith Cox. But in spite of never having traveled, he was a very happy boy. Only—sometimes he lost his temper and sulked because his two older brothers, Milo and Matthew, seemed to think that he was still just a baby, and left him to play with his sisters, Hannah, who was a fat little girl with fat flaxen braids, and Narcissa Clementina, who was a fatter little girl, with fatter and more flaxen braids. And although Benjie loved Hannah and Narcissa Clementina, he himself had left off wearing skirts years ago. He was also of the opinion that this world is a man's world, and that he was well on the way toward being a man himself.

One day in September a neighbor of Grandmother's came riding to Randolph County, where Benjie lived. His name was Peter Kersey, and he was an Elder of the Deep River Monthly Meeting, over in Guilford County, where Grandmother lived. He had come on business of his own, but he stopped at Benjie's house, and had dinner there, and he left a letter from Grandmother. Although this letter was addressed to the whole family, Benjie heard and remembered only one amazing paragraph.

"I want Benjie to come and spend the winter with me," wrote Grandmother. "The schoolhouse is only a mile through the woods, so that it will be right smart easier for him here than at home. Tell him that I am lonely since his grandfather died, and that I need a manbody to look after me and keep me company."

"A manbody!"

Benjie looked at Milo and Matthew. And then he threw out his chest, and stiffened his neck and thrust his hands in his pockets. For Milo and Matthew were staring at him in quite a surprised manner, as if to say, "Look here! Who's *this* Grandmother is calling a 'manbody'? Surely not little Benjie!"

And Milo, who was thirteen, said, *"I* could go, Mother."

And Matthew, who was eleven, said, "Maybe she meant *me,* Mother."

But Mother said, "No, it's Benjie Grandmother wants, and it's Benjie who shall go."

So perhaps it is not surprising that Benjie felt there was no one in all of North Carolina quite as important as Benjamin Bartholomew Barnett. Unless it might be the Governor. But—"a manbody"! Well, wasn't he eight years old now? Of *course* he could look after Grandmother!

So the very next morning, quite early, Benjie dressed himself for the journey to Guilford County. He put on the tow shirt and breeches that Mother had woven from the coarse part of the flax and then tailored into a neat suit. He put on the shoes and stockings that in the summer time he wore only to Meeting. And after breakfast he put on the round straw hat that had first been Milo's, and then Matthew's, and now had descended to Benjie.

It had been a store hat, and Milo had been extremely proud of it. Matthew had been a little less proud of it, and Benjie was not proud of it at all. He wore it without thinking much about it, though sometimes it did occur to him that it would be nice to have a hat that had never belonged to any one else. But you must endure hand-me-downs, if you happen to be the third boy in the family.

During the hat's descent from brother to brother, its edges had become torn and frayed, but Mother had bound them very neatly all around with a strip of gray flannel. There was a torn place in the crown, too, which she had darned with knitting yarn into a kind of design, just as if it were intended to be that way. This morning, preparing to go to Grandmother's, Benjie was too excited to give the hat a thought.

The time came to depart. Benjie's father slung Peter Kersey's saddle-bags over the horse's saddle, for Peter kindly consented to have Benjie's few belongings packed into one of the bags. Then Benjie was hoisted up. Benjie's mother thought her son looked very small indeed behind Peter's broad back. Her lips trembled as she waved farewell, and Benjie, much to his surprise, suddenly felt as if he might be going to cry if Peter didn't hurry off at once. Which of course would have been very strange behavior for "a manbody".

So Peter Kersey and Benjamin Bartholomew Barnett rode away to Guilford County, to Grandmother's house.

Benjie liked living at Grandmother's from the moment of his arrival. In the first place he loved his grandmother. In the second place, in Grandmother's house he was the only boy. He was important and not just Milo and Matthew's little brother. Grandmother treated him as if she really considered him "a manbody", or at least well on the way.

In the third place, out of the iron pots slung over the hearth fire, and from the big outdoor oven on baking days, there came the most savory and delicious foods, for Grandmother was as famous for her cooking as she was for her thrifty ways. The molasses cookies were even bigger and browner and better than Benjie remembered.

Grandmother lived in a comfortable old house built of great, hand-hewn timbers. The oaken floors were always well scrubbed, the hand woven coverlets and rugs always bright, the pewter always gleaming, and Grandmother herself, in kerchief and cap, as neat as a plump little sparrow.

Though Grandmother lived in great comfort on her fertile farm, she was very careful and thrifty. People respected her for it, too, but sometimes they would smile, and say, "as thrifty as Friend Judith Cox." Grandmother had worn her best bonnet to Meeting every First Day for twelve years, but it was just as stiff and neat as it was the day she had carried it home from the bonnetmaker's so long ago. Grandmother expected it to last her the remainder of her days. Her best silk dress and her second-best delaine were folded away in old linen when she wasn't wearing one or the other of them. Her shawls had not a hole in them. Her white kerchiefs lasted an amazingly long time. In the house there were chests and boxes and barrels and old trunks full of things Grandmother would never dream of casting aside. She considered it a grievous sin to throw even a pin away, and in her sewing box there was a certain needle for which she had a great attachment. She showed it to Benjie. "I have been using this same needle for eight years! I made one of thy baby dresses with it." And she added:

"Thee must always be careful of what thee has, Benjie. 'Wilful waste, woeful want.' If thee will think upon that, thee will understand what it means. Waste is an abomination in the sight of the Lord."

In the evenings, while Grandmother knitted busily, she and Benjie would play riddles and guessing games, and Grandmother would tell stories. Benjie would read his lessons to Grandmother, too. She always seemed to enjoy them much better than he did. Afterward Grandmother would read a chapter from the big Bible. Then early to bed, and the long, long night of sleep.

So Benjie was a happy boy, and felt sure that his winter with Grandmother was going to be a great success.

"Am I looking after thee and keeping thee company, like thee said in thy letter, Grandmother?" asked Benjie.

"Thee is very satisfactory," answered Grandmother. "Thee is a regular little manbody."

Every First Day, which was Sunday, Hamish hitched the horse to the carriage. Grandmother put on her best bonnet and one of her good dresses and her softest, finest kerchief. Benjie cleaned his shoes and scrubbed his cheeks and put on his tow suit and the straw hat bound round with the gray flannel. He and Grandmother climbed into the carriage. Grandmother took up the reins, clicked to the horse, and off they went to Meeting.

When they arrived at the meeting-house, Grandmother patted Benjie's shoulder, and said, "Now thee be a good boy, Grandson," which was rather unnecessary, as Benjie behaved himself very well indeed. He may have squirmed a little when his feet went to sleep, or when the day was warm and his tow breeches scratched him, but that was all.

Then he and Grandmother parted, for Grandmother must sit on the women's side of the meeting-house with the women and girls, and Benjie must sit with the men on the men's side. He felt very grown-up sitting there without his father and Milo and Matthew, as at home, and for several First Days this was enough to keep Benjie completely satisfied throughout the long silent meeting. For when Benjie was a little boy, the Friends had no music at their religious services, and only rarely did they have preaching. Children must "wait in stillness upon the Lord," as their elders did, and receive comfort and strength through silent meditation and prayer.

On a certain October morning Benjie and Grandmother went to Meeting. There never was a more perfect day. The long needles of the pines glittered in the golden sunlight. The red and golden leaves fluttered lazily down from the trees that were all red and golden. Through the open windows of the meeting-house Benjie could hear the horses moving lazily and stamping at their hitching-racks. From afar came the whistle of quail. For the first time Benjie felt fidgety. The coarse stuff of his clothing made him itch, and although no one paid him any attention, he knew that he must not scratch. The world outside seemed to be saying, "Come out, Benjie. Come out and play in the golden morning."

Benjie kept hearing this soft and golden voice, and as there seemed no probability of the Meeting ever coming to an end, and as the prickles on his legs seemed to be getting worse, he arose at last from his place, very softly. He squeezed past several large knees, whose owners looked at him gravely from under their broad hats. But Benjie knew that they scarcely saw him, for their thoughts were far removed from worldly things. He tiptoed down the aisle of the men's side and out into the meeting-house grounds.

The stillness outside was almost as deep as it had been in the meeting-house, a charmed and golden stillness, and Benjie, now that he had come, scarcely knew what to do with himself. It was very queer, but he didn't itch a bit any more. He looked about and felt lonely. The world seemed an empty golden shell, with no one in it but the horses and a stranger named Benjamin Bartholomew Barnett. Oh, dear, what ever made him come? How shocked and sorry Grandmother would be if she knew he had run away from Meeting! A little lump came into Benjie's throat when he thought of Grandmother, whom he loved so much, and who loved him. Forlornly he wandered to the fence and began to stroke the noses of the horses, since there was no joy for him in the lovely day, after all. He gathered handfuls of grass for them. They nosed him eagerly.

And then a most surprising thing happened. For all

of a sudden Benjie heard a loud crunching noise. His head was jerked violently sidewise. A damp breath blew through his hair, and he looked up to see an old white horse at his shoulder. And he had Benjie's hat in his mouth. He was chewing with all his might and main. He was chewing up Benjie's hat!

"Ow!" cried Benjie. "Gimme my hat!" He reached up as far as he could and began tugging at the object that was no longer a hat, but a crushed and mangled fragment. A long strip of gray flannel hung from the horse's mouth. Bits of straw fell to the ground. The hat was gone, all but one little piece in Benjie's hand—the hat that had been a fine store hat, the hat that had once been Milo's pride, that had been worn less proudly by Matthew, and was, until a moment ago, Benjie's only hat.

Oh, the mean old horse! The meanest old horse in the world! What could Benjie do? He couldn't slip back into Meeting and sit with uncovered head. That was unthinkable, for the Friends wore their hats throughout the Meeting. What would Grandmother say when she found that Benjie had not only "played hooky" from Meeting, but had lost his hat as well? "Wilful waste, woeful want," that's what Grandmother would say. Oh, she would think him a very bad boy! Well, he was, although he hadn't really meant to be. Losing his hat was a punishment for stealing away from Meeting. At last Benjie climbed up into Grandmother's carriage, with the one remnant of his hat in his hand, and made himself as small as possible.

Presently the people began coming slowly out of the

meeting-house, looking refreshed and calm and cheerful. They shook hands with each other in the autumn sunshine. There was a pleasant hum of talk.

Benjie screwed himself into a tighter knot on the carriage seat, but kept a weather eye open for Grandmother.' Yes, there she was! Beloved Grandmother, folded so neatly into her shawl, her face placid and rosy in its neat frame of bonnet. There! She was looking for him! Oh, dear! Benjie turned his head away sadly. He couldn't bear to see Grandmother looking for the *good* boy that should have come out of the meeting-house with all the good people when Meeting broke.

And then he heard the soft rustle of Grandmother's skirts. He felt her near him.

"Why, Benjie-boy!" she cried. "Is thee ill? Did thee have to leave the Meeting?"

"No, Grandmother," answered Benjie. He turned and looked at her, full of misery. "I didn't have to leave. Just see what happened, Grandmother." He held out the piece of straw. "An old horse chewed up my hat!"

"Thy hat! Benjie! Does thee mean to say that a horse reached into the meeting-house and took the very hat off thy head? Never did I hear the like!" And as Grandmother climbed into the carriage she looked about indignantly as if to say, "Where is that rude creature that ate the hat off the grandson of Judith Cox?"

"Oh, no, Grandmother!" Benjie could not help smiling a little at the impossible picture that Grandmother had imagined. Nothing short of a giraffe could have reached into the meeting-house.

"No, Grandmother," he went on. "I did leave Meeting. It's a nice day, and my pants scratched me, and my feet were going to sleep, and before I thought what I was doing, I was walking out of Meeting."

"Benjamin Bartholomew Barnett!" exclaimed Grandmother. "Thee left Meeting just because thee was fidgety?"

"But I didn't have a bit good time, Grandmother!" cried Benjie hastily. "I wished and wished I hadn't come. And then the old horse grabbed my hat. If he'd just waited a minute I'd have given him some nice grass. I was taking turns feeding them all grass. But he couldn't wait—the old greedy!"

"A just punishment for thee, Benjie," declared Grandmother. "Now thee has no hat. And thee sinned besides." Grandmother shook her head sorrowfully.

"Maybe next year the hat would've been too small for me, Grandmother," suggested Benjie.

"That does not alter the situation, Grandson. Some other boy could have worn it."

The remainder of the ride home was very quiet. Dinner was very quiet. But later, while Benjie leaned against Grandmother's chair, and stroked Jerushy's soft old feathers, Grandmother told him stories. She told him of his great-grandfather, whose home had been on Nantucket Island, but who had spent most of his life at sea, for he had been a whaling master. "A very good man," said Grandmother. "He held a silent meeting on his ship every First and Fourth Days, just as if he were in the meeting-house at home." She told Benjie of his great-uncle, who had once lain in prison for many weeks, because he refused to bear arms against his fellowman.

She spoke of Benjie's great-great-grandfather, who had lived in England before sailing to America as a young man, and who had been able to tell his children of the days when George Fox, the great founder of the Society of Friends, used to come to his father's house in that English village where he lived as a boy.

And Grandmother said, "The good people before thee were God-fearing people. *They* had no worldly thoughts at Meeting. None of them would ever have strayed away from Meeting at the slightest excuse, as thee did, Benjamin."

And she looked at Benjie, and Benjie looked at her. It was a long moment, and when it was over, it seemed that Benjie and his grandmother loved each other even more than ever. And Grandmother reached into her deep pocket, and brought forth a handful of peanuts, and she and Benjie broke them and ate them.

After supper, and six o'clock, when First Day was over, and Benjie was getting ready for bed, he saw Grandmother's eyes begin to twinkle. Her rosy face grew rosier. She held her apron up to her mouth, and she began to shake all over. Grandmother was laughing! It made Benjie laugh to see Grandmother laughing so hard. And when she had calmed down and wiped her eyes, and tucked Benjie into bed, she looked down at him, and she said, "Don't thee be thinking that I considered it funny of thee to run away from Meeting, Benjamin Bartholomew Barnett. It's just the idea of that old horse chewing up thy hat. All of a sudden it struck my funny bone."

By Mabel Leigh Hunt

THERESA FOLLOWS THE CROPS

Perched on the roof of the old car were a scraggly goat, a chicken coop, and ten-year-old Theresa. Inside were Papa, Mama, Grandma and her two brothers. On the sides were pots and pans, bedding and odds and ends of furniture and tools. Wherever there was a harvest, there was the Gomez family.

FROM THE TOP of an old rattly car, came a soft Mexican voice singing a made-up tune to the motion of the lurching machine:

> "In our old Chevrolita
>   All tumbled down and old,
>   From Montebello California to
>   Yakima we go.

January to June,
June to January!
In our old Chevrolita
Papa, Mama, Grandma,
Jose, Alberto, Theresa,
We all follow the fruit
Follow the fruit!
Oh, the yellow oranges,
Oh, the sweet cantaloupes!
Oh, the tomato so red,
The cotton so white,
The grapes so scented,
And the berries like wine!
Apples, peaches, pears and prunes,
Apricots and cherries.
Chopping lettuce, topping beets,
Picking, planting, harvesting
With almost never a roof over our heads,
We follow the crops in our old Chevrolita."

The song with no particular tune or rhyme was made up of bits of Theresa Gomez's life. Perched on the roof of the old car were a scraggly goat, a chicken coop and ten-year-old Theresa. Inside were Papa, Mama, Grandma and her two brothers. On the sides were pots and pans, bedding and odds and ends of furniture and tools. Wherever there was a harvest, there was the Gomez family. They and thousands like them traveled like that from California to Washington. The tune and words that Theresa invented were sad because what Theresa wanted more than anything in the world was to live in a house that never moved, a white house with flowers and grass around it. She wanted to go to school from that house that never moved, dressed in a real dress with big, splashy flowers printed over it.

Her song and dream were broken into by a voice. "There is that Mexican family. Now, Betty, you must keep away from them if they camp at the same place we do."

Theresa looked at the passing car. It, too, carried a family that followed the crops, but their car was quite new, with pots, pans and bedding in a trailer behind. Inside was a little girl about Theresa's age with yellow hair and fair skin. She was dressed in a faded, clean dress with a pattern of poppies all over it. Theresa turned her back on the road. Her face flushed. It was like this wherever they went. Betty or Mary or Peggy would never talk with her. She remembered the day she had gone to an American school. Papa had not wanted her to go. He had been angry that she couldn't find work in the orchard. The children had run away from her, too. How could Theresa tell the teacher how long she would be there? She was cross when she answered, "I don't know, we follow the crops." And the children had laughed. Theresa never went back.

Theresa's pleasant dream was over. There were the orchards on both sides. The cars along the road were turning in at a gate. From her perch on top of the car Theresa could see horrid wooden barracks where the families were supposed to live. No flowers and no white —only ugly, long wooden shelters.

Papa signed at the office for his family of workers, and then began building a shelter. Papa would not live in barracks. He found a spot near a tree and with two

big packing cases and long, tangled vines made a *ramada,*
or shelter, for the Gomezes. In an hour or two there
were clothes drying on the branches, corn cakes on the
outdoor stove and boxes standing around for chairs.

From somewhere Theresa heard a familiar voice.
"Those Mexicans are right alongside of us, Betty. Remember what I said." Theresa's face burned.

That afternoon Theresa sat holding Alberto in her
arms, looking in terror at his red spotted face and chest.
Everyone was in the orchard picking fruit. Theresa had
tied a rag around Alberto's waist to keep the disease
from spreading, as her grandmother had told her to do,
but Mrs. Corsi, their Italian neighbor, had wandered
toward her from the barracks and called out, "Scarlatina? Bambino sick? I getta lady. She fix the bambino."

Theresa sat with tears in her eyes; tears for the baby
and tears for herself. The remarks that Betty's mother
had made hurt and added to her fright about Alberto.
She was afraid they would all lose their jobs if sickness
were discovered and then they would be hungry. Theresa
squeezed Alberto until he whimpered and scowled at
the lady in white who soon appeared.

"What is this for?" the nurse asked as she took Alberto from Theresa and unwound the rag from the
baby's body. Theresa shook her head but did not answer.
She was sure the nurse would laugh. But the nurse did
not laugh when Theresa finally told her, simply patted
her hand and smiled.

"Is Alberto sick with scarlatina?" Theresa asked.
"Mrs. Corsi says yes."

"No, these spots are hives. Maybe it's his food. Does he eat what you do?" the nurse asked. Theresa shook her head for yes. She became shy and frightened. She shooed away the flies while she watched the nurse's strong fingers. Then she picked up a little bottle with bright red stain in it marked "Mercurochrome."

"Do you go to school here?" the nurse asked as she began to bathe the baby.

"No, we just came today. Is there school?" Theresa's face grew serious. "Americans don't like me in school. I don't want to go."

"Look here, there is a school not far from this orchard. You know there is a nursery in the camp for babies like Alberto. Suppose you get a clean dress, fix your hair and go to school tomorrow," the nurse said.

Just then Theresa's father came up and the nurse said to him, "You know children of Theresa's age must be in school. She is too small to work in the orchard and you will be here for six weeks." That made Papa very angry.

Hot and cold with joy and fear Theresa looked at the bottle in her hand and an idea came to her. She asked if she might keep it. The nurse nodded and Theresa hid the bottle in her blouse.

Papa would not talk with Theresa as she started getting supper. Then she washed her dress of bleached flour sacks. Meanwhile the whole family had assembled. Papa was shrieking out the news to them. Why should Theresa go to school? The Americans didn't really want her and soon she would be old enough to work in the orchards. Now everybody could hear. Theresa heard Betty's mother say, "The Mexicans are at it again. It's a wonder they don't kill each other."

Theresa just waited until it was quieter and then said, "Nurse says it's the law and I am going tomorrow." They grumbled as they ate their supper and Papa did not play on the little guitar which went with him everywhere.

Theresa was so excited she couldn't sit still. Maybe in this school the children would be nice to her. She knew how to dance and sing. She knew lots of Mexican songs. She had even cut out a picture of the great Diego Rivera's paintings from a paper she had found. She had tried to copy them. Maybe, oh maybe, the Americanos would like what she could do and for six weeks she would be happy.

While Papa smoked away without a word and Mama sat half asleep, Theresa took the small bottle from her blouse and began to make a design on her dress. From somewhere in her memory she brought forth a pattern that was not American, not Mexican, but the two together. With the little glass stick in the bottle, she made hundreds of small red dots on the crinkled muslin until they looked almost like needlework. Then she washed her black hair and gave herself a sponge bath.

All night Theresa tossed. Toward morning she got up very quietly, dressed, tidied her hair and with her shoes in her hand made her way out of the camp. A bright light was still burning in the office. Next to it was a strange building she hadn't noticed before. Peeking in, she decided it must be the nursery for there were little cots and little tables and chairs. She found her way to the road and sat there for two hours watching the sun rise higher and higher.

The camp was awake now so Theresa looked around for a place where nobody could see her. A big rock and thick bushes looked safe. Pretty soon she heard children's voices and then—then she heard Papa's voice talking very loud to someone. Who was it? The nurse, of course. She could hear Betty's voice too. Nearer and nearer they came but in a few minutes she couldn't hear Papa any more. He must have gone back. Then the bus came along.

Theresa saw about twelve children and the nurse getting into the old bus. Just as the last one climbed up the back steps, she dashed out and climbed in too. Her heart beat very hard but no one seemed to notice her. Theresa was the only Mexican child on the bus. She held her Diego Rivera picture very tight and said nothing.

In the school office the girl in charge smiled at her. This was better. Then the nurse came over to Theresa and said, "I thought we had lost you. Your father is angry but don't worry. I think everything will be all right when I have more time to explain things to him. It's kind of hard getting used to a new country."

Theresa and Betty were taken into another room. There were no other children because it was so early. Theresa didn't know that only the camp children got up at five every day. A young woman came into the room where the two girls were sitting not saying a word to each other. "You are from the camp, aren't you?" she asked. They nodded. Betty did not look at Theresa. The teacher took them down a long hallway into a room with pictures all around it and curtains at the windows and lots of small seats.

"Theresa, did you embroider your dress? It is very pretty," the teacher said.

"I painted it," Theresa almost whispered. Betty's eyes were glued to the decorated sacks. When the other girls and boys came in they did not make faces at Theresa. They just sat down and waited for the teacher to begin.

"Children, this is Betty Marsh and Theresa Gomez." The teacher took Theresa by the hand and squeezed it in a friendly fashion. "I hope Theresa won't mind my saying this to you, but the lovely pattern on this dress she is wearing, she made all by herself, and the design is like the ones I showed you yesterday, remember?"

Theresa could feel a warm friendly spirit come toward her. Betty leaned forward and whispered, "I like it, too. You look nice." Theresa had won something that no one could take away from her ever. It was as big as anything that had ever happened to her—just this— Americans being nice to her.

By Clara Lambert

MY SONG YANKEE DOODLE

Hing giggled and laughed as he was told to wear the clothes; the white stockings, the blue satin shoes, the silk trousers bound at the ankles, and the beautiful blue blouse.

Jin-wai closed his eyes tightly as his father put on the long gown that he said was the proper thing for a scholar to wear. And he squirmed as the round black cap with a button on the top was adjusted on his head. "Very proud father," said Fong. . . . "You will do me great honor, my sons. Come home after the celebration is over, and we shall have a feast to celebrate my sons' first appearance in public as Chinese citizens."

"WHAT IS THIS, my son?" asked Fong, viewing with distrust the sealed envelope from the American school which Jin-Wai handed him.

"An invitation to a party," replied Jin-Wai unhappily.

Fong beamed. "Better—much better—than a note from your teacher suggesting you go immediately to the doctor to have your tonsils removed, which is painful to you and expensive to me."

"I wrote the invitation myself," said Jin-Wai. "Teacher told me what to say."

"How nice," said Fong, breaking the seal of the letter. He handed it to Mrs. Fong. She couldn't read English, but looked it over carefully, and echoing the sentiments of her husband, said, "How nice!"

"I shall translate it for you," said Fong. "It says that our honorable presence—yours and mine—is requested at Pageant of all Nations to be held at two o'clock next Wednesday at the American school three blocks away where my unworthy son sits all day in classes trying to learn the American language, so when he becomes a man he can do much big business with the Americans in their American way."

The letter didn't say exactly that, but Jin-Wai knew his father enjoyed his little joke. Mrs. Fong nodded her head happily. It was the first invitation to attend a party she had received since the Fong family had moved last summer from Chinatown to this "faraway foreign city called the Bronx." She had no intention of attending as she never left the house, thus displaying the proper Chinese modesty in a woman. But she had been invited. That was a social triumph. To her there was more pleasure in receiving an invitation than in attending.

"Party—party—party!" cried Hing, the four-year-old baby brother, his little face beaming with delight. But then he was very young and had not yet learned to control his emotions. The invitation, however, neither pleased nor delighted Jin-Wai. The thought of the party terrified him.

"Tell me more about it," suggested Fong.

This was what Jin-Wai had been expecting and dreading. But his father had instructed him in the ways of truthfulness as explained by the philosophers, and he knew by heart "The Five Principles of Filial Duty." A disobedient son is a disgrace to a Chinese father. It makes him lose "face."

So with eyes downcast and hands folded in his lap, Jin-Wai spoke. "The idea is my teacher's," he said. That completely absolved him from any blame in thinking up such a thoroughly stupid and embarrassing thing. "Wednesday is a day of celebration for my teacher."

"A feast?" asked his mother.

"No, honorable mother. A celebration, but we don't eat."

"The Americans at their celebrations make very long speeches and eat very little," explained Fong. "Why this celebration?"

"Because my teacher says all winter long she's been

having us sing songs and do dances and now she cele-
brates that we've learned the songs and do the dances.
So she says we invite our honorable parents to celebrate
with her. She says she is proud of us, and we make our
honorable parents proud, too. She says the school does
this every year and now the time has come again."

"How nice," murmured Fong.

"She says there is more to it than even that, also. She
says this is a great big free country but it wasn't once,
and now it is. And she say it's a free country because so
many different people come here with many different
ideas. Many foreigners from many foreign lands, but we
all belong to one country now and are all alike, and so
we put on costumes of our native country and sing American songs and show we are all one big happy family
even though we come from different countries, and it's
teacher's idea but I think it's silly."

Fong scratched his chin and said nothing.

"Teacher says that I—" Jin-Wai paused. How he
hated to tell this next. "Teacher says each child should
come dressed in costume of his own country, but I don't
think it is a good idea."

Fong frowned. "A man should never be ashamed of
the proper dress of his own country."

Jin-Wai knew that perfectly. Yet how could he explain how he felt to his father? His father didn't have
to go day after day to the American school. He wasn't
laughed at and called names. It had been difficult from
the very first day. He was the only Chinese boy in the
classroom and he wanted so much to make friends. He
wanted to be like the American boys, play the games

they did, and understand all the beautiful swear words they used so humorously.

So after school he stepped over to a group of boys and said, "Howdy?"

And the boys turned and looked him over critically. "Hi, Chink," said one.

Then, "Chink! Chink! Chink!" they all began to yell. Jin-Wai, without another word, turned and fled. It wasn't until he reached the corner out of hearing distance that he stopped and wiped the tears of shame from his eyes.

After that he made no more attempts to be friendly, but kept to himself. And even though the boys still called him "Chink," he had learned to control his tears and keep his face perfectly expressionless, lest they see how much they were hurting him.

And now his father thought it would be nice to wear a Chinese costume at the "Celebration." How could he? The boys would laugh at him more than ever, and yell a lot more, too.

Then, to his dismay his father said, "I think it very good if you take your younger brother, Jin-Hing, with you to the party. He has never been, and it will be a new experience for him."

"Party—party—party!" cried Hing.

"He is *only* four years old."

"One is never too young to learn," responded Fong. "He will not disgrace you. When one is the father of two sons, one looks with humble but becoming pride upon their appearance in public dressed in the costume of their native country." Jin-Wai went to bed that night sad at heart.

Had Jin-Wai been an American boy he would have argued with his father, pleaded, made threats, stormed, and done everything possible to keep from being "dressed up." But being Chinese and trained in obedience, had his father told him to cut off his hand—he would probably have hesitated a moment—and then obeyed. Better to lose a hand than to cause your honorable parent to lose face.

His father had spoken, and also Hing was keenly anticipating the party. He would not disappoint either one of them. It was the first burden of manliness placed upon him. And while he tossed all night in the restless slumber, he knew he would go through with it and never utter one word of complaint.

But the next day he suffered from self-pity. He was sorry he was Chinese. He wished he could be like other boys, accepted as one of them, and not be looked upon as being different. Didn't he like to go roller-skating, too? Didn't he like to play marbles? And didn't he know some fancy swear words he could use on proper occasions? He could even show the boys some new games, if they would let him.

Wednesday came as usual. School was dismissed early after the morning session so the children could go home and dress.

Jin-Wai's mother had gotten the clothes from a box where they had been packed away in sweet smelling herbs. And his father stopped work in the laundry to assist and give instructions. Hing giggled and laughed as he was told to wear the clothes; the white stockings, the black satin shoes, the silk trousers bound at the ankles, and the beautiful blue blouse.

Jin-Wai closed his eyes tightly as his father put on the long gown that he said was the proper thing for a scholar to wear. And he squirmed as the round black cap with a button on the top was adjusted on his head.

"Very proud father," said Fong. "Very proud, although I am lacking in modesty to say so. You will do me great honor, my sons. Come home after the celebration is over, and we shall have a feast to celebrate my sons' first appearance in public as Chinese citizens."

"Proud?" thought Jin-Wai. His father didn't have to walk through the streets wearing skirts like a girl. He didn't have to have everybody look at him and laugh. And when Hing knew what jibes and jeers were awaiting him he wouldn't be smiling so happily either.

Taking Hing by the hand, Jin-Wai trotted out onto the street. His father and mother stood in the doorway and waved their hands. Jin-Wai looked neither to the right nor the left, but trudged manfully forward, pulling Hing along after him.

"Too fast! Too fast!" said Hing, who had short legs and had to give a little jump every now and then to catch up.

But Jin-Wai paid no attention. As he drew near the school it wasn't half as bad as he thought it would be. Other boys all dressed up were going into the school, and they were all too busy with their mothers standing about fussing over details of their attire to pay any attention to him. He found his seat in the class-room and pulled

Hing up beside him. As the other boys took their places Jin-Wai looked straight ahead and kept saying to himself, "I am obeying my father. I am obeying my father." The only consoling thought he had.

The exercises were to be held in the assembly hall. It wasn't until they were marching to join the children from the other class-rooms that Jin-Wai's teacher saw him. She had been fluttering around trying to calm the excited mothers and keep the boys from mussing their costumes.

"Why, Jin-Wai!" she said, breathlessly. "I didn't know you were planning to come dressed up. How nice you look. And is this your brother? Isn't he cute. Dear, dear—we'll have to think up something for you to do. I wish I'd known." And she dashed ahead to separate two boys who had started to fight.

So she hadn't expected him to come dressed up! In vain, had been his suffering of the past few days. He could have stayed away, and he wouldn't have been missed. And now Miss Teacher suggested he do something. He wished the schoolhouse would burn down— right to the ground—this very minute, and everybody in it, including himself.

Seats were reserved down front for the children. The proud mothers sat in the back.

The program started with everyone singing, "My Country 'Tis of Thee." Then the school orchestra played what was called a medley of popular airs. And as each group went upon the stage to perform, the orchestra sounded forth with a few bars of the national anthem of their country.

Five little Scotch boys danced to the tune of "The Campbells Are Coming." Jin-Wai felt a little happier when he saw that they, too, were wearing skirts. Thank goodness his bare legs were not being displayed to the public.

A group of Italian children sang several of their folk songs. Some Finnish boys did a drill. The Spanish boys and girls danced to clicking castanets. And so on until all the nationalities had performed. As each group finished they lined up on the stage. Only Jin-Wai and his brother remained in the auditorium.

He heard his teacher say, "I didn't expect. I didn't rehearse anything." Then the lady whom he knew to be Number One Teacher replied. "He will be so disappointed if he can't come up with the others."

Jin-Wai shuddered. Disappointed? Not he. He was hoping he wouldn't be noticed. But his teacher bent over him and whispered. "Wouldn't you like to go up on the platform with the others? Just walk around so everyone can see how nice you look. We don't know what melody to play. We haven't practised the Chinese national anthem, if there is one."

The pride of centuries of a race of proud ancestors came to Jin-Wai's assistance at this crucial moment. Just because he was a Chinese didn't mean he didn't know the proper thing to do. "Play 'Yankee Doodle,'" he said. "Me take that tune."

A whispered consultation was held with the pianist, and as "Yankee Doodle" was pounded out upon the piano, Jin-Wai, holding Hing by the hand, marched upon the stage. There was a burst of applause. For Jin-

Wai carried himself with much dignity, walked so proudly, and had such perfect self-possession that he won the heart of all the mothers. He faced the audience.

"He's going to do something," whispered the teacher.

Jin-Wai bowed. And Hing, properly trained to do as his brother did in public, folded his hands in front of his round little tummy and bowed too. Suddenly Jin-Wai felt proud and happy. Proud he was wearing his Chinese dress. It was beautiful. Much more beautiful than the homemade costumes the other children were wearing. Silk, his was. Not cheesecloth nor cheap material. He wasn't afraid any longer.

He took one step forward and began to recite in Chinese. The audience listened amused but pleased. When he finished he bowed again. And Hing bowed too. Then Jin-Wai took Hing by the hand and led him to a place on the stage by the side of the other boys of his classroom. There was a loud burst of applause from the audience.

While the orchestra played another number, there was a hurried consultation among the teachers. Then Jin-Wai saw his teacher come upon the stage.

"The prize this afternoon for the best costume and the nicest performance by unanimous choice goes to Jin-Wai Fong, our Chinese neighbor. Come here, Jin-Wai."

Jin-Wai, still holding Hing by the hand, stepped forward. "What was it you said in Chinese?" asked the teacher.

"I said 'The Five Principles of Filial Duty' by Mr. Confucius. It means you should always obey your parents and do exactly as they tell you to do even though it does not seem to you to be the thing for you to do."

Cheers came from the audience at these words so touchingly expressed. The mothers present understood and applauded vigorously. Then the teacher handed Jin-Wai the prize—a nice book full of pictures of the Presidents and their wives. Jin-Wai bowed low.

"Present?" asked Hing.

For a moment Jin-Wai paused. He had no right to accept this prize. He had not won it because of anything he had wanted to do. He had made no effort of his own. He was not entitled to it. And if he accepted the prize and ever in his own thought felt pride, he would to himself forever lose face.

So he turned to Hing and placed the prize in his hands. Let Hing have all the honor. Let him be the one tonight to boast to their honorable father. Then Jin-Wai smiled happily. He had done the proper thing—saved his face.

He took his place again with his classmates. The teacher pulled a rope, and the American flag concealed in the space above the stage unfurled and hovered over the children as they all began to sing, "The Star Spangled Banner."

"Hi, kid," said the boy next to Jin-Wai under his breath, and smiled when he said it.

"Hi, yourself," said Jin-Wai. His heart began to thump happily. The first friendly word he had had. Maybe his father did know what was best. Maybe he should always do things in the approved Chinese way— his way. Maybe that was the right way to understanding and friendliness.

By Carl Glick

QUEEN OF SUMMER

*They did not go all the way down to the houses. . . .
But part way down the hill they met a little Syrian girl,
tending a goat. She wore a long skirt like a woman's, and
ear rings, and a scarf. Her hair hung in long black braids
tied with red at the ends. Her eyes danced, and she had
dimples when she smiled at Betsy, Tacy, and Tib. They
had found out that her name was Naifi.*

BETSY AND TACY and Tib were three little girls who
were friends. Betsy and Tacy lived on Hill Street, which
ran straight up into a green hill and stopped. The small

yellow cottage where Betsy Ray lived, was the last house on that side of the street, and the rambling white house opposite where Tacy Kelly lived, was the last house on that side. These two houses ended the street, and after that came the hill. Tib Muller lived just around the corner; near enough to come to play every day.

Tib was the same age as Betsy and Tacy. They were all ten years old. Tacy was the tallest; she had long red ringlets and freckles and thin legs. Tib was the smallest; she was little and dainty with round blue eyes and a fluff of yellow hair. Betsy was the middle-sized one. She had plump legs and short brown braids which stuck out behind her ears. Her smile showed teeth that were parted in the middle, and Betsy was almost always smiling.

Betsy and Tacy and Tib never quarreled. They sometimes quarreled with Julia and Katie, though. Julia and Katie were Betsy's and Tacy's big sisters; they were twelve years old. This is the story of one of their quarrels. Most of the quarrels were in fun, but this was a real one. It ended with making up and with crowning a queen.

It all started when they began to plan to crown a Queen of Summer on Betsy's side lawn. Betsy and Tacy and Tib wanted Tib to be queen. Julia and Katie wanted Julia to be queen.

"I have it," Betsy's father said. "We'll settle this in the good old American way. By the vote."

"But papa," said Julia, "that wouldn't do. Katie and I would vote for me, and Betsy and Tacy and Tib would vote for Tib."

"Let your friends vote," answered Mr. Ray. "Let the

neighborhood vote. Take two sheets of foolscap and at the top of one write, 'We, the undersigned, want Tib Muller for queen of summer.' And at the top of the other one write, 'We, the undersigned, want Julia Ray for queen.' Then take your papers and go out after votes, and may the best man win."

It was a wonderful idea. Everyone thought that the quarrel was over. But it wasn't.

At first, getting the votes was fun. The two groups rushed down Hill Street, running into all the houses. Mr. Ray had said they were to go no farther downtown than Lincoln Park, but before they reached Lincoln Park Julia and Katie found an Ice Cream Social where they got so many votes that Betsy and Tacy and Tib were afraid they could never catch up. Then Betsy had an idea.

"We can't go beyond Lincoln Park," she said. "All right. We'll turn around and go back, and we'll just keep on going."

"But Betsy," said Tib, "there's no sense in that. We'll come to the Big Hill."

"And we'll just keep on going," Betsy repeated.

Tacy's eyes began to sparkle, and in a moment Tib's began to sparkle too.

"You mean we should go to Little Syria," said Tacy, and Betsy nodded.

They had discovered Little Syria just a few weeks before. Of course they had always known that there was such a place. Little Syria was a street of small houses and big vegetable gardens and strange dark people who spoke broken English and came to Hill Street sometimes peddling garden stuff and laces and embroidered cloths. Betsy and Tacy and Tib had visited Little Syria when out buggy riding with their fathers and mothers. They had not known that they could reach it by walking over their own Big Hill.

But that was what happened. One day when they were playing up on the Big Hill they had gone farther than they usually went. They had ome to a part of the hill that was new to them, and climbed out on a high, rocky ridge. Below, spread out in the sunlight, was a strange, wide, beautiful valley, with a row of tiny houses in the center.

"That looks like Little Syria," Tib had said. And going closer they had found to their great surprise that it was.

They did not go all the way down to the houses, the day they discovered it. But part way down the hill they met a little Syrian girl, tending a goat. She wore a long skirt like a woman's, and ear rings, and a scarf. Her hair hung in long black braids tied with red at the ends. Her shoes were red, too, and under her dress she wore bloomers down to her ankles. Her eyes danced, and she had dimples when she smiled at Betsy, Tacy, and Tib. They had found out that her name was Naifi.

"We'll see Naifi again if we go to Little Syria," Tib cried now.

It was a daring trip, but they made it. They did not tell anyone where they were going; they just took a picnic and went. They had their picnic on the big flat rock and ran down the hill to Little Syria.

They found Naifi living in one of the little houses

with her father, her grandfather and her grandmother. The tall, dignified grandfather was smoking a curious pipe that stood on the floor, with a long tube leading to his mouth. The small bright-eyed grandmother was pounding something with a mallet, in a hollowed-out block of marble.

"She is making kibbee," explained Naifi's dark-haired young father. "That is meat she is pounding; it is good lean lamb."

The grandmother could not speak any English, but Naifi had already learned a little. She still wore ear rings, but her long skirts were gone now, and she wore quite an ordinary short dress and ordinary shoes and stockings.

"She is now a little American girl," her father said proudly.

With Naifi guiding them, Betsy, Tacy, and Tib went to every one of the little Syrian houses. They saw people drinking coffee, poured from long-handled copper pots into tiny cups. They saw women baking flat round loaves of bread and other women making embroidery, and men playing cards. They saw a boy playing a long reed flute . . . a munjaira, Naifi said it was. They saw everything there was to be seen and they met everyone and everyone signed. Most of them wrote from right to left.

"That is Arabic writing," one of the Syrians explained. "The Syrian language is Arabic."

This Arabic writing caused a great deal of trouble. When Betsy, Tacy, and Tib got home and told where they had been, Julia and Katie were disappointed and angry, for they thought they had votes enough so that Julia could be queen. But they were willing to give in and let Tib be queen because they had promised that the one who got the most votes would win. When they saw that Arabic writing, however, they felt differently about it. Katie looked at their list and cried, "You don't expect us to count this, I hope."

"It's Arabic," Betsy explained.

"Arabic!" cried Julia. "You might have just scrawled it yourselves for all we know."

"You might have let a chicken run over the paper," said Katie. "You have to throw out these names that aren't English."

"We won't!"

"You must!"

"We won't!"

"You've got to!"

That was the way the quarrel went until Mrs. Ray came out and called Julia and Betsy into the house, and Mrs. Kelly called Katie and Tacy in, and Tib went home, crying. Everybody felt like crying. It was a very bad quarrel.

Julia and Betsy in their house, and Katie and Tacy in theirs, and Tib in her house around the corner, all felt very badly.

After Julia and Betsy went to bed, Betsy began to cry. Then from the other side of the bed she heard a sound. It was a sob, a perfectly gigantic sob.

"Betsy!" cried Julia, and she came rolling over and hugged Betsy tight. "I'm sorry."

"I'm sorry, too," Betsy wept.

"I don't want to be queen of summer," Julia sobbed. "I want Tib to be queen."

"But Tib doesn't want to be queen, I know," wept Betsy, "if it makes you and Katie feel badly."

So they made up, and at Tacy's house it was just the same, and all along Tib had wanted to give in. But the trouble was that now nobody wanted to be queen of summer. Julia said that Tib must be queen, and Tib said that Julia must be queen. Neither one would give in, and yet somebody had to be queen. There were beautiful pink and green streamers all made for the coronation.

Mr. Ray wasn't worried about this kind of a quarrel. Besides, he knew that he had some news that would end it. He called them all up on the porch.

"I heard something yesterday," he said, "that will interest you very much. There's a real princess in town."

"A real princess!" came an astonished chorus.

"She's from the old country. She's of the blood royal," answered Mr. Ray.

"Is she down at the hotel?" asked Julia.

"No, but she's right here in town. How would you like to go to see her and ask her to be queen of summer?"

"Oh, we'd like it! We'd like it! Where is she?"

"You never could guess, so I'll tell you. She's in Little Syria. Imagine," he said to Betsy, Tacy, and Tib, "having a princess right under your nose and not recognizing her."

"What's her name?"

"Her name," said Mr. Ray, "is Naifi."

Betsy, Tacy, and Tib almost fell off the stairs.

"Naifi! But papa," cried Betsy, "she can't be. Naifi's a perfectly darling little girl, but she's just a plain little girl like us."

"No, she is a princess," Mr. Ray replied impressively and explained.

One of the Syrians had come into his shoe store the day before and started talking about his country. You could read about that country in the Bible, Mr. Ray said. Most Syrians are Mohammedans, and Syria was under the control of the Mohammedan Turks, but the Deep Valley Syrians were Christians.

"They came to America for much the same reason that our Pilgrim fathers came. They want to be free from oppression and religious persecution," Mr. Ray said. He went on:

"Most of them come from the Lebanon district. You've heard about Lebanon, I'm sure. King Solomon's temple was built from the cedars of Lebanon. Cedars still grow on those wild hills, and in the ravines and valleys some brave groups of people still keep their loyalty to their native Syrian princes . . . in spite of the Turks. Emirs, these princes are called, and their daughters and grand-daughters are Emiras, or princesses. Naifi's grandfather is an Emir of Lebanon, and Naifi is an Emira."

Through this long explanation Betsy, Tacy, and Tib had sat perfectly still, stunned with surprise. Their little friend Naifi was a princess! But when Mr. Ray finished they jumped up eagerly and asked if they might go to invite Naifi to be queen of summer. Julia and Katie wanted to go, too, and Betsy, Tacy, and Tib were glad to take them.

They all climbed the hill to the high rocky point that looked down on Little Syria; then they ran down into the valley to the row of little houses, and into Naifi's house.

Naifi and her father and her grandfather and grandmother were very glad to see them. But to the surprise of
the girls, Naifi's father didn't seem to like the idea of her
being a queen.

"No, no," he said, shaking his head. "I do not want
my Naifi to play a Syrian Emira. She is forgetting about
such things. You are an American now; are you not, my
heart, my eyes?"

Naifi nodded until her braids swung up and down.
She stood very straight, and her eyes were bright. "American," she said.

"American," said her grandfather, the old Emir of
Lebanon, striking his breast.

"American," said his wife. For even the old grandmother knew the word "American."

Something in the way they said "American" gave
Betsy an idea. She jumped from her chair.

"Of course," she cried. "But this is to be an American
celebration. It is an American queen and a queen of summer we want Naifi to be."

"It is?" asked Naifi's father, looking puzzled.

Tacy followed Betsy's lead like lightning. "We're going to have a big flag up, red, white and blue," she said.

Julia and Katie fell into line. "I'm going to sing 'The
Star Spangled Banner,'" said Julia. "And Katie is going
to recite Lincoln's Gettysburg Address."

"It's almost the Fourth of July, you know," Tib said.

Naifi's father translated all they said to the grandfather and the grandmother. They all talked in Arabic
excitedly, waving their arms. Smiles broke over their
faces, and Naifi's father put his hand on her head.

"She may go," he said. "I will bring her myself. I start tomorrow on a trip with my horse and buggy, selling the linens and laces. But first I will bring her to your house, to be your American queen."

So Naifi was crowned queen of summer next day.

She was crowned on the Rays' side lawn under one of the two young maples; it was just the right size. Pink and green streamers wound around the tree up to the lowest branch, and from that point chains of flowers ran to either side of Mr. Ray's armchair. It was a big leather armchair. It made a fine throne.

A large American flag overhung all, and small American flags were stuck into the ground in a half circle behind the throne. Flags which were ordinarily stored away in closets and brought out only on patriotic holidays had been produced by dozens to make Naifi's coronation strictly American.

Tacy's brother Paul and Tib's brother Freddie borrowed flags all up and down Hill Street, while Betsy's little sister Margaret and Tib's little brother Hobbie picked flowers on the hill and Betsy and Tacy and Tib wove garlands and Julia and Katie decorated. Everything was done without the smallest disagreement, and the mothers were so pleased that Mrs. Ray made lemonade, and Mrs. Kelly baked a cake, and Mrs. Muller baked cookies. Even a coronation needs refreshments.

When the decorating was finished, the children went out to invite people. All the neighbors were invited, and by half past two o'clock the lawn was full of people.

Grown-ups sat on the lawn in chairs but the children kept racing to the Rays' front steps to look down Hill

Street. They were pretty worked up about a princess coming. At last they saw an unfamiliar horse, a buggy loaded with satchels. It was Naifi's father bringing Naifi to the Rays' house.

He stopped at the hitching block and jumped out and pulled off his hat. The sun shone on his glistening hair. He lifted Naifi out of the buggy, and his face was proud. He pointed to the big American flag.

"Look at that, my heart!" he said.

The children swooped down upon them.

Naifi was a princess out of the Arabian Nights. Betsy could not have invented one more lovely. A cloud of chiffon floated about her face. Her mouth was hidden, but her dark eyes were sparkling. They were rimmed with sooty black.

Her dress was long and full-skirted, like the one she had worn the day they saw her first. But this one was of soft rich cashmere, purple in color and embroidered with gold. The short jacket was gold-embroidered, too. Bloomers were tied at her ankles above little slippers of gold. She was laden with jewelry . . . bracelets, rings, ear rings . . .

"Naifi! You're wonderful! You're beautiful!" cried the children.

"Hel-lo," said Naifi. "Hel-lo, hel-lo."

Mrs. Ray asked her father to stay, but he said that he had to go. He drove down Hill Street with a proud smiling face.

The children hurried Naifi into the Rays' parlor. There the parade assembled. Mrs. Ray was going to play the piano for it. On the lawn the other mothers and the guests waited expectantly. The sun shone down, and the air smelled of roses.

Mrs. Ray played a rousing march. It was named "Pomp and Circumstance." She played it with spirit. The procession streamed out of the door to the porch, down the porch steps, over the lawn.

First came Margaret and Hobbie waving Flags. They waved them in time to the music. Next came Paul and Freddie in their best suits. They were pages. Pages walked straight, and tried not to smile. Then came Betsy and Tacy. They scattered flowers as gracefully as they knew how. They scattered the flowers picked that morning on the hill, columbines and daisies and the scarlet Indian paintbrush.

Treading on the flowers came Naifi, dimples flashing. And just behind walked Tib, holding the edge of Naifi's dress. Julia and Katie came last of all, bearing a pillow with a crown of flowers upon it.

Betsy's mother played three or four crashing chords. Naifi seated herself on the throne. The rest seated themselves on the grass. Julia rose and swept her brown curls almost to the ground in a curtsy.

"Your Majesty!" she said in her sweet voice. "We will now endeavor to entertain you."

Mrs. Ray began to play a special dance Tib knew. Tib jumped up, picked her skirt up by the edges and made a pirouette. Then she danced; beautifully, too.

After Tib's dance, which was loudly applauded, Betsy and Tacy sang the Cat Duet. This was a funny duet they had sung in school one time. They were loudly applauded, too.

Katie recited the Gettysburg Address, and when she had finished, she and Julia knelt before the queen of summer. They held the cushion high and Tib lifted the crown of flowers. As she put it on Naifi's head, Mrs. Ray, inside the house, began to play "Hearts and Flowers."

Julia went up and stood on the porch steps, looking solemn. Paul and Freddie handed out flags. Then Mrs. Ray switched to "The Star Spangled Banner." Everyone stood up, of course, and Julia sang. At the end of a verse she smiled suddenly and asked everyone to sing. Everyone sang "The Star Spangled Banner" and waved flags. Naifi's eyes were something to watch then. Bright as diamonds, they looked about the lawn at the tossing banners.

After that it was just a party with plenty of lemonade, cookies, and cake. But the coronation of an American queen was what everyone remembered.

"I'm almost glad we had that awful quarrel," Tib said later. "It was such fun finding a princess down in Little Syria."

By Maud Hart Lovelace

WHO BUILT THE BRIDGE?

Many Americans had built that new bridge. Americans from many lands. Some had come to America a short time ago. They still carried memories and habits from the land they left. Others had never known any land except these United States. But their grandfathers . . . or their great-great-great-grandfathers had once come over from Europe or Africa or Asia, all except the Indians. New Americans and old Americans . . . workers of many kinds had built that great bridge.

THE NEW BRIDGE was finished. On each side of the big river stood the broad stone bases. From each stone base rose a high, slender steel tower. The steel beams and cross beams made a pattern against the blue sky. Between the two high slender steel towers hung two great cables in a long swooping, lovely curve. Far away those cables looked like threads from a spider's web. Near by they looked thick; each really was three feet thick and made of hundreds of smaller ones of twisted wire. Even so, the cables didn't look strong enough to hold up a road for automobiles. Yet there was the road, hung from the great cables by hundreds of smaller straight ones. Today that road was to be opened. Today the first automobiles were to cross the new bridge. For the new bridge was finished.

The town was excited. The town was proud. Now the townspeople would be able to whiz across the big river in a few minutes. Why, now you could live over on the other side in the open country with grass and trees and get to your work in the town on time. The farmers on the other side of the town were excited. They were proud. Why, now you could load your truck with vegetables in the early morning and get them over to the market in a jiffy. No wonder that the morning assemblies in the town schools were going to talk about the bridge. Some classes were even going to the opening of the bridge. They were going to hear the mayor speak and to see the first two autos cross—a town auto starting from one side and a farm auto from the other side. No wonder the morning paper had a picture of the beautiful bridge on the front page and carried big headlines:

OPENING OF NEW BRIDGE
BUILT BY THE TOWN AND STATE
AJAX CONSTRUCTION CO. BUILDS ANOTHER GREAT BRIDGE

Yes, in a way the town and the state and the construction company built the bridge. But not with their hands. Whose hands had built the bridge, anyway? There were many children in the town who knew. Hadn't their fathers worked on it?

The two Caruso children knew. Their father and mother had come from Italy. Maria Caruso was in the third grade. She had large black eyes and long, black, curly hair. Her brother Luigi was in the fifth grade. He had large black eyes and short, black, curly hair. Both children had been born in America. They had never seen Italy with their eyes, but they had seen it often through the stories their father and mother had told them. For both their father and mother talked a lot of their old home, particularly at supper time. Then the family sat around the table with its bright flowered cloth and ate a big bowl of spaghetti and grated cheese. Maria and Luigi knew only an American city. But as their parents talked, the children could see a little Italian town. They knew how the stone quarry looked behind the town. They knew just how carefully the stones from that quarry had been fitted into the walls of many of the town's houses and even into the walls of the town church. For had not their father fitted many of these stones himself with his strong skillful hands?

"Yessa, yessa," their father would say, shaking his head with its curly gray hair. "I work with stone in Italia. Then I come to America. Now I am American. I work with stone in America. I help build the stone walls in the big bridge. You look at my walls. Every stone go in the right place. I help make good strong walls for the big bridge." Yes, the Caruso children were excited and proud that the new bridge was finished. Was not their father's stone work a part of that bridge?

And the Votipka children, too, knew who had helped build the bridge. Indeed they always called it "Father's bridge." Those steel towers that made a pattern against the sky—those were "Father's towers." For their father was a member of the steel riveters' team. Once as a boy in Bohemia, their father had known nothing of steel. He had known only the houses which his father had built in a Bohemian town. But those houses were made of strong wooden beams with broad wood boards for walls and sometimes even straw-thatched roofs.

Their father often told them how queer the high houses in New York had looked to his boy's eyes when he stared at them from the ship's deck and from Ellis Island. "How could houses be strong enough to stand up so high?" he had asked. He was told that their beams were made of steel. "Steel!" And then and there the little boy from Bohemia had decided he would grow up and be a steel worker. He would build houses and bridges of steel in this new country that was to be his home.

And in time this actually happened. He became an American and learned to be a skillful worker in steel. He learned sureness of foot. He didn't get dizzy out on a steel beam. Yes, the little Bohemian boy was now a grown man with a family of his own. Now he was a member of the riveting team that had built the new bridge.

And that was what Jan Votipka, his oldest boy, now hoped he would be someday. Should he be a "spider boy" and walk on high beams with a bag of rivets over his shoulder? Or should he stand on some high scaffold and heat rivets in his charcoal fire and throw the red-hot rivet to a man on the next beam? Sometimes when Jan threw a ball out on the baseball field, he imagined he was throwing a hot rivet high in the air. Or best of all, he would be the man who caught the rivet in a pail and picked it up with tongs and put it, still red-hot, into the hole. You had to be quick, you had to be sure, you had to get the rivet just right, so that the next man could drive it in quickly with the riveting machine. That's what his father did—caught the hot rivets and put them in place. For months Jan had heard the "rat-a-tat-tat" of the riveting machines as the slender steel towers rose higher and higher. And each time Jan had said to himself, "Father has put in another hot rivet. Someday, I'll be doing that myself."

Now here on the front page of the morning paper was a picture of Father's steel towers. Jan looked at it proudly. And so did all the other little Votipkas.

In another part of the town, in the Mulligan kitchen, big and little Mike were looking at the picture of the new bridge in the morning paper. Little Mike was only five. But that was old enough to know that big Mike, his father, was the smartest man on earth. That was old enough to know that the big bridge could never have been built without his father's help. "Show me where you worked?" asked little Mike, leaning over the paper on big Mike's knee.

"Now, isn't it an extraordinary thing, Mike boy," went on big Mike, "that we Americans can build what-ever we want to nowadays. Take this bridge, now," and he tapped the picture with a strong thick finger. "Our townspeople take a squint across the big river and they say to themselves, says they, 'Now wouldn't it be fine to drive right across the river?' So they get a smart man to draw some fancy pictures of a fine bridge and would you believe it, my son, those pictures show just what your father and other sandhogs should do. So then our townspeople says to themselves, says they, 'Shoot!' and we all begin to work and, before you know it, there is the morning paper saying the new bridge is to open this very day. We Americans are an extraordinary people, Mike boy, if we haven't just built another gr-r-r-rreat bridge."

So it was in many families that morning. Booker T. Washington and Lulu Belle Washington knew that their father had helped drill the rock on the two sides of the river so that the steel towers could be anchored deep in the rock. They, too, grinned at the picture of the new bridge till their teeth showed white in their brown faces. It was their bridge, too.

And the Pulaski children knew that their father had helped mix the concrete in the huge concrete mixers. They knew that the bridge could not have stood up so big and strong without the cement to anchor the steel beams and cables. And the Macpherson children well remembered the days when their father's tugboat carried first one steel cable and then another giant cable across the river. They had watched the little tug puffing and puffing as the great cable trailed behind it in the water. They felt that the bridge could not have been built without their Scotch father and they were right.

Yes, Americans had built another great bridge. Not only the town and state, not only the construction company, but many Americans had built that new bridge. Americans from many lands. Some had come to America a short time ago. They still carried memories and habits from the land they had left. Others had never known any land except these United States. But their grandfathers or their great-grandfathers or their great-great-great-grandfathers had once come over from Europe or Africa or Asia, all except the Indians. New Americans and old Americans; workers in stone, workers in cement, workers in steel, sandhogs, tugboat captains and bridge engineers; nearby townspeople and faraway steel workers, miners and railroad men—workers of many kinds built that great bridge. The great new road across the big river was the work of many Americans—to be used by all.

By Lucy Sprague Mitchell

THE CONTEST

"What would you do if you had a thousand dollars?"
Janey asked suddenly. . . .

And Lupe rose further in her regard when she con-
tinued the game by asking: "What would you do?"

Janey's answer was ready.

"I'd have a house built with rooms in it for all of us,
not counting the kitchen. And it would be all light inside
and clean, and there would be water pipes . . . so you
could just turn them off and on whenever you wanted to.
And on one of the walls there would be a shelf for the
willow plate, and we would stay in it always."

THOUGH IT WAS barely six o'clock in the morning, the Larkin shack was in a fever of activity. Most of it was caused by Janey, who kept running out to peer at the sky and to rush back with the report that, "There isn't a cloud as big as my hand anywhere. It isn't going to rain after all, and I'm glad, I'm glad, because rain would spoil everything."

"You'd better calm down and eat your breakfast or we won't get around in time to go with your father," Mrs. Larkin warned her, and Janey finally paused at the table long enough to eat her portion of fried salt pork and corn bread.

She had good reason to be excited, for this was the day of the Wasco County Cotton Picking Contest. All the pickers who had qualified by making a record of more than three hundred pounds of cotton picked in a single day were to vie with one another for first places in the picking contest. Mr. Larkin had qualified, along with seventy-five others, and at seven o'clock would go to the field to start the nine hours of grueling work in an effort to win one of the cash prizes. And the prizes were worth working for. If he won first place, he would receive one hundred and twenty-five dollars, in addition to which he would be paid the regular wage of ninety cents a hundred pounds for the actual picking. If he won second place, he would claim seventy-five dollars, and third would bring fifty dollars. There were lesser amounts for fourth, fifth, and sixth places, but Janey hadn't bothered to consider them. Dad couldn't rate less than third. Suppose he should come in first! They would be almost rich. Janey paused with her mouth full of corn bread to speculate on the things that one hundred and twenty-five dollars would bring them, and so alluring were the splendors before her mind's eye, that she might have sat there the rest of the morning if Mrs. Larkin hadn't goaded her again into making haste.

Across the road, there was a light in the Romero house. Every picker was allowed a swamper, or helper, and Mr. Larkin had asked Manuel Romero to assist him. It was agreed that if he won either of the first three prizes, Manuel would receive ten dollars for his work, five dollars if Mr. Larkin came in fourth, fifth, or sixth, and nothing at all if he lost altogether. Manuel was quite willing to take his chances with his neighbor. Both families were to attend the contest in a body. To Janey, it was the most exciting thing that had ever happened to them. Never before had Dad competed in such a contest, and her anxiety over the outcome was almost more than she could stand.

"Oh, Dad," she stopped to exclaim as they were going out the door, "suppose you don't win anything at all!"

Until this moment she had never seriously considered such an unpleasant possibility. But now that the time for starting the contest was actually here, the ugly thought would intrude itself in spite of all she could do to push it from her.

"Suppose you don't win anything at all?" she repeated.

"Well, in that case, I'll have my day's wages, and at the rate I'm going to pick that won't be anything to sneeze at."

Janey giggled, feeling better at once. Dad had such a

funny way of saying things sometimes. Of course he'd
win. First place too, more than likely. She had been silly
to think anything else even for a minute.

But later, as with Lupe she walked to the edge of the
field where the pickers were spread out awaiting the
starting gun, she again felt a slight qualm of doubt.
Seventy-six men stood there, each facing a row of gleaming cotton, Dad with the rest, his long picking sack
around his waist and trailing out for several feet behind
him. Somehow Dad looked awfully like just anybody.
He didn't look a bit like the best cotton picker in Wasco
County. But then, neither did any of the others. They
looked like very ordinary men, their stature dwarfed a
little by that wide field. But their eyes had a new eagerness this morning, and their faces were strangely alert.
A newcomer dropped suddenly into that place would
have known instantly something important was about to
happen.

It was a perfect autumn day with a little mistiness on
the horizon which the climbing sun had not yet shone
away. The blue bowl of the sky fitted neatly onto the edge
of the reaching land with no ragged edges to show where
land and sky were joined unless you counted the distant
blue willows where the river ran. There was a hush over
everything, for voices were swallowed up in that vast
space, and when the gun cracked to announce the start of
the contest, it sounded more like the bark of a toy pistol
than a real gun. But as one man, the pickers bent to their
work, so Janey decided it was a real gun she had heard.
She left Lupe and sidled up beside Mrs. Larkin, slipping
a hand into hers.

"Oh, Mom, I do so terribly want Dad to win. Do you think he will?"

Mrs. Larkin held Janey's hand close and watched the pickers for a few seconds before she replied, and then she said slowly: "Nobody knows, daughter. He'll just have to do the best he can and take his chances with the rest. I guess that's the way all life is, mostly."

Janey pondered the sober words, sensing rather than realizing a great wisdom in them. They were almost like words she had come on in the Bible. Mom talked like that sometimes. And sometimes, as now, she seemed far off, like God. You never thought of teasing or playing with Mom the way you did with Dad. Mom was different. She it was who made you do the things you should and spoke words that made you think. There were things close locked in Mom that Janey had longed lately to discover, and felt sure she never would. But Janey knew that without her she and Dad would be as useless as cotton plants without the sun.

The men had picked down the long rows, weighed in and dumped their bags of cotton, and were working back to the place from which they had started. Janey and Lupe ran to meet them. More and more people had come to watch the picking, crowds were following the men, and traffic officers had arrived to keep the onlookers from hindering the workers.

Lupe moved away from one burly officer, eying with suspicion the gun swinging at his hip.

"Come on," said Janey impatiently, "what are you afraid of?"

"Him," with a nod toward the officer.

"Afraid of a motor cop?" asked Janey, in amazement. "He won't hurt you. Lots of times when the car gets something wrong with it and we get stuck on the road, a motor cop comes along and tries to help us fix it."

"They arrest people," declared Lupe firmly.

"Sure they do when you're breaking a law, or something. But they'll all right, honest." Janey was a little disgusted with Lupe.

"I betcha you're a-scared to go up and say something to him," challenged Lupe, still doubtful in spite of Janey's reassurances.

"I am not," replied Janey, coming down hard on the last word, and striking out to where the officer in question was chatting with a knot of sightseers.

Janey waited until she caught his eye, and grinned at him.

"Hello, young sprout, how's tricks?" he demanded.

"My dad's in the contest," announced Janey.

"No foolin'?" asked the officer. "Which one is he?"

"That one." Janey flung out an arm, and moved closer to the officer. Out of the tail of her eye, she could see Lupe approaching cautiously.

"So, that's your dad? Say, he's no slouch. I've been watching him for the last few minutes and he can sure pick cotton."

At this, Janey longed to throw her arms around the officer's sunburned neck, but wasn't quite sure such an action would be within the law. Instead she just beamed happily, and trotted along beside him as he started down the field. Lupe came trotting along behind.

Suddenly, without warning, the officer stopped in his

long stride and the little Mexican girl ran smack into him.

"Hey, what's going on here?" he cried, grabbing her by the shoulders and grinning down into the scared face. "Tryin' to rush me, or something?"

Poor Lupe. It was well that the man was holding her in a firm grip or she would have fallen to the ground, for her legs were limp under her. Her eyes were enormous pools of black terror in her graying face and she looked as if her last minute had come. Janey could hardly keep from laughing, but liked Lupe too well to ridicule her thus openly. Instead, she said:

"Lupe's afraid of cops, but she shouldn't be, should she?"

"Heck, no," replied the officer. "I've got two kids at home and I'll tell you something if you promise not to breathe it to a soul." He released Lupe and gave a quick look around as if he were actually afraid someone might overhear him. The two little girls bent close. "Those kids of mine don't mind me worth a cent," confessed the big man, "but don't you ever let that out. Now skedaddle, I've got work to do."

"You see," said Janey, as she watched the broad back with its Sam Browne belt drawing away from them, "you see. Cops aren't anything to be afraid of."

But Lupe still looked a little unconvinced.

The hours dragged on, the sun rode high in the heavens, and still the men's swift fingers moved over the green plants, sweeping the cotton into the picking sacks. Time and time again the sacks were weighed and their fluffy contents dumped into the trucks until their high sides bulged with the snowy loads. The pickers snatched a hasty lunch, hardly halting in their work, and the afternoon wore on. The final outcome of the race could be guessed at now. Mr. Larkin was well in the lead of most of the field. Only one man seemed to challenge his chances at first place. This one was a huge Negro whose big black hands moved with unerring deftness and with lightning speed. Good-naturedly he chaffed at his white rival whenever they were within hailing distance of each other, and Mr. Larkin replied in kind.

Janey, almost worn out with the day's excitement, was sitting with Lupe in the Larkin car.

"What would you do if you had a thousand dollars?" Janey asked suddenly.

Money prizes had occupied so much of her mind all day that now it was easy to let her dreams of wealth lift her thoughts above mere possible sums to wholly fantastic amounts.

Lupe took a moment to consider the question, then answered: "If I had a thousand dollars, I'd buy an automobile. It would be light yellow with shining wheels. And it would have red leather on the inside, and two horns. And I'd drive it anytime I wanted to."

Lupe's eyes fairly glowed as she contemplated the splendid vision. Janey glanced at her with surprise and satisfaction. It was something to have discovered there were things in Lupe's mind that weren't just everyday things, even if they were only yellow automobiles. And Lupe rose further in her regard when she continued the game by asking: "What would you do?"

Janey's answer was ready.

"I'd have a house built with rooms in it for all of us, not counting the kitchen. And it would be all light inside and clean, and there would be water pipes right inside the house, so you could just turn them off and on whenever you wanted to. And on one of the walls there would be a shelf for the willow plate, and we would stay in it always and. . . ."

But what further wonders Janey's dream house was to have remained forever a mystery, for just then a gun went off for the second time that day. The contest was over.

Pell-mell, the two girls scrambled out of the car and began racing for the field. A crowd was gathering swiftly around the trucks, tired men running jerkily from the field if they were sure they had placed somewhere near the top. The others came more slowly to claim their day's wages.

In a few minutes the tension would be ended and the prize money paid out. Janey saw her father with Manuel Romero at his side standing in a group of men while the weights were being checked. The crowd was quiet, eager to catch the first word of the results. At last it came. A name was called out, a shout went up and the big colored man stepped forward, his sweating face split by a wide and gleaming smile. So Dad hadn't won first place after all. For a moment Janey felt as if she must run away, as if she couldn't endure the strain of waiting for the other results. She looked toward her father and wondered how he could appear so calm and could go on talking quietly with Manuel just as if this were no different from the end of any other day's work. But even as she watched him, she heard another name called. It sounded like "Larkin," only she might have been mistaken. But no, now Dad was moving forward, and men were slapping him on the back. It was, it was Larkin. Dad had won second place and seventy-five dollars!

Janey didn't know she had been leaping up and down until she felt a hand on her shoulder. "You'll thump yourself right down to China if you keep that up." Janey looked up to see Mom smiling down at her. Actually smiling.

"Oh, Mom!" cried Janey, flinging both arms around her waist and pressing her face against her. "I'm afraid I'll *bust.*"

"It wouldn't surprise me a bit if you went off, just like a firecracker," came the calm voice above her. "Here comes your father; we'd better start for the car."

The next day Mr. Larkin, instead of going to work, took his family into Fresno to make some much-needed purchases now that there was a little extra money at hand. First of all, the car needed four new tires. Of course they wouldn't be brand-new ones, but at the second-hand dealers' they would find some that were much better than those already on the wheels, and these must be found before any other things were bought. For with a family like the Larkins, a car was the most important thing they owned. Without it, their means of earning a livelihood would be at an end, since everything depended on their ability to keep up with the harvests. Without a car in fairly good operating condition, they would be helpless. Janey understood this quite as well as her father and

mother and only permitted herself to hope a little wist-
fully as they rolled along the highway that there would
be something left over after the tires were bought. Janey
wanted a new coat.

It took nearly two hours to buy the tires. Janey hadn't
realized there were so many second-hand tire shops in the
world, and Mr. Larkin called at every one of them and
bargained carefully before finally making up his mind
to do business. Then there was further delay while the
old tires were removed and the others, which the man
assured them were practically as good as new, were in-
stalled. By that time it was nearly noon and Janey was
good and hungry.

"Let's leave the car right here, and do the rest of our
shopping on foot," Dad suggested.

"Might as well," Mom seconded, and so they did.

Janey couldn't remember when she had last walked
along a street like this with automobiles coming and going and street cars clanging past. There were windows so
filled with fascinating things she almost forgot she was
hungry until suddenly the fragrance of cooked food was
wafted to her as a man swung open the door of a restau-
rant just ahead of them and stepped out onto the street.
Coming abreast of the place, Janey flattened her nose
against the large front window and peered inside. She
saw a long counter with stools in front of it and white-
uniformed women setting plates of steaming food before
waiting customers. It all looked simply delicious and
Janey longed to go inside. Just then she heard Dad's
voice behind her and could hardly believe her ears.

"What do you say we go inside and sample their stuff?" he was saying.

With one bound Janey was through the door and wriggling onto a stool before the long counter. A waitress slapped a menu down before her and Janey lost herself in the long list of delectable foods which on this day were being offered. Never had she read anything more interesting than that menu. Once, twice, thrice she went down the list. It was as thrilling as *King Arthur* and the Bible all rolled into one. She heard Dad give his order, then Mom. Now it was her turn; the waitress was standing impatiently before her, pencil poised, and still Janey couldn't make up her mind. Should she have roast beef and mashed potatoes, or veal stew with "homemade" noodles?

"Come, come," said Mom at last, "name one and look at the rest. We can't stay here all day."

"Roast beef," said Janey and sighed. For the rest of the day she would be regretting that veal stew. If only she had room enough and time enough and money enough to eat it all! To start right at the top of the menu card and eat her way clear to the bottom! It would be wonderful!

But the roast beef when it came was so good that Janey forgot all about the other things, and when they had finished and Dad paid the bill she was further gratified to observe that there were still quite a few pieces of currency left in the buckskin bag.

Once again they began to walk along the noisy street until they came to a large store with windows jammed full of all sorts of things. There were clothes to wear and pots to cook in and even chairs to sit in all mixed up together in a nice convenient way so that you could see at a glance just what the store had to offer. And everything in the window had a neat sign on it stating exactly just what each thing cost.

Into this store went Mr. and Mrs. Larkin with Janey close at their heels. Now Mom had paused at a counter and was asking a question of the young lady behind it, and the young lady was nodding toward a far corner of the store. Janey hadn't tried to overhear what they said, but she couldn't help catching the word "coat," and now the young lady was smiling down at her in a special knowing sort of way. And Janey's head began to spin with a high hope. Breathlessly she followed in the wake of Dad and Mom as they sauntered slowly in the direction the clerk had indicated.

And now there could be no doubt. They had arrived at the corner at last and there before Janey's dancing blue eyes were rows upon rows of tall racks with dozens upon dozens of coats hanging from them and every coat had been made to fit some little girl.

A clerk was coming toward them with eyebrows lifted in a politely questioning way. With a practiced, sweeping glance she took in Janey's skinny form, the dress just barely reaching to her knees and the sleeves of her shabby jacket ending two inches above her wrists.

"We want a coat for this girl," Mom was saying. "Something under ten dollars."

The clerk moved toward a rack. "These are eight-seventy-five," she said; "you'll find them a real value at that price."

Dad turned to Janey. "There you are, young one," he said. "Take your pick."

But it wasn't as simple as all that. No, indeed. Janey went around and around the rack, trying first to decide on the color. At length she settled on blue. Then she had to try on one after another to decide which style she liked best, and when that hurdle had been safely got over, they had to find one that was large enough to allow her to grow into it during the next few years, and still not so large that she would look ridiculous in it now. Finally a compromise was reached and Janey became the proud owner of a blue woolly new coat that came way down below her knees and well down over her hands, but which was warm and, to her eyes at least, beautiful.

After buying a few more things, such as overalls and shirts, quite unexciting, they started for home. They had managed well, for the car had new, or almost new, tires, Janey had a brand-new coat, and there was still some money left over in the buckskin bag.

By Doris Gates

THE COSTUME PARTY

"Do you know that your dress is just like the one my mother used to wear in Poland?" the stranger asked Aniela. "I come from Lowicz, too. . . . The colors in that striped skirt are from Mother Earth herself."

THE DAY FOR the "project" and the party had arrived at last. As Aniela went down the hill to school, she saw boys and girls coming from every direction, each in the costume of the country he was going to tell about. Most of them wore the dress their parents had brought from the old country, and they carried in baskets the special food each was to bring. Aniela wondered if they would like the *pączki* Mama had made. She wondered if someone else would tell about the famous people of Poland. She hoped Cecilia wouldn't know about the story of the coffee and the crescent rolls, for Cecilia's name came before Aniela's on the board, and she would tell her story of Poland first.

Then Aniela remembered about the map of Poland Tadek had drawn, and the Christmas carol he had decorated. No one would have anything nicer than that! How proud she was to show everyone what Tadek could do! Ever since that time when she had been kept home with a broken leg, she had thought Tadek could do wonderful things, for he had kept her amused by drawing pictures. Together they had laughed at his funny drawings of Babcia's clucking hens, of Papa playing the organ at church, of Rosie the mine mule with her long ears, and all the other funny things they could think of. If only Tad could learn to paint and draw as he wanted to do, he wouldn't have to work so hard in the mine. Aniela sighed, then remembered the party and hurried on to school.

The singing was lustier than ever that morning. The "rocket's red glare" pierced the roof! It was hard to make arithmetic seem important, and spelling was even duller than before, but at last they were over.

Miss Bauer held up her hand for quiet.

"Now, boys and girls," she said, "you have all done so well in taking an interest in our plan that I think we shall begin to work it out right now. You have brought so much food that I am sure there is enough for another whole class so let us invite Miss Sadowska and her boys and girls, shall we?" Miss Bauer sent Aniela with the invitation. It took a little while to get all the children seated. Some sat two in a seat, some sat on the floor around the room.

"If we try," Miss Bauer began again, "I am sure we can be quiet enough to have our party and our lesson all at once." She opened a covered basket and showed them half-moon pies she had brought and told how the recipe had been handed down from mother to daughter for generations.

"And I have brought enough for everyone!" she said, smiling. "But pie is better for the last, so let us begin with some other food.

"Now, Michael, you are first on the list. Will you begin? Didn't I see a basket on your arm? You chose Slovakia, didn't you?"

"Yes, Miss Bauer," said Michael, answering both questions at once. "My mother sent some sheep's milk cheese that she knows how to make."

"That will be very good," said Miss Bauer. "Did anyone bring bread?"

Cecilia had rye bread and Aniela had her crescent rolls.

"Perhaps the rye bread will be best for this cheese, and since it is soft we can spread it with the knife I brought." Cecilia passed her basket of bread, and Aniela followed with the jar of cheese while Michael began his story.

Michael looked very handsome in his sheepskin coat embroidered in bright colors, and with his broad red belt. Into the belt was thrust a hatchet. He began to speak.

"This is the way my father used to dress when he lived in the old country in the Carpathian mountains in Slovakia. This hatchet was used for clearing the way and for helping climbing. It is always kept bright and sharp ready for use, my father says."

He held up the hatchet. Then he reached into his basket and brought out several things that looked strange and interesting and went on.

"My father says that the men and boys of his part of the country were skilled in wire work and made curious things of it. He says they used to go about the country among the peasants selling these things and mending broken dishes. Like this, see!" He held up a plate, around which was woven a close pattern of fine wire. It was so carefully done that it looked as if the plate had been made that way in the beginning.

"This plate was broken into a dozen pieces," he said. "Yet you cannot see a crack." He looked around very proud. All the boys and girls were so interested that they even stopped eating.

Then Michael held up a queer-looking contraption that was also made of woven wire.

"This is one of the things the wire boys sell. It is a mousetrap. No mouse can run free to eat up the food when one of these is in the house!" Everybody laughed. Then Michael said:

"My father taught me a song about the wire boys, and Aniela's father helped me to put it into English. Shall I sing it?" Michael was one of the choir boys, so he didn't mind singing.

"Why, that would be splendid!" said Miss Bauer. "Stand up and sing out so we can all hear the words." And here they are:

> "This is the wire man,
> He wires the dishes.
> Who gives him a penny
> Will gain his good wishes.

> "This little wire boy
> Everyone hears his hail,
> Because he cries all the day,
> 'Mousetraps for sale!'

> "This little wire boy
> Comes from the mountain height.
> All the day he wanders,
> But he sleeps at night."

Everybody put down the bread and cheese to clap their hands. Aniela remembered hearing Babcia tell about the wire boys and how they mended her pots and dishes.

Then it was Sue's turn. Her costume was bright with embroidery, too. A kerchief covered her head as it did Aniela's. In her basket she had brought honey and sausage and bread.

She began to speak.

"My dress is from Bohemia," she said, then told where Bohemia lay in Europe and the countries that bounded it. She told how well kept the farms were and how fine the cities. She took out of her basket a beautiful little pitcher of ruby glass that her mother had brought from Bohemia where it was made.

"My father told me that some of the most beautiful glass in the world comes from Bohemia." She held the little pitcher up for all to see.

Then she said: "Aniela's papa lent me a copy of our Bohemian song. Shall I sing it?"

"Oh, yes, please do," said Miss Bauer.

In her native tongue Sue sang "Where Is My Home?" Then Aniela knew what it was Sue had come to see Papa about. She could understand most of the words, because they were much like Polish words.

It was Alice's turn next. Alice had currant tea buns in her basket. She was dressed in her Sunday best and had her prettiest hair ribbon on. She had chosen England for her country. She told of what fine silver plate comes from England; what good, hand-woven cloth is made from the wool they raise there. She told of the beautiful dishes that are made in England, and how the old patterns for the dishes were brought from China three hundred years ago, and that is why it is called "chinaware." She told the story Miss Patterson had helped her find about the willow pattern that has been used a great deal and that we all know.

Bronwyn had chosen Wales. She had brought little meat pies, which Miss Bauer divided so there would be enough to go around. Bronwyn wore a thick, stiff dress of close-woven wool.

"It is good for keeping out the damp and cold," she said. "It is always damp and foggy some part of the day in Wales where we used to live."

She wore a kerchief crossed over her breast and a checked apron. On her head was a frilled white cap, on top of which was a steeple-crowned hat.

"And when the weather was very bad," she went on, "we did this." She put on a great cape with an enormous hood that could be pulled up over steeple-crowned hat and all. Aniela thought she looked like the pictures of Mother Goose that she had seen in the first grade room.

Bronwyn told how her father had been a miner in Wales, as he was in America; how proud he was of his own mining tools, and how the miners all depended on him. She told about the fine stone houses they had lived in. How they were built close together and went up and up the steep streets.

"A little like Pennsylvania houses," she said, "only—different." Everybody laughed, even Bronwyn herself.

She told how they had come to America because wages had gone so low in their country and her father hoped for a better living here. When she described how the daffodils grew on the hillside in the spring, her chin trembled, because it made her homesick. She sat down. Then she remembered her cockle basket and got up again to tell how she used to visit her grandmother near the sea and gather cockles on the shore. She said that cockles were small shellfish very good to eat.

"I am sure we should all love to go to Wales," said Miss Bauer. "That was a very good story, Bronwyn.

"Now, Cecelia, it is your turn. Didn't I see something

else in your basket?" Cecilia brought out the pink slices
of ham that were supposed to have been eaten with the
rye bread, but Miss Bauer told Aniela to pass her
crescent rolls instead. What a feast it was!

Cecelia looked just as pretty as Aniela thought she
would. She wore the Krakowiak costume. The top part
was a little jacket cut in tabs about the waist, with
spangles sewed to the edge and around the square neck.
Underneath the jacket was a white blouse with full
sleeves like Aniela's. But the skirt, instead of being of
striped wool, was of fine white material, with ribbons of
every color running around the deep hem. She wore red
boots laced high, and on her head a wreath of flowers,
with more ribbons streaming.

She told a great deal about the city of Kraków and
about the dragon that Krakus killed. How he used to eat
more and more people and animals until he was fed a
sheepskin stuffed with sulphur, then he drank and drank
of the river Vistula until he burst.

Then Cecilia read how Poland had always been a
place of safety for those who were in trouble, how during
the time called the Reformation, books were allowed to
be printed when they were forbidden in other countries
of Europe. She told of the University of Kraków and
that it was one of the oldest in central Europe, about the
wonderful cathedral of Kraków, the palaces and the gardens.

Aniela began to think it hardly worth while to tell
what she knew, but she and Cecilia and Michael danced
the Krakowiak, as they had learned it at the Saturday
school, and Miss Sadowska looked pleased.

While the boys and girls were clapping, Aniela went back to her seat to get her things ready, for her name was next on the board.

She got out her copybook, in which was the Christmas carol, the story about her costume, and the one about the coffee and the crescent rolls. She spread out the map and waited to be called upon. Before the room was quiet again, someone knocked at the door.

Miss Bauer held up her hand for silence and went to see who it was. A strange man stood there. To Aniela, he looked like the man who had visited Father Witkowski at Christmas time and who came to the Saturday school entertainment. He talked in a low tone to Miss Bauer for a moment, then sat down near Miss Sadowska, whom he seemed to know.

"We have company, boys and girls, and I know you will want to share our party with him. Then, shall we go right on? Aniela, I think you are next," Miss Bauer said, as she arranged some of the food on a paper napkin for the stranger. Aniela wished she didn't have to tell her story with the strange man there, but he looked so friendly, and seemed to be having such a good time, that she began by opening her basket to bring out the *pączki*. Mama had made more than enough. The bottom of the basket was filled with the luscious-looking doughnuts. Miss Bauer took the basket to pass it around.

"My Mamusia came from the province of Lowicz, in the very heart of Poland. That is why my dress is like this instead of like Cecilia's. See! This is where it is," she held up the map and pointed out where Lowicz lay. Then she read the paper Father had helped her prepare, telling the meaning of her peasant's costume. She pointed out the yellow for the wheatfields, the brown for the plowed furrows, and the black for the rich bottom land. The green was for grass where the cattle stood all day in the sun. The darker green was for hedgerows of small trees and shrubs where the rabbits hide and the birds have their nests.

Then she read what Miss Patterson had helped her find out about Chopin the composer, and Paderewski, the great pianist, and how Stanislaw had heard him play in Philadelphia! Of course she remembered to tell about *Kościuszko.* She read what Father had told her about the victory of the Poles in a battle against the Turks.

"You see," she went on, "the Turks would have taken all of Europe if Jan Sobieski, Good King John, had not been so good a general. Poland was then a strong country, and the Turks could not get beyond her borders. But during this time, she had fought many wars to keep her freedom. She had fought Sweden and Russia as well as the Turks.

"The Turks had reached into Austria and were threatening the city of Vienna when the Emperor sought help from Poland. King John was no longer young, and he was weary of wars, but the Austrians begged his help, so he consented to go to their aid. When the Turks heard that Sobieski was on his way, they fled in terror, leaving behind them great quantities of coffee. Coffee had not been used in that part of Europe before that time.

"A Polish spy had carried information that led to the defeat of the Turks. He had learned their language and their way of living and knew the use of coffee. As a reward for his great service to Austria, the Emperor gave him permission to open the first coffee shop in Vienna. To celebrate the victory, he made rolls to serve with the coffee in the shape of the crescent that to this day is the symbol of Turkey. And that is why we have crescent rolls!" said Aniela as she finished her story. Then she asked Miss Bauer if they could all sing the carol Tadek had decorated, even though Christmas was long past. Many of them knew from having learned it at the Saturday school.

"There is always time for a song," said Miss Bauer.

When they had finished the carol, Miss Bauer called them to attention again.

"Now, boys and girls, there are only a few more to tell their stories. Then it will be time to go home. Gather up all of your things that belong to the lesson, and, Aniela, you can collect them for me to see. I know you have maps and pictures and your stories, and I shall look them over very carefully."

While the last two boys were telling their stories, one about Lithuania and the other about Russia, Miss Bauer and some of the girls passed around the half-moon pies.

The party was nearly over. Aniela sighed. It had been such fun!

Then Miss Bauer spoke to her.

"Aniela, will you stay for a few moments after the others have gone?"

Aniela looked surprised. What could Miss Bauer want her for? Didn't she like her part of the "project"?

Finally Miss Bauer came back to where she sat and said: "Aniela, you have told us many things about Poland that I am sure we should never find in books. We shall think of Poland as our friend more than ever. Come up here to the front of the room. Here is someone who would like to speak to you." She took Aniela by the hand and led her over to Miss Sadowska and the strange visitor.

"Do you know that your dress is just like the one my mother used to wear in Poland?" the stranger asked Aniela. *"I* come from Lowicz, too! And how that dress and kerchief take me back! I am glad you know the meaning of it. The colors in that striped skirt are from Mother Earth herself. When I am painting the picture on the church wall, I shall think of you in that little kerchief." He pinched Aniela's cheek.

Aniela's eyes opened wide. A painter! The very one who was painting the church wall? She could hardly believe it! Then he *was* the man that Father called "that painter fellow"! How she wished that Tadek could be there!

Quick as a wink, she thought, "If he likes my dress, perhaps he will like me, too, and will listen if I tell him about how Tadek wants to draw and paint." She began to say it all at once, as if she were afraid he would get away before she finished.

"My brother—he can draw. He can paint too, if he has paints. He thinks all the time about drawing and painting. He works in the mine and drives Rosie, but nights, when supper is over, he draws pictures. He draws everything!"

She stopped for breath. She looked at Miss Bauer, afraid she had said too much, but Miss Bauer was smil-

ing and handing to the painter the carol they had sung.
The painter was smiling too, and when he saw the carol,
he looked at it for a long time. Then he said:

"So your brother did this?"

Aniela nodded her head. Her words were all gone.

"It is beautiful," said the painter. "But who is
Rosie?"

His eyes twinkled at Aniela.

"Rosie is the mine mule," she answered. "And sometimes she balks."

"Yes, I know about mine mules. I used to drive one
myself. I was just teasing. Now tell me more about this
brother of yours." He looked again at the carol of the
birds. "When he can draw like this, he should find an
easier way to make a living than working in a mine. He
has a real gift. I should like to see this boy. And doesn't
your father play the organ? Doesn't he want your brother
to learn to draw and paint?"

Aniela hung her head. She didn't want to tell the
painter that he thought painting would make a very poor
living. She didn't want to say anything against her dear,
dearest Papa, so she didn't say anything for a moment.
Then:

"Mamusia wants Tadek to paint more than anything,
but Tatuś says he can't earn a good living that way," she
said.

"But a gift like this must not be buried. Perhaps your
daddy is right. There aren't always churches to be
painted. Sometimes painters go hungry. But if that is
what you want most, to draw and paint is like having
food and drink. Something must be done. I shall talk to

this daddy of yours, then we shall see!" He smiled at Aniela.

Something bubbled up inside her. Something wonderful was going to happen! She knew it!

Aniela suddenly felt she must get home. She must tell someone or she would burst! She picked up her basket and her shawl, and without stopping to say "Goodbye," she ran as fast as she could go out of the school and up the street, around the corner and up to the hill toward home.

By Marguerite de Angeli

GIVE ME A RIVER

When she saw the eager faces in her audience, Jenny Lind smiled and bowed and then they cheered and clapped and shouted all over again. . . . Many of her listeners knew the Swedish folk songs on the program, for they had sung them in the old country long before they ever heard of Minnesota Territory, or had thought of making it their home. These she sang so simply, so sweetly, that the men and women in the boats could only wipe their eyes, for they were back again in Sweden, raking hay in a sunny mountain pasture, singing at their work, or dancing and shouting around a Maypole in a remote Swedish village.

JENNY LIND the great singer, the lovely Swedish nightingale, was coming to Stillwater! She was coming on the twenty-third of May to give a concert! The Turngren children told each other it couldn't be true. They had heard stories about her all their lives. . . . "Jenny Lind sings for Queen Victoria" or "Mlle. Lind Opens the Paris Opera." . . . But to have her here in their village on the St. Croix river was almost more than they could bear.

Their friend Louis Liverpool, who lived alone in a little house by the river and knew more songs than you could count, said when he heard the news, "I tell you there's nothing like living by a river. Always somethin' goin' on. Go ahead take the oceans and the lakes, they don't belong to me. Give me a river any day."

As the day of the concert approached the village fairly hummed with preparation. The women cleaned and washed and polished. The men cut weeds along the village paths, mended the wooden sidewalks and painted the store fronts. The children met every afternoon to make Swedish flags to wave when the darling of the great cities of Europe, the idol of every Swedish heart, the beloved Jenny Lind stepped off the gangplank of the packet *Magnolia* which was bringing her up the river.

Margy Turngren painted a wreath of flowers around

the great day on the kitchen calendar and every night
after that she and her four brothers took turns firmly
crossing off the dragging days. When the twenty-second
of May came, she packed her bag and was off to spend
the night with her friend Katy Lou Boyle who lived
with her Aunt Melly at the West Hotel where Jenny
Lind was going to stay. It took them a long time to go to
sleep with so much to think about. When the clock struck
midnight, Katy Lou cuddled into her pillow whispering,
"It's beginning. The twenty-third of May is beginning!"

Early the next morning they jumped out of bed for
this was the day they had been waiting for and there were
many last details to be attended to. They put bowls of
wild roses in the rooms reserved for Jenny Lind. They
made the bed with Aunt Melly's own hand-woven sheets
and pillow shams. They went back again and again to be
sure no speck of dust had appeared, that no wrinkle had
found its way onto the bed, that no petal had fallen to
give the room an untidy look. Here, they told each other,
Jenny Lind would lay her pretty head, there she would
hang her lovely clothes, here she would walk up and
down rehearsing.

Just before lunch Aunt Melly let them go out. The
streets were exciting. Children hurried towards the concert hall with arms full of flowers; men followed with
milk-cans full of water; the volunteers rolled out the
fire engine; the boys rubbed the brass once more and tied
on bunches of blue and yellow flowers because it was
going to lead the parade from the dock to the hotel.
There were shouts of laughter everywhere.

Margy and Katy Lou loitered along the streets watching the ladies decorate the hall, listening to the men talking on the street corners. When they heard the coach from St. Paul come rattling down the hill they turned reluctantly back towards the hotel, for Aunt Melly had warned them lunch would be early. A boy throwing dodgers ran by in a great hurry.

"Wash your hands," Aunt Melly called. "What has struck you, Katy Lou? You look as if you'd seen a ghost."

Katy Lou walked across to the dining room table holding out one of the dodgers. "Jenny Lind isn't coming," she said bleakly. "The *Magnolia's* stuck on a sandbar."

No words can describe the heartbreaking disappointment which engulfed the two girls when they realized the awful truth. Jenny Lind wasn't coming. There would be no parade, no concert. They ate part of their lunch and then asked to be excused. They climbed to the cupola on top of the hotel and spent the afternoon sharing with each other their sad little comments on the whole affair. There was nothing they wanted to do, nowhere they wanted to go, for no matter how you looked at it, any substitute plan was an anti-climax.

While they were eating their supper that night, the dining room door opened and a red-faced young man stepped in.

"What do you want?" Aunt Melly asked.

"Captain Boyle's compliments," said the boy, presenting a letter. Aunt Melly opened it and read it out loud:

"Dear Melly

Miss Lind is greatly upset over our mishap. She says she will give as much of her concert as possible to any who are able to get down here. She leaves tomorrow morning on a down packet so it will have to be tonight, if at all. Please pass this word around.

Sincerely

JAMES BOYLE."

There was a moment's silence and then Aunt Melly said, "I'm not going to be beaten when I have a chance to hear Jenny Lind sing."

"What're you going to do?"

"I'm going to find the *Magnolia* and I'm going to take you and Margy with me if it's the last thing on earth I do."

The girls threw their arms around each other.

"Now, then," Aunt Melly went on. "Katy Lou, you take this letter and hand it to Mr. Applegate. He was chairman and I saw him going home half an hour ago. Hand it to him and then come straight back here. Margy, run as fast as you can to Louis Liverpool. You know where he lives. Tell him to meet us at the levee with his bateau. Stay with him. I'll bring you a shawl."

The news in Captain Boyle's letter spread rapidly through the town so that when Aunt Melly and Katy Lou reached the levee an excited crowd had already gathered there. Mr. Applegate had his family with him; the four Turngren boys left with the chief of the fire department. The people on the levee waved and shouted as each boat disappeared in the black night.

Louis and Margy were waiting in the long bateau. He stood erect holding a flare over his head while the others took their places, then he took up his oars and they swung into the current and were off with the rest. A whippoor-will called sharply over and over but otherwise there were no sounds on the river but the squeak squeak of the oar-locks and the drip and splash of the water from the oars. The air was cool and the shawls Aunt Melly had provided were wrapped around the two girls. Occasionally their boat was near one of the others but then it would pull ahead, or they would, and they were alone again on the dark river.

After an hour or so, the river widened, the bluffs grew higher and they could see several boats on either side of them with rowers bending to their oars. Someone was singing one of the old Bellman songs about a butterfly. The girls peered ahead in the dark while the bateau cut through the water and the oars splashed and dipped, splashed and dipped, pulling downstream under the marvelous summer sky.

"Look!" Aunt Melly said suddenly. "Straight ahead on the left."

"Oh," said Katy Lou with a shiver. "Is that the *Magnolia?*"

There she was to be sure, gaudiest of river packets, stuck on a sand-bar, as helpless as a wagon with three wheels. But to the girls she was beautiful, nevertheless, and exciting and magnificent. Her gangplank had been swung out ahead ready to be lowered when they tied up at Stillwater. Her lights, her gold trimmings, the bright reflections rippling across the water, gave her the appearance of a fabulous fairy-tale ship, overtaken for the moment by mortal disaster. As Louis's bateau drew nearer, the *Magnolia's* sides towered above them like white cliffs. The ship's bell struck softly. Other boats joined them, moving mysteriously out of the darkness.

Captain Boyle, standing by the rail, shouted through his megaphone, "Tie your boats together, so you won't float away. Miss Lind prefers to come out here to sing. Everybody stand by." Ropes were thrown overboard and quickly passed from one boat to another, oars were shipped, while the women and children made themselves comfortable with cushions and shawls.

At last a door on the lower deck opened and in the bright light that streamed out they could see Captain Boyle leading by the hand a smiling young woman, whom they knew at once to be none other than the great Jenny Lind herself. She was dressed in a gown of pink silk crepe, with a low-cut bodice and long ruffles of black lace. A tiny wreath of flowers crowned her hair. As the Captain led her forward shout after shout went up from the people in the boats. They clapped and cheered and shouted, they waved handkerchiefs and shouted and cheered again. But Katy Lou and Margy could only stare with eyes that grew rounder and wider, as the lovely creature smiled and waved at them. Were they really there, looking at Jenny Lind, waiting to hear her sing, or would they wake up in a moment and find it was all a dream and they just had time to get to school?

When she saw the eager faces in her audience, Jenny Lind smiled and bowed and then they cheered and clapped and shouted all over again. Presently, however, two deckhands passed out the programs which had been printed for the Stillwater concert and when all was quiet, she folded her hands, raised her head, and began to sing, softly at first, then, gradually letting out her voice, she gave them all she had. Those who heard her that night could never fully describe the beauty of her voice nor the qualities that made her famous, but they never forgot how she looked nor what she sang.

Many of her listeners knew the Swedish folk songs on the program, for they had sung them in the old country long before they ever heard of Minnesota Territory, or had thought of making it their home. These she sang so simply, so sweetly, that the men and women in the boats could only wipe their eyes, for they were back again in Sweden, raking hay in a sunny mountain pasture, singing at their work, or dancing and shouting around a Maypole in a remote Swedish village.

At the end of an hour she nodded to the Captain, and presently two negroes appeared carrying a banjo and a fiddle, seating themselves on the gangplank behind her. Then the beloved Swedish nightingale, the great Jenny Lind, turned to her audience with a gesture which drew together those in boats, the others below or behind her, making them one with her and her music, the woods, the dark river, and the starry sky.

"Come my friends," she said, "there is one more song and you must sing it with me. We will make music together before I go." The fiddle and the banjo gave the opening notes, and Jenny Lind began to sing. Louis Liverpool was the first to join her, standing up in his bateau with his hat held against his chest and his face turned up towards hers. The children followed and one by one the whole group joined in until they were all singing:

" 'Mid pleasures and palaces though we may roam,
  Be it ever so humble, there's no place like home;
  A charm from the skies seems to hallow us there
  Which sought through the world is ne'er met with elsewhere.
  Home, home, home sweet home,
  Be it ever so humble, there's no place like home."

When they had sung the last verse, she bowed again and again, leaned over the rail to take the flowers Lars Turngren handed her, then turned to the Captain with a smile and leaning on his arm, disappeared through the cabin door.

The listeners in the boats looked at each other, hardly able to believe they had really seen Jenny Lind. As the boats turned towards home, they fell into a long line which wound back and forth through the bright reflections, while the children looking back, chanted over and over, "Come back Jenny Lind. Come back Jenny Lind."

Louis Liverpool nodded his head. "My heart is singing something too," he said. "Remember this, you can take the lakes and oceans—how many times have I told you they don't belong to me—give me a river any day."

By Elizabeth Palmer

HOUSE OF THE SINGING WINDOWS

"Mother, are there then goblins—real goblins—*in this Iowa where we go?"*

His mother had laughed. "No, Johann! Thy great-uncle speaks of a different kind of goblin. . . . He means only the strange customs we will meet, the unfamiliar people, the new language."

Well, Johann's heart was young and strong, but now it hid a deep, growing worry. Oh, he didn't fear the new language . . . but strangers . . . other boys his age . . .

JOHANN RIEHL LAY flat on his stomach behind the low stone wall and peeked out cautiously at the children going by.

There were two of them . . . a boy who might match Johann's own nine years, and a girl a little younger. Every morning they passed Johann's home on their way to the white frame house down the road, and every morning Johann lay breathlessly behind the stone wall and watched them.

"Goblins!" he whispered when they were safely gone. "Hobgoblins!"

They weren't of course and Johann knew it. But the word had a special meaning for Johann.

Way back in Bavaria, across the sea, Johann's great-uncle Fritz had used it when Johann's father and mother had urged him to come with them to America.

"Nein, nein!" he'd shaken his head positively. "Once I have been there and that is enough. I am too old to go fighting hobgoblins now!"

Johann's eyes had nearly bulged from his head. He had followed his mother to the kitchen, words sputtering out of him like corn popping.

"Mother, are there then goblins—*real goblins*—in this Iowa where we go?"

His mother had laughed. "No, Johann! Thy great-uncle speaks of a different kind of goblin, one that needs no tickling spear to scare the old and timid. He means only the strange customs we will meet, the unfamiliar people, the new language. To him, those are as fearsome as goblins, and he has no longer the young stout heart to beat them off."

Well, Johann's heart was young and strong, but now it hid a deep, growing worry. Oh, he didn't fear the new language—hadn't he spent a whole year learning it painstakingly from the Englishwoman across town? But strangers . . . other boys his age. . . .

He'd asked his great-uncle about it, very casually to show that it didn't really matter.

"The American *junge,* Uncle Fritz, the boys and girls over there—they were not so different from me, hein?"

Under his great bushy eyebrows, his great-uncle's eyes had twinkled secretly. "Ach, such creatures! They do nothing but play baseball and eat apple-pie and ice-cream and dream of being cowboys! And their talk, it is outlandish! 'Holy jumping catfish' they say. And 'Nuts!'"

Johann was quite subdued during the rest of the preparations for their journey. Baseball. Ice-cream. Cowboys. Holy jumping catfish. Anxiously, he said the strange words over and over, struggling with their meaning.

It was March when they embarked—Johann, his mother, his father, and the twenty-two canaries Mother could not leave behind. The voyage was wintry and dismal, across a sea as grey with fog as Johann's own heart. But Spring reached America almost as soon as the Riehls did, and Johann thought the bewildering number of miles they crossed to Iowa were like layers to a towering cake, each layer more richly plummed with beauty than the last.

Oh, this was a good land, a fine, generous, strong

land. Johann loved it already. If only—if only its people loved *him!*

For the first week, he didn't have to find out about that, though. Mother kept him too busy. They scrubbed and polished every inch of the snug farmhouse that was to be their home. It was an old, old house, built of stout, warm-hued stone, and in it Johann could almost believe himself back in Bavaria. Mother had set up her many little pots of vines against the living-room and kitchen walls by the staircase; she had spread the familiar braided and crocheted rugs over the floors. Father had taken time off from planting to screen the front windows inside and out (the sills were more than a foot deep), and now the windows made fine big cages for the twenty-two canaries.

"Next week," Mother decided briskly, "thou must start to school, Johann, with the other *kinder!*"

Johann's heart dropped straight to his hiking boots. School. Strange American children like the two who passed his hiding-place each morning. Now surely Johann was up against the biggest goblin of them all?

Soon after eight o'clock, the following Monday morning, Johann's mother pronounced him ready for school. His hair was slicked flat under the little pancake of a beret; his short tight jacket and brief pants were freshly pressed. His bare knees, like his hands and face, shone pink with scrubbing.

"Now shall thy father go with thee, Johann?" his mother asked kindly. "Or I?"

"Nein, neither!" Johann said hastily. "Let me go alone, Mother!"

"Alone?" she looked at him doubtfully. "You have the school report, *hein?* And the letter from the schoolmaster? . . . Ah, well, go then, little one."

Once outside, Johann circled quickly to the barn.

His heart beat furiously fast; if he hadn't been nine-going-on ten, he'd have almost thought he was scared. Soon now he must face the American children—do battle with his biggest goblin—but oh, joy, he had found the right uniform for his fight!

He had discovered it yesterday, quite by accident, hanging dusty and forgotten on a hook in the barn . . . a tattered, enormous pair of overalls!

Just such a garment, though smaller, had the boy worn who'd passed Johann's house each day . . . so different a looking garment from Johann's own clothes that Johann had been sick at heart.

But now—

Diligently, Johann smacked and smoothed the precious overalls, pinning them to his size with many, many safety pins. Perhaps Mother could have cut them down to fit, but Johann hadn't told her of his prize. She'd worry because there was no money this Spring to replace his foreign clothes.

The overalls bulked a little oddly when he was finished, but even so, Johann decided anxiously, they looked better, more American than his own suit. Carefully he hung his jacket and cap on the hook, and ventured at last out into the road.

Ahead of him walked the girl and boy.

The boy was first to hear the scuffle of Johann's boots in the gravel. He looked back and stopped, staring at

Johann unblinkingly the whole minute it took Johann
to overtake them.

Then, finally, he spoke. "Hi!"

The careful "how-do-you-do" Johann had learned
from the Englishwoman choked in his throat. He swallowed hard, and faintly echoed, "Hi."

"You going to school?"

Johann nodded. They fell into step.

"My name's Peter Janus, and this here's Paula.
What's your name?"

"Jo—" Inspiration struck Johann, and boldly he
chopped off the balance. "Joe Riehl."

Johann gestured back toward the stone farmhouse.
The little girl squealed suddenly, "Oh Peter, he lives
in the house with the singing windows! I *told* you somebody nice must live there!"

Peter looked more sharply at Johann. "They said
some Germans bought that. You German?"

Johann took a deep breath and mustered the words
well in his mind before trying them. "Holy jumping catfish, no! I'm American!"

They reached the schoolhouse. Peter led Johann up
to the teacher's desk. "We gotta new boy, Miss Iverson.
His name's Joe. Joe—what did you say?"

"Riehl."

Miss Iverson held out her hand. "Hello, Joe. We're
glad to have you." She had a smiling face and corn-
yellow hair, and Johann knew instantly that he wanted
to please her above all else.

There was no time then to find out what class Johann
would belong to. He took a seat in the back of the room

and listened and looked with all his might. Here all about him were American children, real Americans. Already they accepted Johann as one of them. But if they found out he *wasn't*—

When the recess bell rang, Peter came straight to Johann. "Whatcha want to play?"

Johann plunged bravely. "Baseball."

"Baseball, huh?" Peter's face brightened. "What's *your* act—pitch or catch?"

Johann gulped. His eyes roved wildly in search of help. Miss Iverson chose just that moment to come up to them and say, "You run out and play, Peter. Joe's had recess all morning, and now I must find out what class to put him in."

"Now, Joe," she went on briskly, drawing paper and pencil toward her, "have you a report card from your last school?"

Automatically, Johann reached into his pants pocket beneath the tremendous overalls. Then his hand stopped; his face became a picture of woe.

"You forgot it?" Miss Iverson smiled. "Well, never mind. Tomorrow will do. Now what subjects were you studying this year?"

Johann brought his hand out of his pocket guiltily, leaving the report card where it was. His mind was a whirl of giddy fireworks, and all he knew clearly was that he *couldn't* show that record from a foreign school. He just couldn't.

"Reading, I suppose?" Miss Iverson prompted him. "Geography?"

"Oh, *ja!*" Johann said hastily. "And Script and

French and Political Science—" He stopped short, silenced by the puzzled look in Miss Iverson's eyes. Now what had he said wrong?

Slowly, Miss Iverson pushed the paper away from her. "I believe we'll wait for the report card after all," she said with a friendly nod of dismissal. "I'll put you with Peter today."

Johann drew a mighty breath of relief. For today, then he was safe. Tomorrow was a goblin he'd not battle till it came.

The rest of the morning went smoothly. Johann recited with Peter's Reading class, and found the words he'd learned from the Englishwoman quite adequate. His sums were correctly done, too, and he went out to lunch very satisfied with himself.

Peter sprawled beside him in a shady corner of the schoolground. When Johann opened his basket and got out the fat roll with the good *leberwurst* inside, Peter's eyes popped greedily. "Oh, boy! You got hot dogs, huh?"

Johann looked curiously at his sandwich and then nodded violently. "Sure. Hot Dogs. You want one?"

He gave Peter a roll, and Peter said generously, "Here, you can have my pie!"

Johann took it gingerly. It had thin flaky crust top and bottom, and it tasted not unlike his mother's *apfeltorte*. Johann gobbled it down to the last bite and sighed contentedly. These American ways, they weren't so hard to take!

The afternoon got off to a bad start. Miss Iverson opened it by talking about a party. Apparently it was to be quite a party, the last event of the school year, and the children must have discussed it often from the way everybody chattered at once. Peter leaned over to whisper noisily, "It's gonna to be fun! An all-American party. Our folks are comin' and everything!"

Johann's heart curled into a tight little ball. All-American. Then it would be just for those who were completely American. Johann felt suddenly cold and left out; he could never pass for an all-American, never!

Afternoon classes didn't go as well as the morning ones. Johann stumbled badly in Spelling, and in History he could only stand dumb. Then, shockingly it was recess again and Peter was pushing a great long sort of club into his hand and shouting, "First bat! Joe's first bat!"

He was shoved and jostled into an awkward position facing a boy with a ball. Johann's eyes were huge and black with fright; he didn't know what was coming next. But it turned out to be the ball that was coming—coming right at him and fast!

Johann gave a startled yelp and put up the strange club to ward it off. The ball cracked briskly against it and shot back over the big boy's head. Everybody was yelling and screeching in a deafening way. Urgent hands pushed Johann wildly. "Run, Joe! RUN!"

What had he done? What must he run from? His pounding heart took his breath away; he tried to force more speed into his trembling legs. Something tangled with his feet and almost threw him. An open pin pricked sharply at his heaving side; he felt his overall slipping, slipping from his shoulders, and the tangle was growing more desperate around his feet.

But still he ran, and still urgent hands thrust at him, turning him in a big circle until suddenly he tripped and fell flat, right where he'd started.

"Yay! Home-run!"

Johann thought his poor ears would split. Peter pounded him on the back. He tried earnestly to get up, and now the cause of his tangle was hopelessly apparent. The pins in his overall legs had come loose. Terrible lengths of blue denim, like rolls of elephant flesh, cascaded around his ankles. Even the sides of the suit gaped open limply.

The roar around him was sharpened by laughter. "Hey!" the big boy who'd thrown the ball howled. "You shrinkin' or somethin', kid?"

But suddenly Peter was squared away before the big boy like a bristling terrier. "Maybe he likes his clothes that way, see? Maybe he likes room to grow! You wanna make something of it?"

The recess bell cut across the argument. Peter hurried back to Johann and helped him with the pins. "Don't you give a hoot about that ol' smarty!" Peter said strongly. "You are swell!"

The spreading warmth around Johann's heart was damped out coldly at four o'clock when Miss Iverson closed the schoolhouse door and joined Johann and Peter and Paula.

"I believe I will just walk home with you," she told Johann companionably. "It'll be a good time to pick up your report card!"

Johann couldn't say a word. All his words were strangled inside him. A last desperate hope loosened his tongue. "I'll go ahead!" he stammered. "I—I'll tell Mother you're coming!"

He tore away from them faster even than he'd made the home-run. Panting, he crossed the fields, flung open the front door. "Mother! Mother! They are coming!"

His mother hurried anxiously out of the kitchen, wiping her hands on her big apron. "What is it, boy? Who comes?"

"The teacher, Mother! Oh, you must hurry, hurry— make yourself fine in the good dress—talk only the American—oh, Mother, you do understand, don't you? They are coming!"

"Ja, ja!" She ran up the steps, too rushed and bewildered to notice Johann's strange costume. He trotted swiftly back to meet the others and slow their pace. Now if Mother put on the American dress Uncle Fritz had bought her when he was here—oh, it was just a kitchen work dress, but it was *American!*—maybe, even yet, his secret would still be safe.

Slowly, slowly, Johann guided the trio through his front gate.

"See, Miss Iverson!" Paula cried. "See the windows!"

"Oh, beautiful!" Miss Iverson exclaimed, and then she repeated softly, "Beautiful. . . ."

But her voice was different, and she wasn't looking at the windows now. Johann followed her glance to the front door.

His Mother stood there. Her face was flushed pink from hurry, but its gentle dignity was undisturbed. She had done what her son asked: she had put on her finest

. . . the full, embroidered skirt and tiny jacket, the fine-tucked floating-sleeved blouse of her Sunday best back in Bavaria. Proudly, now, she held out her hands to them while her eyes went shyly to Johann for approval, and she said in her careful English,

"Welcome!"

Johann's throat choked with a great love for her. Oh, it didn't matter that she'd torn his poor secret wide open! She'd tried hard to please him . . . they'd just better like her! They'd just better!

Fiercely he strode to her side and faced them. "Miss Iverson, this is my mother, Frau Riehl!" And just so there'd be no mistake, he added defiantly, "And my name's not Joe, either. It's Johann!"

But oddly, nobody seemed much concerned. Paula and Peter had run over to look at the canaries, and Miss Iverson said casually, "I daresay it will be Joe soon enough. The boys will see to that." She started to follow his mother into the house.

Johann said bewilderedly, "But we're not Americans like you. We come from across the sea—"

Miss Iverson smiled. "Don't we all, Joe? Isn't that what America is, a gathering place for everybody with the courage to cross the sea and find it? Why, that's why our country is big and strong, Joe, because it takes big, strong people to leave all that's dear and familiar behind them, and to strike out to find a new world! People like you and your parents . . . like Peter's grandfather who came from Greece, like my own mother and father who left their home in Norway. Oh, you'll see us all, dressed in our own particular Old World clothes at the all-

American party! Your mother must be sure to come and wear that lovely costume."

Johann's head was swimming with happiness. "But the all-American . . . I thought it meant . . ."

"Just that we, who were Norse and Greek and German, are all Americans now, Joe—that's what it means." Miss Iverson went on into the house, and Johann swung around open-armed to Peter and Paula.

"Come on in!" he invited warmly. "The windows look much prettier from inside!"

Proudly he ushered them into his home, and sunshine poured into his heart through a thousand singing windows.

By Nan Gilbert

HATSUNO'S GREAT-GRANDMOTHER

Dinner was Japanese American. Seven Nodas—and Grandmother—crowded around an ordinary American table; but the utensils were chopsticks instead of knives and forks. The fish soup and the pickled radish were Japanese; the pakkai *were American spareribs and the fluffy white rice was international. Bread and butter were pure American, and the dessert was Japanese gelatine, too firm to quiver. "It is not so nervous as American jelly," Harry said.*

Only Grandmother seemed all Japanese.

HATSUNO NODA WALKED alone in the crowd of girls and boys pouring out of school. She held her head so straight that her chubby black braids spatted her trim shoulders, and her step was so brisk that you would have thought she enjoyed walking by herself. Hatsuno could not bear to let anyone guess how lonesome she felt in the gay throng.

Brother Harry and six-year-old brother Teddy were deep in clumps of their schoolmates, but the girls from Hattie's class streamed by her without pausing. Behind her Patty White, whom she liked best of all, skipped along between Sue and Phyllis, giggling and talking. Hattie wondered what they were talking about. Often they were chattering about Hattie's secret dream; but today it sounded as if they were discussing the Mother's Day tea next month. This morning the teacher had appointed Patty chairman of the decorating committee.

Hattie could have helped decorate. Her slim fingers knew how to fold amazing Japanese paper birds, flowers, dolls. And at the old school the teacher would have had her do colored drawings on the blackboard, along with Tommy Lin, who was Chinese, and Consuelo, who was Mexican. The three drew better than any of the "plain Americans." But in this new school, where almost all were "plain Americans," no one knew what Hattie's fingers could do.

No, the girls were not talking about the tea.

"If you join now," Patty was saying, "you can go up to camp this summer—"

Oh, if only Patty were saying it to Hatsuno! But she wasn't. She broke off as she danced past with the others.

"Hi, Hattie!" she called, wrinkling her tiptilted nose in a smile and tossing back her thistledown curls.

Hattie smiled a small, stiff smile, though she ached to shout "Hi!" and fall in step with Patty. Then maybe Patty would think to ask her.

"Join"—"camp": those words were the keys to one of Hattie's dearest dreams.

Hatsuno had never been in the mountains. All her life she had lived where she could see them, stretching like a purple wall across the end of the dingy downtown street. They were beautiful, with snow-capped peaks shining pink and lavender and gold in the sunrise, and Hatsuno had always longed to explore them; but though they looked so near, they were miles and miles away.

The new school had given her hope. In the new school there was a Camp Fire group; and every summer it spent a few days at a camp far up in the mountains. Hattie had seen pictures of its bark-covered lodges climbing steeply among the tall evergreens beside a sparkling stream. She had heard Patty tell of the campfires and the horse-back rides. For Patty was a Camp Fire girl, and Patty's mother was the Guardian of the group. Yet, friendly though Patty was, she never spoke of Hattie's joining. And Hattie was far too shy to bring up the subject.

In her old home she had not been so shy; but the old house had grown too small, and they had had to move to a larger one. Hattie, the first Noda baby, had been followed by five boys, and, as Harry said, each child shrunk the house a little bit more. This spring brought not only a new baby but a new grandmother, and the house was as small as Hattie's year-before-last coat. Even Mother couldn't let out its hems enough to make it do.

Mother could manage almost anything. During the depression, when Father was out of work, Mother had kept the children neat as wax and even stylish. She was always up, working, when Hattie woke in the morning, always up, mending and making over, when Hattie went to sleep at night. Mother was proud that even in the bad years Denver had few Japanese Americans "on relief": almost as few as in jail.

Even Mother could not stretch the house enough for the new baby and Great-Grandmother. So the Nodas had moved, uprooting the children from neighborhood and school. The new school was pleasant; Hattie's teacher, Miss Bender, was lovely; Patty White was the gayest, prettiest girl Hattie had ever met. But Hattie didn't fit in.

So here she was, walking home alone, with Camp Fire and the mountains as far away as ever. Teddy overtook her, making noises like a machine gun—like a railway train—like an airplane. Teddy's face was as round as a button, his eyes as black as coal, his teeth as white as rice.

"Last one home's a lame duck!" he chirped at her.

She did not hurry as she once would have done. Home was a changed place now; changed by Grandmother as well as by the new house.

Though Great-Grandmother had come from Japan ten years ago, Hattie had never seen her till this month. Great-Grandmother had lived with Aunt Kiku in San

Francisco, until Aunt Kiku's death had left Grandmother alone.

She was not at all what Hattie had expected; not at all like grandmothers in books, comfortable, plump people who loved to spoil their grandchildren. No, Grandmother was not that kind.

Hattie slowly opened the door, which still quivered from Teddy's banging it. Little gray Grandmother sat stiffly erect, only her head bent toward the sock she was darning, her small feet dangling.

"How do you do, Grandmother?" said Hattie.

"How do you do, Elder Daughter?" Grandmother responded. There is no easy way to say "granddaughter" in Japanese.

Under their folded lids Grandmother's eyes traveled down Hattie. Hattie, feeling prickly, smoothed her hair, straightened her collar, twitched her checked skirt, and finally shifted her weight to one knee as Grandmother reached her feet.

"A cold day for bare legs," Grandmother observed. Hattie thought her look added, *And a great girl twelve years old should wear long stockings.*

Self-consciously Hattie's eyes pulled free from Grandmother's. "Oh," she cried, "Dicky's climbed on the piano again." She ran over and replaced the box of satiny white wood in which her latest—and last—doll always stood on view, fairly safe from the six boys. It was an enchanting doll, with glossy black hair and a silk kimono. "The other boys at least keep off the piano," Hattie scolded, "but not Dicky."

Grandmother's cool eyes seemed to say, *Boys have*

to be excused, since they're so much more important than girls. And why should a great girl of twelve care about dolls?

Hattie hurried on into the good-smelling kitchen. "Mother," she complained, "Grandmother doesn't understand that we're Americans, not Japanese. I bet she'd like me to flop down on my knees and bump my head on the floor the way you used to have to, and say, 'Honorable Grandmother, I have returned.'"

"Wash your hands," said Mother, "and help me get dinner on the table."

Hattie slapped her shoes down hard, as she went to the sink to wash. She wished her heels weren't rubber; they didn't make enough noise to express her feelings.

"Of course you will give proper courtesy to the old," Mother said quietly.

"Why? She doesn't even like me." The question was useless. Hattie had grown up knowing that politeness to the old was as much a law as honesty, industry, self-control—and minding parents.

Mother only said, "Stop and buy grapefruit on your way from school. Be sure to pick out heavy ones."

"Of course," Hattie grumbled. Hadn't she known how to choose good fruit and vegetables since she was nine?

Dinner was Japanese American. Seven Nodas—and Grandmother—crowded round an ordinary American table; but the utensils were chopsticks instead of knives and forks. The fish soup and the pickled radish were Japanese; the *pakkai* were American spareribs and the fluffy white rice was international. Bread and butter were pure American, and the dessert was Japanese gelatine, too firm to quiver. "It's not so nervous as American jelly," Harry said, and made Teddy laugh till his eyes went shut.

Only Grandmother seemed all Japanese: in the way she sipped her soup and tea, with a noise that was polite in Japan but not in America; in the way she refused bread and butter; in the way she greeted an old neighbor of the Nodas', who came in as they were finishing the meal.

Grandmother shuffled across the room, toeing in, because for sixty-five of her seventy-five years she had worn clogs; and she bowed the deep bow of old Japan, her withered hands sliding down to her knees. Why couldn't Grandmother be more American?

The neighbor had come to remind them that tonight was the festival called Buddha's Birthday. Grandmother's eyes brightened at the news. But Mother apologized: she could not go with Grandmother, for Saburo the new baby was feverish, and she could never bear to leave her babies when they were sick. Father? He had to work tonight. Thoughtfully Grandmother looked at Hattie. Hattie excused herself and hurried back to school.

Right up to the time school opened, she kept seeing Grandmother's eyes brighten and grow dull. If Hattie had been with Patty and the others on the schoolground, as she longed to be, she might have forgotten Grandmother. But sitting lonesomely at her desk, pretending to read, she could not forget.

Maybe it was good, after all, to have a rule about being kind to old people whether they like you or not.

Hattie thought of Mother, taking care of her and her brothers when they were young and helpless. How dreadful if, when Mother grew old and helpless, they did not take turn about and care for her! Hattie frowned at her book, thinking.

"Mad, Hattie? My, but you're scowling!" teased Patty, pausing as she came in from the schoolground.

Hattie shook her head and smiled. If only Patty would sit down beside her and say the thrilling words, "Oh Hattie, wouldn't you like to join Camp Fire?" If she would even say, "Can't you come over after school?"

But after school Hattie walked home alone, as usual, stopping for the grapefruit on her way. When she had put them in the home cooler, she hunted up Grandmother, and ducked her head in a shy bow. "Grandmother," she said, "if you want to go to Buddha's Birthday tonight, I'm sure Mother will let Harry and me go with you."

The Nodas were Methodists, so the Buddhist church was strange to Hattie and Harry. Tonight it was crowded, and all through the program small children trotted in and out and climbed over people's feet, with nobody minding. There were songs and dances and pantomimes, graceful kimonos, stately poses, dignified steps; and voices in the high falsetto which was the proper tone for Japanese actors, but which gave Hattie a funny, embarrassed feeling. "Such squeaky doors!" Harry whispered comically.

Coming home by street-car and bus, the three arrived so late that the house was all sleeping. Harry bade Grandmother good-night and stumbled drowsily to his room, but Grandmother lingered, eyes bright and cheeks flushed.

Hattie hunted for something to say. "The dancing was lovely," she said. "And the kimonos."

"I have one old kimono," Grandmother said, turning toward her door. With Hattie at her heels, she opened a dresser drawer and took out a silken bundle which she unfolded and held out, smiling faintly at Hattie's gasp of admiration.

"Chrysanthemums, for your aunt's name, Kiku, Chrysanthemum," said Grandmother. Gorgeous blossoms in many rich colors grew across the heavy blue crepe. "It was the only one she saved from the great San Francisco fire. She wrapped it round one of her doll boxes." Grandmother motioned toward the drawer and a white wood box that lay there.

"Could I see?" Hattie stuttered.

"You may," Grandmother answered.

When Hattie slid open the box the breath of the Orient puffed out into her nostrils. She lifted the bag that protected the doll's hair and face, and gazed at the miniature lady, exquisitely moulded, and robed in brocades, padded, corded, embroidered. Clasping the box to her breast with one hand, Hattie pulled out a chair for Grandmother. "I don't know much about the doll festival," she coaxed shyly. "Here in Denver we don't."

She curled up on the floor at Grandmother's feet. "O Kiku San brought her doll set with her," Grandmother said, "when she married and came to America. This one is more than a hundred years old. We were taught to take care of things. The girls' festival—O Hina Matsuri—was a great day. It was play, but it taught us history and manners."

Looking from the doll to Grandmother, Hattie listened with all her might. She missed some words, for the Japanese the Nodas used at home was simple, and, to Hattie's relief, there had been no Japanese Language School for some years now. Still, she could follow the story, and it made pictures for her in the quiet night: little-girl-Grandmother wearing enchanting kimonos, in charming rooms carpeted with cushiony mats; spending long hours learning to serve tea just so, to arrange flowers just so, to paint the difficult Japanese letters just so; learning to hold her face and voice calm no matter how she felt. Girl-Grandmother, writing poems with her friends and going to view the full moon, valuing beauty above riches. Grandmother, hearing about America, and longing to go where life was free for women. Grandmother, never able to come until she was too old to fit herself into this new land.

When the parlor clock struck one, Grandmother stopped short. "A girl of twelve should be asleep!" she said severely.

Next morning Hattie wondered if she had dreamed that companionable midnight visit, for Grandmother looked coldly at Hattie's bare knees and said, "Since you must run and jump like a boy, I suppose those ugly short clothes are necessary." But even while Hattie was biting her lip uncomfortably, Grandmother added, "Hatsuno, the chrysanthemum kimono and the doll are to be yours. After all, you are our only girl."

Home was beginning to seem homelike again.

That was fortunate for Hattie, since neighborhood and school were still strange. It was a relief to go back to their old district on Sundays, to the Japanese Methodist Church. And once Mother took the older children to an evening carnival at their old school. On the way they stopped at the store where they used to buy Japanese food, dishes, cloth. Clean and bright itself, it was jammed in among grimy second-hand stores and pawn shops. It was queer, Hattie thought, but no matter how clean people were, or what good citizens, if they happened to be born Chinese or Japanese or Mexican, they were expected to live down on these dirty, crowded streets, with the trucks roaring past. Yes, the new neighborhood and school were far pleasanter than the old— if only Hatsuno could fit in.

As Mother's Day approached, Hattie felt lonelier than ever. When she came into school two days before the tea, Patty, Sue and Phyllis were huddled round the teacher's desk. Miss Bender smiled approvingly at Hattie, who was already top student in Seventh Grade. Patty smiled, too, and looked at her expectantly. Hattie's heart thumped with the wish to push herself in amongst them. But how could she? She smoothed her starched skirt under her, sat down, and pretended to clean out her desk.

"It's such a late spring," Miss Bender was saying, "the lilacs aren't out. But I'll bring sprays of cherry-blossoms. And we must find out how many mothers to expect. I hope your mother is coming, Hattie."

"No, ma'am," Hattie said soberly. "The baby has chickenpox, and Mother just won't leave a sick baby."

"Haven't you an aunt or grandmother who could come in her place?"

Oh, dear! Grandmother would be so different from the rest. What would Patty think of her? Then Hattie's head came up. "I'll ask Great-Grandmother," she said.

She thought Grandmother would refuse. She hoped Grandmother would refuse. Instead, Grandmother asked, "Every girl should have mother or grandmother at this tea?"

"Yes, Grandmother."

"And your mother will not leave the baby. Elder daughter, you went with me to Buddha's Birthday. I go with you to school."

Hattie swallowed a lump in her throat. Grandmother was doing this because she thought Hattie wished it. Tea —Grandmother would sip it in Japanese fashion. Would she notice if the girls giggled? She would hide the fact if she did. Hattie thought of Grandmother's long training in the concealment of pain or disappointment. Well, that was a good heritage for anybody. Hattie would use it now. "Thank you, Grandmother," she said. "I will come and get you Friday, after school."

When the two came into the schoolroom that afternoon, the mothers were all there and having their tea, and it seemed to Hattie that everyone stopped talking and turned to gaze. Well, she and Grandmother must look pretty funny, Hattie thought.

Hattie was dressed like the other girls, in white sweater and short white skirt, her white anklets folded neatly above her oxfords, and her black hair out of its braids and done in another favorite style of the season. Grandmother, as short and slim as Hattie, wore a dress nicely made over from a kimono, but looking a little strange; and her gray hair was combed straight back from the withered little face with its slanting eyes.

Politely Hattie introduced Miss Bender to Grandmother, and pulled up one of the visitors' chairs, since Grandmother had never been to tea where people stood up and balanced the dishes on their hands. Patty brought her a plate, Phyllis the sandwiches, Sue a cup of tea. Then Patty returned, pulling her mother after her. "Mom," she said, "here's Hattie. And here's her great-grandma." Patty dropped her mother's hand and stood beaming.

Hattie looked anxiously at Grandmother. She could not speak a word of English, nor the others a word of Japanese. But instead of words, Seventh Grade and its mothers were bringing sandwiches and cakes till Grandmother's plate was heaped. And Grandmother sat there, as stately and self-possessed and smiling as if she went to seven teas a week.

Hattie studied her more closely. Others might think Grandmother's little face a mask, but Hattie saw that the eyes were bright again, and that the wrinkled cheeks were pink. Grandmother liked it! Grandmother felt happy and at home!

Maybe even a great-grandmother could be lonesome, especially when she was too old to learn the ways of a new land. Thinking so happily of Grandmother that she forgot all about her own shyness, Hattie squeezed Patty's arm, just as she might have squeezed Teddy's on some rare occasion when he was sweet instead of maddening.

Patty squeezed back—quickly, as if she had been waiting for the chance. "Mother!" she stuttered, in a voice that matched her gay fluff of curls. "Mother, I think maybe I was mistaken. I think Hattie might like to—" She looked eagerly up into her mother's questioning eyes—"You ask her, Mother!" she begged.

"About Camp Fire? Hattie, would you like to join our Camp Fire group?"

Hattie was silent from pure joy and astonishment.

"If I got your name in this week," Mrs. White continued, "you could go to camp with us. A camp in the mountains; do you know about it?"

"Oh, yes, ma'am, *I know*," Hattie said with shining eyes. "Oh, yes, ma'am!"

By Florence Crannell Means

TWO NAMESAKES

Dona Josefa, the grandmother, sat on the low adobe hearth that ran out on both sides of the fireplace in the corner. . . . There was a thick sheepskin on the floor at her feet. Pancho sank down on it and gazed into the fire. His grandmother smiled at him.

"It has been a great day, has it not, little man? Paco is indeed a good burro and he will serve you well."

"I'm glad you like him too, Grandmother," Pancho answered. "Did you notice the star on his forehead and the cross on his shoulders?"

"Indeed I noticed them Panchito, and I wonder if you know what those marks mean?"

"You said you would tell me. Could you, now?"

PANCHO YAWNED AND rubbed his eyes with a brown fist, wondering why he, the sleepy-head, was the first to awake. Morning sounds and the rosy edge of a crisp day in autumn were just beginning to come through the little deep window above his bed. El Commendador, the rooster, crowed impatiently, commanding the sun and everybody else to get up and get busy, although it was not yet time for the world to wake up. There was a fluttery chirping of birds in the big cottonwood tree, and the distant bark of a dog, taken up by every dog in the village, even Tito.

These were just the usual sounds. They never roused Pancho. There must be something else.

There was an odd lightness in the middle of him. A fiesta feeling. He felt like taking a deep breath to hold himself down. To be sure, it was the day of his patron and name saint, San Francisco de Assisi. Was that enough to wake him?

Suddenly a new sound reached his ears. He held his breath. A soft, muzzling whinny—just a whispery sound, but very plain.

Could it be?

Pancho fairly fell out of bed and tumbled to open the door.

Ay, Dios! It was! Spell-bound, he stood gazing, bare brown toes curling with delight on the worn door-sill. The door opened on a placita, or courtyard, the adobe rooms of the house closing around it on three sides, the corrals out beyond in the back. Over the low adobe wall of the corral, Pancho could see Susana, the gray burro, and beside her, a new baby burro, the most enchanting and lovable little creature Pancho had ever seen. His little burro. His very own, because Papa had promised him that if Susana's baby came on Pancho's feast day, it should be his.

Dona Sus—the gray docile, patient Sus, stood looking at her son. She glanced at Pancho and back at the baby, as though saying, "Here he is, young master, but only look at him. He is as gay as the little buds that come to the willows in the spring: he is as soft as the fur of the rabbits your brothers have caught to make the cover for your baby brother, may his health prosper: he has four shining hooves, surely as dainty as the slippers of the señorita who passed this way yesterday. And pray observe the white star on his forehead, and the cross of black across his chubby shoulders. He is no ordinary beast, and he is yours to command. Use him well." Susana bowed her head as though saluting Pancho, and softly nudged the baby.

Pancho had reached the wall and was over it in a bound. Strangely enough the little burro did not dart away, but let his new master put his arms around him and hold his. soft cunning head in his arms. Pancho almost cried for joy. He was a true namesake of his gentle patron saint. He loved all the creatures about him, especially the babies. El Chico, his own baby brother, came first, then the clumsy puppies, and soft tumbling kittens. The frolicsome kids of the sedate goats, and even little pigs, were appealing, and the down chicks that always made him think of white and yellow flowers walking about. But next to El Chico came a baby burro as the most amusing and lovable baby thing on earth. Pancho had dreamed of him for weeks, and now here he was, warm and furry in his arms.

A name for him. Why, of course, born today, he must be named also for San Francisco, who had talked to the birds and beasts and called them his little brothers. It was fitting that they should all be brothers, the gentle saint, a boy with a tender heart, and a little new-born animal.

Pancho held one of the furry ears, and whispered into it. "You are mine, little brother. My name is Francisco Hernandez, but I am called Pancho for short. And your name is also Francisco, and Hernandez, too. You will be called Paco for short so that we shall be known apart. And we will be comrades. I will take good care of you and we will go someday to the mountains. Look, Paco, the sun is coming up and it is our feast day."

Just then the sun did come up over the distant mountains. It lit up all the peaks and shone on the aspens that were just turning to gold. It came down into the valley, to the village of Coronado, a cluster of adobe houses gathered together along the little stream, surrounded by fields and corrals. With the sun everything came to life, and Pancho smelled the sharp, aromatic smoke of cedar and piñon that was beginning to come lazily out of the chimneys to float in blue wisps in the quiet morning air. People were getting up. They must see his Paco.

He scampered toward the house, calling, "Come! Come quickly and see my burro! He is the most beautiful baby burro that was ever born, and he is mine, because

Papa said if he were born today he should be mine, and he is mine." He leapt into the air and gave a quivering shriek of joy that brought everyone out of the house.

Pancho's father, Don Antonio Hernandez, came out first. His eyes twinkled as Pancho danced around him.

"Are you sure he was born since midnight, Pancho?" he said, as though dubious about legal ownership.

"Of course, Papa. I heard him just a little while ago. I am sure it was the first sound he made. You said I could have him."

"Well, since he was able to wake you up, I think he should be yours. What are you going to call him?"

"Paco, Papa, for San Francisco and me."

Ricardo, the tall brother, who was Pancho's idea of just what a young man should be, came out just then.

"See that you take good care of him, Panchito. We'll need a lot of help with the crops next year."

Juan, the second brother, strolled out saying it would be hard to tell two little burros apart, especially with the same name. Pancho paid no attention.

Dolores and Lucita were next. Lucita, who was younger than Pancho, chirped and danced about, exclaiming over Paco's bright dark eyes and his polished little hooves, but Dolores, the older sister, just came close and gently stroked the long ears.

Pancho saw Mama at the door with El Chico in her arms. He ran to her, took the baby and carried him carefully to Paco. The baby cooed with joy when he got his fists in the soft fur of the little burro's wide jowls. What fun to have the whole Hernandez family there admiring his prize! But where was the little grandmother? Pancho saw her standing in the doorway. He gave the baby to Mama and ran to help his grandmother through the gate.

"Yes, Pancho, he is a very fine beast. I shall tell you something about him tonight."

"But come," Mama said, "it is getting late. We must eat before the tortillas are burned."

He could scarcely bear to leave Paco so soon. Dashing in, he seized a tortilla, which is a thin cake made with corn meal, and wrapped it around some of the beans in the big pot. Mama had to call him back to drink some milk. Then he saw his other presents. A cigar box for his trinkets that the girls had covered with bright bits of paper, the warm woolen scarf he had seen his mother and his grandmother working on. And there was a splendid knife that his brothers had given him.

"It is too much," Pancho said. "My burro was enough."

Ricardo and some of his friends were starting early for Santa Fe with a wagon-load of corn and wool to sell. They planned to stay overnight and see some of the celebration in honor of San Francisco who was patron saint of the capital. But for once, Pancho did not even ask to go. He would rather stay with Paco.

What a waste of time to go to school with Paco waiting in the corral! But at last he was free to race home to his pet.

When it grew dark Pancho's father went with him to see that the straw was sufficient in the adobe shelter, and the gate of the corral fastened securely. Dona Sus and her son were sleepy and willing to be left alone. Pancho begged to sleep out there with them. No, he couldn't sleep out in the corral, nor could he bring Paco in the house to sleep with him.

When they came into the kitchen the lamp was on the table and Mama and the girls were clearing up after the supper. Lucita tripped to and fro, the light catching in her brown curls, as she put the dishes away in the tall carved cupboard that had been in the house longer than any of them. Dolores sat near the lamp picking over frijoles, the good beans that are eaten every day in the year. More of them simmered gently in the olla, an earthen pot, on the hearth.

"Don't forget the cheese and milk, Lucita," Mama said. Lucita trotted with them into the little cold storeroom. Juan had milked the goats as a special favor, while Pancho was busy with Paco.

Dona Josefa, the grandmother, sat on the low adobe hearth that ran out on both sides of the fireplace in the corner. The sticks of piñon and cedar wood that stood on and in the fireplace burned brightly, shooting out sparks and popping like firecrackers. She was busy as usual, braiding strips of cloth into a rug. The hard adobe floor was covered with these rugs, big square ones and little round ones. There was a thick sheepskin on the floor at her feet. Pancho sank down on it and gazed into the fire. His grandmother smiled at him.

"It has been a great day, has it not, little man? Paco is indeed a good animal and he will serve you well."

"I'm glad you like him too, Grandmother," Pancho answered. "Did you notice the star on his forehead and the cross on his shoulders?"

"Indeed I noticed them, Panchito, and I wonder if you know what those marks mean?"

"You said you would tell me. Could you, now?"

Lucita hurried to put the last dishes away and came to sit near the fire. A story was the one thing that would keep her still. Dolores listened as she sorted the frijoles, her dark eyes dreamy.

"Well, then, you should know that not all burros have the star in the middle of the forehead," she began. "It is plain that Paco is descended from those fortunate animals that stood near the manger in the stable at Bethlehem the night Our Lord was born. You remember that the brightest of all stars shone that night above the holy Mother and Babe. It is said that the oxen and sheep and burros knelt in wonder and adoration, and because they were the first worshipers, they were marked with a star."

"Of course Paco comes from that stock," Pancho said with a sigh of satisfaction. "He is such a lovable little beast."

"There is a reason for that, too," Dona Josefa went on. "A great danger threatened Our Lord when He was but a babe."

"I remember," Dolores said slowly. "And an angel was sent to tell Our Lady and San José to take Him far away so that He would be safe."

"Yes, San José found a mother burro for Our Lady to ride upon and the little colt had to go, too. All the way on that long journey the Mother and Babe played with the little burro and delighted in him. That made him even more lovable. How else could it be?"

"But what about the black cross, Granny dear?" Lucita asked.

"It is very plain, even now," Pancho said proudly. "It goes down his back, and right across his shoulders and even down his forelegs."

"That is a sadder story, my children," said Dona Josefa. "Many years after the journey that the Holy Family made, Our Lord came up to Jerusalem, as you know, and he rode into the city on still another burro. That was a proud day for the humble beast. This Señor was the first who had ever ridden on his back. There were palms spread on the road, and singing and a great welcome.

"After the procession he lost the Señor whose gentle touch had made him happy. For days he was always looking for Him. And one day he saw Him. He was carrying a great cross of wood, stumbling and falling beneath its weight."

"Even a burro would know that was wrong," said Dolores.

"Yes, but crowds of people just stood watching and did not help Him. They would not even let the burro pass to take the cross upon his shoulders as he tried to do."

"But because he wanted to," Lucita said quickly, so that she could be the one to finish the story, "his shoulders twitched and he was marked right then with the cross."

"Yes, it is a badge of honor too," said the little grandmother. "You see, this is why the burros are so patient and humble. Three times they have been honored above the other beasts."

"But Paco is going to be treated with the honor that he deserves," Pancho said stoutly. "You'll see. He is worth it."

"Time for bed, children, if the story is finished," Mama called.

Lucita looked up hopefully, although she was sleepy.

"That is all for tonight, little greedy one," said Dona Josefa.

"Then a thousand thanks, and goodnight."

Pancho lingered a moment for extra thanks and his grandmother's blessing.

By Helen Laughlin Marshall

MACARONI

AN AMERICAN TUNE

*The little Italian boy looked down at the American boys
and tried to grin in a friendly way. He said, "You know
that my name is not Macaroni. It is Gasparino, and you
know that my dog is named Musso." He spoke English
slowly and carefully but very well. His dog could bark
in English too. Just as well as that American dog at the
foot of the steps.*

'A LITTLE BOY, about seven years old, with his small
shaggy dog at his heels came out from the door of his
father's violin shop, closing it carefully behind him. The
shop was on the first floor of an old brownstone house
in New York City, and the little boy stood with his dog

at the top of the steps which led down to the sidewalk. He looked with wistful dark eyes up and down the street.

It was a warm spring afternoon. School was out for the day. Up and down the lively sunny street children were playing. The girls were skipping rope or sitting on the curb tossing jacks. The boys were playing ball, or running after one another, yelling loudly as boys do when they are happy.

At the bottom of the steps there were three boys and a dog playing with a red ball. When they looked up and saw the little dark, curly-headed boy with his shaggy dog, they began to snicker. The thin freckled lad shouted, "Oh! look at the Italians!" The little fat boy shrieked, "Hey! foreigners!" And the red-haired boy yelled, "Here come Macaroni and his Dago dog."

The little Italian boy looked down at the American boys and tried to grin in a friendly way. He said, "You know that my name is not Macaroni. It is Gasparino, and you know that my dog is named Musso." He spoke English slowly and **carefully** but very well. His dog could bark in English too. Just as well as that American dog at the foot of the steps.

But the three boys shouted louder than before. "Macaroni! Macaroni! Macaroni! And his Dago dog!"

Gasparino started down the steps with his fists clenched. Musso came too, growling. The boys and their dog turned and ran, hooting and laughing up the street.

Gasparino did not run after them. He sat down on the lowest stone step with Musso close beside him. He felt very lonely and unhappy, and so his dog felt lonely and unhappy too.

It was not the nickname "Macaroni" he minded so much as the fact that it was not an American sort of nickname. All those three boys running up the street had nicknames. They were called "Red-Head," "Skinny" and "Fatty." But they were called those names in a kindly way. What hurt little Gasparino was the unkind, unfriendly way in which they yelled "Macaroni" and "foreigner" at him, just because he had happened to be born in Italy.

And wasn't his dog just as good as an American dog? He put out his hand and patted the dog's head. He wondered why it was that the boys did not understand that an Italian was just a boy, like other boys, and liked to do the same things that they liked to do. He liked to whittle things out of wood. He liked to play ball, and run pellmell down the street with his dog at his heels just as they were doing. Well, he had Musso anyway!

Musso stood up and began to wag his tail. A plump lady wearing nose glasses had stopped in front of Gasparino and was smiling down at him. Gasparino got up politely. It was his teacher and she held out a book to him. "Here are the American songs I promised you," she said.

"I thank you," said Gasparino politely and he bowed low and kissed her hand. Gasparino had been taught the manners that are polite in the Italian way. In Italy it is the dignified and polite thing for a man or boy to kiss a lady's hand. It is simply a custom there, just as shaking hands is a custom in America.

It seemed a funny custom to Red-Head and Skinny and Fatty. They stood peering around the corner of the steps next door. They shook with laughter and as soon as the teacher had walked away and was out of hearing, Red-Head came mincing and prancing past Gasparino saying in a sing-song voice, "Sissy, sissy, Macaroni, sissy."

Next came Skinny holding out his trouser legs as if they were a skirt. He said in a shrill voice, "Macaroni, kiss-a-da hand-a, kiss-a da teacher's hand-a." Then came the smallest boy, Fatty. He pretended to dance and repeated the awful word, "Sissy, sissy, sissy." Last of all came the American dog who yapped a "Wop! Wop!" at Musso.

It was too much. Musso growled and showed his teeth. Gasparino raised his two clenched fists and there surely would have been a fight if, at that moment, the crooked-nosed man had not appeared.

He came hurriedly down the street and raised his fist threateningly. "Scat! You," he said, and the three boys ran away.

This crooked-nosed man was an odd looking person. He was unshaved and was dressed in a shabby long-tailed coat, and he wore an old hat down over his eyes. He glared down at Gasparino.

"American boys are hoodlums," he said, "and America is a crude country."

Gasparino turned red with indignation. "They are not hoodlums," he said, "and America is a great and wonderful country."

The crooked-nosed man shrugged his crooked shoulders and turned away to stop before the shop window and look at the violins and cellos displayed there.

Gasparino sat down again on the step and tried to look at his book of songs. Musso stuck his cold nose into his hand and whined. Gasparino put his face down close to the dog and whispered, "I wish I were an American boy. I wish you were an American dog. Oh, Musso, how long will it take us to become really sure-enough Americans?"

It was not six months since Gasparino had arrived in the United States, with his father, who made and mended the finest violins, and his mother, who mixed and cooked the finest macaroni.

They had not moved into an Italian neighborhood as most Italians do when they come to this country. They wanted their son to play and grow up among American children, so that he could learn American ways and grow up a fine American.

So Gasparino, with his father and mother, had searched and searched until they found this block which had seemed a thoroughly American neighborhood. They had found a first floor for rent in an old brownstone house. This house was number "5" and directly across the street from it stood a gray stone church with a cross on its steeple.

Gasparino's father had stood and stared, first at the house marked number "5" and then at the church across the street. He said, "It is what, in this country, they call a hunch."

"What is this hunch?" Gasparino had asked. "And is it good?"

"It is very good, this hunch," replied Gasparino's father positively, "because the greatest violin maker in the whole world, Antonio Stradivari, also lived opposite a church and his house was also number five."

"But that was a long time ago, wasn't it?"

"Nearly three hundred years ago, my son."

"And it was not in this country."

"No, my son, it was in a little village in Italy called Cremona, that Antonio Stradivari lived. He lived at number five opposite a church."

"Just as we shall do," said Gasparino's mother walking up the steps and ringing the bell.

So they came to live on the first floor of this old house. The large front room the father used for his violin shop. Here he sat before his work bench day after day, making new violins and mending old ones. The three small back rooms were where they lived. In them the smiling mother mended and sewed, and cooked the macaroni that Gasparino loved. There was also a back yard in which Gasparino and his father had planted flowers. It was all very snug and comfortable. Oh, it was a fine thing to be in America!

America was a fine, brave, free country. It was just the place for a boy to grow up and become someone important. Gasparino should be very happy here, playing and learning from these fine American boys.

But it had not turned out that way. The boys had not seemed to understand, that, no matter where a boy comes from, he is just like other boys. Now, after six months, they still called him a "foreigner" and his dog a "Dago" dog.

Sitting there on the steps before his father's violin shop, Gasparino felt discouraged. Musso was discouraged too, which meant that his tail did not wag at all. Even when a slinky black cat passed by and spit at him, Musso did not have the spirit to so much as growl at her.

As the cat disappeared around the steps, a musician carrying a black violin case under his arm paused in front of Gasparino, and looked up as if seeking the number of the house.

"It is number five," said Gasparino politely.

"Thank you, my boy," said the musician, "and do you know if the violin maker is inside?"

"He is, and he is my father, and he is the best violin mender in the whole world." Gasparino said this last in a loud voice, hoping that Red-Head and Skinny and Fatty would hear. But they were across the street in front of the church and did not pay any attention.

The tall thin man with the crooked nose did pay attention. He turned around from the shop window where he was standing. He looked, with sharp shrewd eyes at the black violin case, and he smiled an evil crooked smile when he heard the musician say, "I am glad that your father is a good violin mender, for I have here an old very fine and valuable violin to be mended."

"I will take you in," said Gasparino. He got up and his sad-tailed dog got up too. All three went up the steps and into the shop. The crooked-nosed man looked after them and he smiled an evil knowing smile.

In the shop Gasparino always felt happier. If only Red-Head and Skinny and Fatty would come in sometime, they would be sure to like it. It smelled of old wood and spicy varnish and glue.

Gasparino pointed to his father, who sat at a work

bench near the window where the light was good. The musician opened his black case, carefully lifted out the violin and showed Gasparino's father a place in the back of it where a tiny splinter had broken out.

The violin mender took the violin in his own hands with great respect. He turned it over and over, looking at it very carefully.

Then, in great excitement, he cried, "A real Stradivarius! Look, Gasparino, at the scroll work running around the sides. Look at the inlaid ivory! Antonio Stradivarius made a set of instruments like this one for the Spanish Court over two hundred and fifty years ago!"

"Bravo!" cried the musician much pleased. "You do indeed know violins."

"It is my business to know," said the violin maker modestly.

Gasparino looked at his father proudly. How smart his father was. It was plain to see that this distinguished musician admired and respected his father too, and did not mind at all his being a foreigner.

"You can mend it, my precious violin?" the musician asked anxiously.

"As well as ever," replied Gasparino's father. "I shall pick out a good piece of old seasoned wood which will match perfectly the grain of the wood in the back of the violin. After it is varnished you will not be able to see where it is mended. And the varnish, I shall cook it myself, not cook it too much for that would make the tone wooly and rough. Just right it shall be cooked, as Antonio Stradivari himself would have done it." And he pointed to a shelf on which stood bottles of golden liquid from which to make varnish. There were chunks of glue there also, and pieces of old wood.

The violin maker began to look closely, through a magnifying glass, at the crack in the violin. The musician walked about the shop. Gasparino pointed out to him the old violins hanging on the hooks, the unstrung bows, the odd special tools, and the many signed photographs of famous violinists for whom his father had done repair work.

"Many interesting things you have here," said the musician.

"Are Italian things as interesting as American things?" asked Gasparino.

"Why, my boy," answered the musician, "interesting things do not belong to any one country. They are neither Italian nor American. They are just interesting things."

"I wish Red-Head and Skinny and Fatty knew that," Gasparino whispered to himself. If only they would come in and just once smell the clean delicious smell of old sweet wood, if only they could listen to his father explain the importance of the right wood for violins. It had to be well seasoned wood, maple, spruce. The older the better. That was why, whenever his father heard of any very old church or monastery in which there had been fine woodwork, being torn down, he would hurry to the place and bring back a few precious pieces.

The wood of a violin had to have a certain tone. The back had to be a perfect mate for the front, in both strength and vibration. His father would hold a piece of fine old wood up to your ear and thump it gently so that it would vibrate and "sing" almost as if it were already a part of a great violin being played by a master. Surely the boys would find that interesting.

The owner of the Stradivarius was just about to leave. He was at the door and turned to say to Gasparino's father, "That violin, you understand, is very valuable."

"You need not fear," said the violin maker, "it will be safe here."

"And may I have it for my concert next week?"

"It will be ready for you."

"I am sure I can depend on anyone who knows violins as well as you do. Good day, sir." And the musician departed.

The violin maker went back to his work bench by the window and began to select his tools. Gasparino came to stand beside him.

"I wish Red-Head could see you fix that violin," said the boy, watching how cleverly the violin maker handled his tools, not seeming to miss in the least bit the forefinger of his right hand, which he had lost in the world war. That was a marvelous story, too. If only the boys would listen to his father's stories, see all the interesting things in the shop, then they would understand that, while being an American was important, there were other interesting and important things as well.

"My son," said the violin maker looking up from his work and smiling, "you see, the hunch, it was good. I get much violin mending, important violin mending to do."

The boy pointed to the cracked violin on the bench. "Is it badly broken?"

"Badly enough to ruin the tone." He picked up the violin, put it under his chin and drew the bow across the strings. "You hear it? The tone is thin and disagreeable because the crack in the back breaks the vibrations."

"Is it the finest violin in the world?" asked Gasparino.

"No, not the finest, although it is a wonderful instrument. But the most famous violin is called 'The Messia'; another is called 'The Cessole'; and another 'The Titian.'"

The boy laughed. "Nicknames, do violins have nicknames like boys?"

"Many of the great violins have what you call nicknames," his father answered, "and they got those names, just as boys do, because of something that happened to them, or because they had some odd thing about them."

"Just the way Red-Head and Skinny and Fatty got their names?"

"Yes, my son, just like that, and the same way you got your nickname, Macaroni."

Gasparino held his head. He could not very well explain to his father that Macaroni was not an American nickname and that an American nickname was what he wanted. But of course his dog, Musso, understood, because he whined a little and stuck his cold nose into Gasparino's hand.

"Is this violin worth a lot of dollars?" asked Gasparino.

"Yes, it is very valuable, just as all well made and beautiful things are valuable. But see, I will trust you to use it. Who knows, my son, some day you may own a fine violin like this one, some day when you are a great musician."

But Gasparino turned moodily away. Outside he could hear the boys yelling and laughing and having all sorts of fun. He was very lonely.

"I don't want to be a great musician," he said. "I want to be an American."

His father understood but did not reply; there are some things that even loving fathers cannot do.

But, after the evening meal, he took Gasparino and Musso back with him into the shop. Sitting down before his bench, he picked up the Spanish Stradivarius, and with his magnifying glass, began closely to examine the crack in its back.

But the little boy was listening to the happy noise of the other boys at play just outside the window and it made him feel very lonely. The boys were playing very hard. It was important that they play very hard so as to have as much fun as possible before their mothers called them to wash their faces and go to bed.

Gasparino particularly watched Red-Head and his American dog, Yank, come rushing down the street. Once more they side-swiped up the steps in front of the shop, and then leaped down again. Red-Head bumped into a man who was standing on the side-walk, gazing into the shop. Gasparino saw with surprise that it was the crooked-nosed man with the black clothes who had spoken to him that afternoon. It looked as if he had been hanging around ever since. Now he came close to the window and peered in at where the violin maker sat directly beneath a strong electric light that hung from the ceiling and was shaded by a green shade. Under this light the valuable violin could be plainly seen and it made Gasparino nervous and afraid. He came away from the window to stand at his father's knee, inside the circle of light thrown by the lamp.

"There is a man outside with a strange look," he said. "He is looking at this violin; he was here this afternoon; maybe he wants to steal this violin."

"It is wrong to think bad thoughts about a man who stops before our window to admire our instruments. They are there to be seen. That is why I have a window to my shop." As he spoke, the violin maker looked up and the man with the crooked nose and shoulder slipped away out of sight.

"Anyway, I'm glad that he has gone," said Gasparino. "He looked as if he wanted to eat the violin. It is very valuable and you know that in America they do have hold-ups."

"Not only in America are there thieves, but do not think more about it. Look at the beauty of the violin. See the graceful curves of the front; it has the satiny surface of the finest human skin. See the varnish which protects the wood from decay."

"Will it ever wear out?" asked the boy.

"There is no reason why it should ever wear out," replied his father. "The tiny cells in the wood, where once the sap ran, are now filled with varnish, making it stronger and protecting it from moisture and decay. It will sing until you will have a little boy of your own, and it will sing to his son and to many sons after that."

"My little boy will be an American," said Gasparino,

"and if the violin sings for him, it will sing 'The Star Spangled Banner,' and the other boys will not call him 'Macaroni.' "

Gasparino's father put his hand on his son's shoulder, "Patience, my son," he said.

At that moment there was a tinkle of the bell that announced the opening of the outside door. They both looked up. The Dago dog, Musso, stiffened up, with his tail still and straight, just as any good American dog would have done. He sniffed the air suspiciously.

The man in the black suit and with the crooked nose was standing just inside the door, leaning back against it. He had one hand in his pocket and it seemed to bulge.

"This is a hold-up," he said in a husky voice. "I want that violin."

Gasparino's father got quickly to his feet, putting the violin behind his back. Musso took a step forward and growled a good understandable American growl.

"Don't move or I'll shoot," said the man. "I want that violin and no fuss about it. Give it to the boy, quick, or I'll shoot him!"

The boy looked up at his father. He knew that his father was a brave man who had been in the great war, but what could he do? The man had a gun in his pocket. The violin maker slowly brought the instrument from behind his back and put it into the boy's hands.

"Bring it here," the robber said.

Again Gasparino looked up at his father, and his father nodded. He did not dare say no, for fear of harm that might come to his son. The boy went forward slowly, holding the violin in both his hands. His faithful dog,

Musso, went with him, step by step, growling an American growl for every foot of the way. When Gasparino came within reach, the robber snatched the violin, opened the door behind him, and started to back out.

Suddenly Musso leaped forward past Gasparino, and dashed right between the man's legs, out through the hallway and onto the front steps, barking wildly.

Outside, up and down the block, people stopped to look, wondering what the dog was barking at so furiously. The boys stopped running, the girls stopped skipping rope, older people stopped talking.

So then, while everybody was looking at the barking dog at the top of the steps, the tall crooked-nosed man burst out of the dark hallway and started to run down the steps. In one hand he held the violin. His hat fell off and behind him came the little foreign boy, Macaroni, who grabbed the man by his coat tail and hung on like a little monkey, shouting, "Thief! Thief! Hold-up! Hold-up! Help! Help!"

For a moment the people in the street, young and old, stood stock-still as people do when they are suddenly very much surprised. Then some one yelled, "Police!" and, for a wonder, one came running from only half a block away. Yank, the American dog, came leaping across the street, as voluntary reinforcement to Musso, the Dago dog. There they both barked and leaped up and down and got fearfully excited in the same language.

The crooked man was holding the violin high over his head with one hand, while with the other he tugged at his coat to get rid of Gasparino. But the boy held on tightly and, when the man tried to push him away, not knowing what else to do, he grabbed the man's hand in his teeth and bit hard. He knew it was not a fair way to fight but then stealing a valuable violin wasn't fair either.

Red-Head and Skinny and Fatty came running to the bottom of the steps and Gasparino saw them out of the corner of his eye. He loosened his bite on the man's hand just long enough to shout to the other boys, "I'm not kissing his hand, I'm biting it!" Then he took a fresh hold with his teeth.

Red-Head did not yell "Sissy" at him. Instead he yelled, "Hold 'im, Macaroni, good boy Macky, hold 'im!"

Then Skinny and Fatty joined in with, "Hold him, Macaroni, hold him Macky, good old Macaroni!"

Gasparino bit harder; the man yelled with pain and forgot to hold the violin high over his head. As he brought it down to defend himself Gasparino snatched the precious instrument away from him and handed it to his father, just as the large Irish policeman arrived and grabbed the crooked-nosed man by the arm.

"Trying to pinch a violin, was ye? Well, it'll be you that gets pinched."

The crooked-nosed man tried to jerk his arm away from the burly policeman. He was shouting in an angry loud voice. "If it hadn't been for the cursed dog, and that wild-cat hanging on my coat tails, I'd a made my get-away. He kicked viciously at Musso who was now prancing about Macaroni.

The policeman looked admiringly at the boy and said, "You ought to be on the police force, sonny. Good work."

Then he turned to the violin maker. "Please come around to the court house in the morning and prefer charges against this roughneck." Then he walked away, holding the crooked-nosed man firmly by the arm.

The crowd gathered around Gasparino. Red-Head, Skinny and Fatty were staring at him with new expressions of admiration.

"Gee!" exclaimed Red-Head. "Geewhittacker! You weren't scared at all, were you, Macaroni?"

"Well, not very much," said Gasparino.

"His dog wasn't scared either," said Skinny. "Gee, did ya see how he came running out first and barking like everything, to let people know a robber was in the house?"

"What kind of a dog is it?" asked Fatty.

"It's an Italian dog," said Macaroni.

"Aw, what's the difference?" said Red-Head. "Christopher Columbus was an Italian, and look, didn't he discover America?"

Gasparino looked down at them from the step on which he had stopped. He began to feel something warm around his heart. The American boys were grinning up at him as if they liked him.

"Gosh!" said Skinny. "That fiddle must be worth a lot of money."

"What kind of a fiddle is it?" asked Fatty.

"It's an Italian violin," said Gasparino, looking him

in the eye, "it was made by the greatest violin maker in the whole world, an Italian."

"Guess there must be some smart foreigners," said Red-Head. "Say, did he whittle it out of wood?"

"Sure he did," answered Gasparino. "And my father also can whittle one."

"Gee!" exclaimed Red-Head. "Your dad must be some whittler."

"I am considered a good whittler," said the violin maker, who had been standing to one side and a little above them on the upper step. He smiled cordially and added, "My son, ask your friends to come in to our shop and watch me whittle."

"Would you like to do so?" asked Gasparino, trembling with eagerness.

"Oh boy! Would we!" shouted Red-Head. "Come on, Yank," and he ran up the steps followed by his dog and Skinny and Fatty. In this order they all followed Gasparino and his father into the shop. The two dogs, Yank and Musso, were the best of friends immediately, like old soldiers who have fought together in the same war. They went snoop-snooping around the floor and Musso as host showed Yank where there were some extra nice smells and then they sniffed courteously at one another.

Gasparino stood still, afraid to say anything. He was so anxious to have this visit a success. He waited to see what the boys would do. He could hardly believe they would not laugh at him and say unkind things, as they always had in the past.

The violin maker went over and sat down at his work

bench under the strong light that swung on a cord down from the ceiling. He called the boys to him in the circle of light thrown down by the powerful lamp. That is, all except Gasparino, who remained by the door, in the shadows, quiet and still with fear that the boys would not be friendly. He was much more afraid of them than he was of the robber.

The violin maker showed the boys his tools and explained what each one was for. He showed them a piece of fine-grained beautiful wood that he said had come out of an old monastery in Italy that was built long before Columbus came to America. On it he had drawn the outline of the shape of a violin. He explained to them that the front of the violin was called the "belly," and that the lovely curve in it was not formed by bending, but by carefully carving it with knife and other tools, so keen that they would cut a hair.

"Jimminy!" exclaimed Red-Head, his eyes bulging with interest and excitement. "It must be fun to whittle something like that!"

"It is fun," replied Gasparino's father.

"Do you have to be an Italian to whittle things like that?" asked Fatty.

"Not at all," smiled the violin maker, picking up a violin bow from the table. "You see this bow? It is one of the finest bows ever made and it was whittled by a Frenchman."

"Honest?" said Red-Head.

"Yes, honest, he was a Frenchman named François Tourte, and before he found out what fun it was to whittle, he was a clockmaker."

"What kind of wood did he use, maple?" asked Fatty.

"No, he whittled his first bows from the staves of an old sugar barrel. But he did not like those bows very much, so he began hunting around in all sorts of queer places to find a better wood. At last he found one that was very stiff and heavy. It had a funny name, it was called 'Fernambuc' wood."

"Never heard of it," said Skinny.

"Guess there's lots of things you never heard of," said Red-Head.

"How many bows could he whittle out of a tree?" asked Skinny.

"Not many. To whittle a really good bow, he had to have a perfectly straight grain in the wood; so sometimes he had to cut up a whole tree, just to whittle a few really good bows."

"What is it strung with?" asked Fatty.

"With long hairs taken from a horse's tail," answered the violin maker, "and they have to be combed out of a live horse's tail, too, and not a dead one."

"If they were taken from a dead horse they wouldn't sound so good, I guess," said Skinny.

"But the strings are made from the guts of a dead cat," said Fatty.

"That's what lots of people think," said the violin maker, "but it is not true; the strings are really made from the guts of a spring lamb, killed in September."

"Italian lambs?" asked Red-Head. As he said it, he turned and grinned at Gasparino, who was still standing alone near the door.

"Not always Italian lambs," laughed the violin maker, "sometimes English lambs, or Spanish lambs, or American lambs."

"Gosh!" exclaimed Red-Head. "It takes a lot of countries, and trees, and horses' tails, and lambs, and things just to play a tune!"

"Can you play a tune?" asked Fatty of the violin maker.

"My son can," he answered.

Red-Head turned with a friendly grin at Gasparino, who was standing in the background. "Aw, come on, Macaroni," he said, "play us a tune."

Gasparino came slowly out of the shadows into the circle of light. He did not say anything as he took the violin from his father and tucked it under his chin. He thought a moment, and then he too grinned back at Red-Head and the others, as if he knew a good joke. Then he began to play a tune that he had been practising in secret ever since he came to America.

For a moment the boys listened with their mouths open, utterly dumbfounded, and then Red-Head yelled, " 'Yankee Doodle!' Macaroni can play 'Yankee Doodle!' " And then he began to sing it.

> "Yankee Doodle went to town,
> A-riding on a pony,
> He stuck a feather in his hat
> And called him Macaroni—"

"Called him Macaroni!" He repeated in glee, "Called him Macaroni! What do you think of that?" He pounded the Italian boy on his back. "Macaroni," he shrieked in delight, "you're the feather in Yankee Doodle's hat!"

"Then I'm an American!" cried Gasparino, with a happy face.

"Sure you are! Isn't your name Macaroni and Macaroni is in the song, 'Yankee Doodle!' Come on, play it again, and let's march!"

Laughing and shouting and singing, with Gasparino in the lead playing the violin, with the dogs barking in the greatest excitement, they marched round and round the shop singing,

> "Yankee Doodle went to town,
> A-riding on a pony,
> He stuck a feather in his hat
> And called him Macaroni—"

By Myna Lockwood

THE ICE SKATES

Debby's teacher said that the Pennsylvania Dutch language reminded her of a lamb stew. There was the German, and that the biggest part, like the meat. Then there was the English, like the big hunks of potato. The sprinkling of Welsh and Irish and French words was like the bits of vegetables in the stew—the beans, and carrots and onions.

The reason that the Pennsylvania Dutch talk was like a lamb stew . . . was because many years ago people left their own countries in Europe and came over to Pennsylvania to live together.

"I DON'T HOPE you've been peeking in the spare room," exclaimed Mom one morning just the week before Christmas. Mom always kept Christmas presents in the spare room, and the door was locked.

Debby was ready to leave for school. She looked guilty, although she had only glanced in quickly when Minnie the Thinnie went into the spare room for an extra blanket for her cold feet. Minnie never stopped shivering now, and her nose was a pale blue.

Debby had been disappointed in not getting a flash of some ice skates. She wanted these more than anything in the world so that she could go with Jerry and the Vogel boys to the quarry to skate.

Now, with Christmas so close, she could scarcely sleep at night, and school days were worse than sulphur and molasses in the spring. All the while Teacher's voice droned patiently on, Debby thought of the rubber bone she had bought for Wasser in Reading, and the beautiful painted dower chest Pop and Mom would give Gertie. Gertie the Flirtie was going to marry Irvin Kunkle, who was nicer than he used to be, for he had brought Debby a box of candy with velvet poinsettias on it.

Debby wasn't looking when Teacher's ruler pointed to the map. She was thinking of the spare room, and wondering if her new skates were hidden in it. She stared out at the dunged fields and the crows and starlings picking a meagre lunch from the frozen ground.

Teacher was looking at her now, but Debby didn't notice.

Oh, Christmas was the very most wonderful time of the year, thought Debby. Easter and the Fair and Hallowe'en and the circus were all very thrilling, but Christmas wasn't a thing which came in the morning and was over when you went to bed.

Christmas began right after Thanksgiving Turkey. For company came then on bleak Sundays—Hattie the Fattie, with her baby (only Debby was TOO YOUNG to change his diapers, and she might stick him with a pin). Or Rude the Dude, with all the little cousins (only Rude the Dude always beat Pop at quoits). Sometimes it was the Weissfinger family that went visiting, now that Pop's work had slackened after the harvest. It was fun to have your Sunday chicken with somebody else. Grandmom Ermentrout or Peter the Eater. It was at Peter the Eater's that you got the best Schmierkase or lemon sponge pie. Debby's mouth watered. . . .

Pop usually replaced broken windows in the winter, or drove in loose nails, or mended machinery so that it would be in good condition for spring. Now, since Thanksgiving, he spent his leisure carving tiny animals and people for the Christmas tree yard, and repaired the play fence which was made of match sticks. Jerry no longer greased squeaky hinges or patched screens. Instead of those dull winter duties, he oiled the train which would run round and round the tree on its oval track, and pasted red tissue paper in the cardboard church windows.

Mom left her socks which she was knitting, and often played the old melodeon in the parlor. It was sweet to hear her high voice singing "Silent Night" and "Come All Ye Faithful". . . .

Teacher was coming down the aisle now, and soon

would be at Debby's desk. Would she use the ruler on Debby's knuckles, the other children wondered? What was it Debby was staring at out in the fields?

"Debby-jiggers!" warned the boy across from her, but she didn't hear him. Her eyes were still dreamy, and she was still thinking of home, and the spare room.

She hoped there would be no more snow, but just ice. She hoped the barnyard would be full of ice, and that the fire would go out and the kitchen door would freeze next time Mom washed it. Then she could keep her Christmas skates on all the time, and skate around as she worked.

"Debby Weissfinger," came Teacher's voice, suddenly as a mole from a hole, "where is Sandwich?"

Debby's mind scrambled for an answer. She had supposed Teacher was talking about Jogerphy, and now it was Food, instead. But lunch time was over long ago.

A paper wad landed saucily on Debby's head and trickled down her nose and plopped onto her desk. She stared at it. The room was very quiet, and full of eyes.

"Sandwich. . . . Have you ever heard of Sandwich?" asked Teacher.

"Yes, Teacher," answered Debby politely.

"Where is Sandwich?" asked Teacher.

"Sandwich iss in my stomach," said Debby, and she didn't mean to be rude.

There was hilarious laughter. Debby's face began to burn and she stared down at the paper wad.

"Children,—children . . . *order*," demanded Teacher. But it was no use. She had to wait until everybody had laughed enough at Debby. Then she said, curiously,

"Debby, I want you to come to the front of the room. I want you to tell us what you think about when you stare out of the window!"

Debby stumbled up to Teacher's desk. Her bright blue eyes were filled with tears, and so that nobody would notice, she gazed at an ink stain on the floor. She wondered if it felt like this to be burned at the stake as a witch. But she knew Teacher wouldn't let her sit down until she had answered.

She couldn't bear to talk about the Skates before the whole school. Supposing she shouldn't get them? She tried quickly to think about something else.

"We're waiting," said the Teacher.

"I was sinking of the Indian lady at the market, in her Indian dress," said Debby.

"An Indian lady at market?" asked Teacher pertly. "What does she do there?"

"Frighten a little mouse under her chair," whispered Reuben Schmidt loudly.

Everybody roared, for they had never heard anything so funny before.

"Order, *please!*" demanded Teacher, whanging her ruler on the desk.

"She sells moccasins and bead things. And herb medicine. It cures everysing," said Debby, still staring at the ink.

"Every*thing*. Not every*sing*," corrected Teacher.

"Everything," repeated Debby, miserably.

"Well, since you're so interested in Indians rather than Sandwich, I'll ask you where the Iroquois tribe lived?"

"I don't know," whispered Debby.

"For shame! You go back to your seat now, Debby Weissfinger, and if I find you looking out of the window again, you will have to stay after school on Christmas Eve!"

Debby crept back to her seat, and hid her face in her folded arms; the tears trickled onto her desk.

But soon everybody had forgotten her, and it was Mamie Kreitzmiller they were laughing at. And very soon after that, school was over, and Debby was jostled into the bus with dozens of others who drew pictures on the frosty windows and called jokes to the driver.

Many of the children were talking about what they wanted for Christmas: bicycles, footballs, candy, pen-knives.

"I'm going to get ice skates," shouted Debby, now slapping back at Danny Ziegenfus, who pulled her hair regularly every day.

But just then the bus stopped and a crowd of boys from school, including Jerry, tumbled out, their ice skates clanging over their shoulders. Without thinking, Debby hurried out after them; just beyond the lane was the quarry. It was glistening in the late afternoon sunshine. It shone like Gertie the Flirtie's diamond ring. Only the ice was much more beautiful.

Jerry was cross.

"You go home!" he cried. "Mom'll give it to you!"

But the bus had gone, and Debby was sliding about on the edge of the ice, pretending that she was Hans Brinker. She watched the boys with a terrible envy while they put on their skates, and hunted for home-made hockey sticks they had hidden behind some brown shrubs the day before.

After a while Mamie Kreitzmiller came with her brother, Herman. She was skinny, and she always had a cold and was sniffling.

Mamie had skates that screwed onto her galoshes. They were an old pair of Herman's, and they were rusty and a little too big. But the skates looked quite perfect to Debby.

When Mamie skated, her ankles caved in, the knees of her snow-suit collided, and she flopped about like a frightened bat. Debby forgot that her fingers and toes were numb from the cold and watched Mamie with breathless excitement. If only Debby had skates, she knew she would be able to do whirls and twirls like that pretty movie girl with the short skirts.

"I can skate," Debby bragged as Mamie came teetering toward her.

Mamie sniffled. "You can't neither," she retorted, and jerked away again.

"I can so. It's easy," shouted Debby, just as Jerry and Herman came swooping past her in a race for the puck. Their skates cut the ice with a saucy sound. Oh, it was awful having to stand and watch everybody skate! Jerry's face was scarlet from the wind, and his jacket was flying open. But Debby had to jump to keep warm, for the sun was going down.

Mamie staggered back and forth in front of her, sniffling loudly to keep her nose from running, and trying to dodge the boys who skated past and around her in their hockey game.

"I betcha I can skate. Betcha a hundred dollars," said Debby, holding her mittens over her ears.

"Betcha two hundred dollars you can't," gasped Mamie, not quite falling.

"Give me your skates and I'll show you," insisted Debby.

Mamie pulled off the skates and Debby fastened them onto her galoshes. They were much too large.

"Chust help me get up," said Debby, "then I go off alone."

Mamie hung on to Debby a few seconds, until she got her balance.

Debby shot forward. The skates were like grease. She caught her breath with sudden fear and delight. This was a new world, this slippery patch of ice . . . And then she fell.

"I told you so!" cried Mamie, trying to pull Debby up.

Debby yanked away from Mamie triumphantly. Her feet shot from under her again. She felt the hard ice slapping at her hands.

"It's all your fault!" cried Debby, hotly. If only Mamie would let her alone, she would be able somehow to skate like that girl in the movies. Oh, it was going to be wonderful fun! She tried to bring her feet together, and just then she felt herself rising up, lightly, onto the slippery blades.

Jerry was holding her under one arm, and Herman Kreitzmiller under the other. They were skating away with her across the hard, gleaming ice, and the wind was taking her breath and making her eyes water.

Jerry was calling "Yike!" and the boys were scrambling out of her way.

Now the skates were like wings! And she was no longer Debby Weissfinger, but somebody magic who would keep going and going until the end of all time.

"Oh," she screamed, "Ohhhh!" as Jerry and Herman skated her along faster and faster. The trees of the Kreitzmiller farm were rushing up to meet her. Then Jerry and Herman gave her a push and let go.

Debby screamed again, this time with fear. For the end of the ice was close. Her legs wobbled and her new world was spinning around.

Now the pond jumped right up and smacked her in the face. Her feet were somewhere in the sky. The sky and her feet rolled over and over one another, and each time the ice slapped her once more in the face. Finally she lay still, twisted like a pretzel. Her blood pounded hotly through her, and she burned and ached. She knew her head must have a crack down the center, like that of her old doll, Janie.

Jerry and Herman were frightened now at the outcome of their joke. They tried to pull Debby together, as if she'd been a marionette, and they yanked off her skates. When she tried to walk, it felt as if her legs were gone.

"I didn't mean nussing wrong," Jerry said with a shaking voice, and he was mopping blood from the crack over Debby's lip.

It felt swollen and puffy, and had a queer taste. She tried hard not to cry.

Jerry was so scared, that Debby couldn't be too angry

with him. He borrowed Herman's bicycle and rode her
home over the frozen, bumpy roads.

"I could skate alone," Debby thought, over and over,
"with skates with shoes on!"

"Don't retch on me," pleaded Jerry, as they turned in
the lane, "or Pop won't let me go skating no more."

Debby giggled, in spite of her aches. "Don't retch
on me, neither," she said, "or Pop won't get me no skates
for Christmas."

They tried to pretend nothing had happened, but
Debby's swollen lip gave away the secret, and they had
to tell Mom about the accident.

"See, now, Luser, I told you how Debby iss TOO
YOUNG for them ice skates," cried Mom, holding a cold
steel knife over Debby's lip to keep the swelling down.

"Vy, shuah," agreed Pop. "Na I see you have right,
Vinie. She *iss* TOO YOUNG." But there was a twinkle in
his eye.

Debby wanted to shout, "I'm *not* TOO YOUNG!" . . .
but Mom had the knife over her lips. Instead she began
to cry. Wouldn't she ever grow up, and be old enough
to do things like other children? Would she always be
TOO YOUNG? Oh, she must do something to show Mom and
Pop that she wasn't really little any more. And she must
hurry and show them before Christmas, so that they
would give her the skates.

"I could skate alone," she thought, "vis skates vis
shoes on."

And she forgot the bumps she had had on the ice,
but she couldn't forget the wonderful sensation that her
feet were wings, and that she was a fairy.

All that week before Christmas, Mom was busy baking. There was no end to the cakes and pies she made. For she would sell many of these at market, and all of the Weissfinger children would be home with all of *their* children to eat the rest of the cakes and pies on Christmas Day.

For weeks before the holidays Minnie and Mom made sand tarts and rock and taffy candies and clear red and yellow animals, in molds. The ginger-bread men that appeared so mysteriously on the Christmas tree were just like the ones that Debby was allowed to press out of the rolled dough with tin shapes. Oh, Debby was allowed to *help* bake the cookies and cakes! But now that she knew how to help, she wanted to bake something of her own, all by herself. She wanted to lean over the oven and push the pan in with her own hands; and she wanted to make the little "try" cakes, and to see with a broom straw if the dough were baked.

If she could only do these things, Mom and Pop would know she wasn't TOO YOUNG for ice skates!

Just the day before Christmas Eve, something peculiar happened.

Mom was finishing the dough for the shoo-fly pies. Debby was watching her. Debby watched Mom after school whenever she had a chance. It was all she could do to keep her hands out of the dough. While she watched Mom, Debby forgot how heavy her heart was. For she was sure now she wouldn't get the skates. Every time she went upstairs she tried to peek through the keyhole of the closed spare room. But she could only see the walnut high-boy.

"Mom, please let me roll out the pie dough!" coaxed Debby. "Please, Mom!"

Then suddenly the telephone rang.

"Aye-yi-yi," exclaimed Mom, with annoyance, for she was full of flour. But she went over to the wall in quite a hurry, Debby thought, and lifted the receiver off the hook.

"Ach, Himmel, I come right off," she said, and hung up.

"Go fetch your Pop from the woods out," she told Debby. "Mach schnell."

Debby was afraid to ask who had telephoned.

She raced out to the barnyard, and yelled, "Pop, Pop!"

He halooed back to her. She could see him coming toward the house, dragging cedar for tomorrow's market. There was market today too; that's where Gertie and Minnie were.

But who had telephoned?

Mom answered the question for her when she came shivering into the kitchen again.

"That was Hattie," Mom said. "She's sick. I go to her."

A dreadful fear clutched at Debby. "Vill she get dead?" she whispered.

"Ach, no," Mom said. "By tomorrow yet she'll be all well again."

Mom threw off her apron and cleaned herself up in a great flurry. But the table was full of pans and dough and all the ingredients Mom had laid out for the cakes.

"Debby, you redd up the kitchen," she ordered. "Put

everysing away neat like. Pop comes home to make suppah."

Pop drove Mom off in the old Ford car.

Debby was left alone. It was a strange feeling. Even Jerry was away, ice skating at the quarry. But Wasser was there, sniffing around the table for crumbs.

The piecrust was there in a big dough ball, and Debby was going to put it in the ground cellar, when the curly feeling came.

She pressed her fingers into the dough. It was deliciously soft. There was the rolling pin. . . . And the crumbs for the top of the shoo-flies. Mom had just made them of flour and spices and butter and brown sugar. Oh, Pop would be so disappointed not to have his shoo-fly for breakfast on Christmas morning!

But it was half ready. . . . Why couldn't she make the rest of it, Debby thought? Now, at last she could show Mom and Pop she wasn't TOO YOUNG. She wasn't TOO YOUNG to bake and she wasn't TOO YOUNG for ice skates. She could feel two hot spots in her cheeks, and she was so excited that she ran over and locked the kitchen door, though it was no use trying to lock the curly feeling out.

Then she rolled out the dough, and filled the pie tins on the table, just as she had seen Mom do. And now she must make the liquid to pour into the crust. Oh, if only she could make the pies before Pop came home! But Pop couldn't be home until late. Hattie lived a long way off.

While she worked she nibbled at some of Mom's oatmeal cookies which cooled on the table. And Wasser kept rubbing against her, begging for just one more!

It was fun to see the molasses in the cup puff up with

the baking soda. If only her fingers wouldn't shake so.
. . . Maybe if she ate just one more oatmeal cooky, she'd
feel steadier. . . . My, it was wonderful to be baking by
one's self. She thought of the fun Mom had, day after
day, when she baked.

Debby put the cupful of soda and molasses in a bowl,
added the hot water from the tea kettle, and wondered
then how much more molasses she would put into the
mixture, for Mom never measured. It must be just right
for Pop! Not too dry, and not too gooey. Just right. . . .
But what was just right? It wasn't the way Mom made
it, Pop always said.

Debby paused with the molasses jug over the crook
of her arm. She poured in as much as Mom used. But
Mom didn't always make eight pies. Eight pies would
take more. . . . A lot more because Pop liked them
gooey. She let the molasses bubble slowly into the bowl,
and then she was just going to stop when Wasser jumped
up on her, and another golden spurt of molasses came
out.

"*Wasser!*" she screamed, spanking him. "Now you
spoiled my pies!"

The angry tears came into her eyes, and dropped
down into the molasses. Debby didn't know what to do.
Should she take some of the molasses away? And how
much? . . .

It was half-past four, and the pies must get into the
oven. She would have to use the mixture the way it was.
She stirred it quickly and poured it into the crust, covering it with crumbs. Then she put all of the pies into the
oven.

If they burned or were no good, Debby knew for sure she would never get the ice skates. But she had to take the chance. . . .

Soon the kitchen smelled sweet with molasses and spice, and Debby stood on a stool and cleaned up all the pots and pans at the sink.

If the cakes did not turn out well, thought Debby, she could run away to Peter the Eater's. . . .

She opened the oven doors dozens of times, watching the pies puff up to their usual fatness, and trying them with a broom straw, and moving them around. Baking was just as exciting as she had thought it would be!

Jerry came home in the early darkness and did his chores at the barn. After they had waited a long time for Pop, Debby and Jerry made their own supper of left-over potato soup, boova shenkel and coconut custard.

Debby told Jerry what she had done, and he promised to keep the secret.

"Aye, but you'll get the hickory stick!" he said, balancing the chow-chow on his head.

In half an hour the pies were baked, and they carried them down to some shelves in the cellar that Mom didn't use very often. Debby covered them with paper, to hide them. But first she and Jerry cut a big slice for themselves. Oh, it was good. It was especially good, thought Debby. It was the best shoo-fly she had ever eaten! The molasses stuck to her teeth, and it was not too dry and not too gooey. Just gooey enough. She couldn't wait for Pop to try it. If only Pop would think it was "just right."

Finally Pop came home alone. Mom would stay all

night with Hattie the Fattie, and tomorrow Hattie would be well again, he said.

Then everything began to happen so fast that Debby was dizzy. The next day was Christmas Eve. Teacher let them out of school early. Ursula the Nursula came home with her arms full of packages, and a sprig of holly on her coat. Mom came back from Hattie's.

"It's a fine big girl at Hattie's," she said. "Twelve pound she veighs!"

Mom was cleaning the turkey and Pop was working in the parlor and wouldn't let anybody come in. Now and then Debby sneaked down to the cellar to look at the pies. They were so beautiful, Debby could hardly keep the secret. . . .

She danced about the house, doing errands for Mom. The house smelled now of pine and the Christmas dinner. Pop and Gertie went to market again, and Debby couldn't bear to go and leave the good smells of Mom's kitchen—but she couldn't bear to stay home either. Christmas market was full of beauty. There were holly wreaths and festoons of crow's-foot, and mistletoe and poinsettias. There were turkeys and ducks and geese, and cranberries the size of marbles. Peoples' baskets overflowed with crisp green celery and bags of nuts and vegetables. Across the aisle from Pop's stall would be a woman selling paper flowers, and brooches and boxes made of shells. You could buy your present there for Pop and Mom.

Before Pop and Gertie came home they would stop at Yeoman's Oyster House and sit at the counter and have a stew. The lights of the city would be blazing, and the Pagoda on the mountain back of Reading would look like a big Christmas tree with its green and red lights. Peoples' noses were scarlet and they huddled down into their mufflers, and when they called "Merry Christmas" to their friends you could see their breaths steaming like a tea-kettle. The bells of the Salvation Army tinkled on the corners, and the street cars clanged with a special frosty sound. Nearly every house had a lighted tree; some of them filled with blue balls, some of them stripped of their needles, the branches wrapped in cotton and trimmed with silver balls. And the shop-windows! How gay with toys—doll beds and sleds, and skates! Skates with white shoes! Like the twirly girl's in the movies.

Debby's heart kept beating as if she were running.

But if she went to market with Pop, she would miss the Belsnickel at Vogels' on Christmas Eve. The Belsnickel was an ugly old man with torn clothes and dirty face who scolded and whipped all the children because they had been bad during the year. But, afterwards, he would have oranges for them, and perhaps a doll, or a ball, and some candy! Last year he had pointed with a long black finger at Debby, and picked her out as the naughtiest child in the crowd. . . .

In the end, Debby decided to go to market.

Debby wakened in the early dawn of Christmas morning. There were holly wreaths and festoons of crow's-foot. She was glad, glad! She listened for Kriss Kringle who might be in the parlor now, laying the skates under the tree. Her room was like an ice-box, and she hurried down to the warm stove of the kitchen to dress. Jerry was there, climbing into his woolen underwear, whistling "Jingle Bells."

"Oh, can't we just peek in the parlor a liddle?" begged Debby.

"Pop says we don't see nussing before breakfast," said Jerry. "Breakfast first, Kriss Kringle after."

"Oh dear," said Debby, that's too long to wait! . . . Come, Cherry, we make breakfast this morning for Mom."

Jerry was only too willing to help, because he was sure there would be a football under the Christmas tree for him. He did a little shuffling dance as he set the table, and carried the bread on his head.

"Cherry—my shoo-fly pies!" cried Debby, scooting off to the cellar.

Mom and Pop came down together, and cried "Merry Christmas," and then Mom saw the shoo-flies right off.

"Ach, Himmel," she exclaimed, turning to Pop, "to sink you shame me and buy shoo-fly at market!"

"You have wrong, Vinie . . . I bring no shoo-fly from market!"

Debby's face shone with the fun of the surprise.

"I make them," she cried. "I make them when you go by Hattie's, Mom!"

"Harreyumma!" exclaimed Pop, and he slapped his knee and laughed and Mom laughed too.

"Hurry, Vinie, vis the coffee, so I can dunk," Pop said. "Aye-yi-yi, but they're fat!"

Debby jumped up and down till her shoes squeaked.

At last the coffee was ready, and Pop ate his ponhaws, and the moment came for the SHOO-FLY.

Pop cut a piece, a very big piece, and the molasses stuck to the knife. Then he dipped the slice in his coffee, and Debby watched without breathing while he ate.

"Ach Debby, wie schoen!" he cried. "Es it gans gut—"

Debby trembled with joy. Maybe this was the happiest moment of her life. "Iss it chust right?" she asked.

"Chust right!" said Pop. "Not too dry—not too wet, chust right!"

"Then I'm not TOO YOUNG," cried Debby, and Mom laughed and laughed.

But Debby couldn't help wondering if her tears falling in the molasses hadn't made the shoo-fly just right, and would she ever be able to make it that way again.

After breakfast they burst into the parlor, and Kriss Kringle had left a TREE, which was pirouetting about on a musical base, and the train was running merrily around on its track, and the smell of pine was like perfume and—

Debby looked wildly round the room. Then she saw THE SKATES. They shone like silver, and they had white shoes.

"My skates . . . I want to skate!" she screamed.

But, no, there were other things to be done Christmas Day before little girls could skate!

There was church, with the men sitting on the sides and the women in the middle. And the lovely, lovely crèche at the altar, with the Mother Mary gazing down at the baby Jesus, and candles shining a soft yellow light about them. . . . Oh, if only those nasty little hard flakes of snow wouldn't come down and cover the ice. . . .

Then the family all coming with their arms full of gifts—Rude the Dude and the little cousins, starched and smiling; Peter the Eater and his family, fat and smiling; Hattie the Fattie's husband, grinning, with a lot of cigars for the men.

And the dinner: turkey, potato filling, cranberries, dried corn, creamed onions, oyster filling, apple sauce, pickled eggs and beets, noodles, pepper cabbage, all of Mom's home-canned vegetables, and many more than seven sweets and seven sours. And the cakes and pies. And Debby's very own shoo-fly. It was the best shoo-fly they had ever eaten, they all said. The very best shoo-fly that had ever been baked.

And after dinner no one was able to move except Debby, who at last was able to go skating with Jerry.

She didn't mind very much that she kept falling, because now that she had skates with shoes on, she knew very soon she would be able to whirl and twirl like that girl in the movies. . . .

At night, after everybody had gone, Mom plunked herself down in a rocking chair in the parlor, and sat looking at the tree.

Debby wondered if she were TOO OLD to sit on Mom's lap. She edged over to her mother who pulled her down; her head hung over Mom's shoulder, and her legs dangled awkwardly over Mom's Sunday silk dress. But Debby was very happy, and she liked it that Mom was humming "Stille Nacht, Heilige Nacht." They rocked and rocked..

Debby stared at the beautiful singing tree, with its pink popcorn strings and clear animal candies. She began to see little things that she had not had time to see before she tried on her skates: a bird in a glass cage, a boy on a sled, a flat wooden boat, a tinsel star, and bright red apples weighing down the branches to the floor.

The train still ran round and round on its track, going nowhere, and the little village under the tree twinkled; Debby loved all the tiny lead people and the carved wooden cows and barn.

Oh, this was so beautiful . . . here before the tree, with Jerry lying on his stomach, fingering his football. Jerry quiet for once in his life. And Pop standing behind them all, with a light in his eyes as bright as the tiny colored bulbs.

Now Mom was humming "Schlof, bubbely, schlof," and Debby's legs and arms were getting heavier, and the tree was blurring as they rocked, and Mom was patting her, just as if she'd been Peter the Eater's baby. . . .

She wasn't any baby. . . . She tried to pull her arms and legs together.

"I'm not TOO YOUNG, am I?" she asked, yawning. "I'm not TOO YOUNG ever again, am I?"

Pop grinned down at her, and munched a little at his tobacco.

"Everysing has an end," Pop said. "Even TOO YOUNG. Everysing has an end . . . except a sausage, and that has two ends!"

By Mildred Jordan

GLOUCESTER BOY

It was the Sunday in June when all the fishing boats were in and the captains and crews gathered in the Square before the church for the ancient crowning ceremony brought over from Portugal by the forefathers of the fishermen of Gloucester.

HERRICK COURT WENT up in several flights of steps with houses on each side. Manuel Madieros lived in the last house on the top floor, and from the kitchen window he could look far out to sea beyond the lighthouse.

Manuel's mother did not look out to sea, for it made her feel sad. When Manuel was a baby and his sister Palmagra was three years old, papa Madieros' boat had not come home from a fishing trip to the Georges Banks.

239

But Manuel watched for his Uncle Joe, and when he saw the schooner *Philomena* coming in he would clatter down the stairs of Herrick Court, across Main Street, and down Union Hill to the wharves.

"Hie, Uncle Joe!" Manuel yelled.

Uncle Joe climbed up on the wharf and said, "Hie, Manuel! Going out with us next trip?"

Manuel wanted to shout "Yes, Uncle Joe!" but he remembered how sad his mother was when he begged to go with Captain Joe on a trip. She wanted him to be a postman, so she would know just where he was at every hour of the day.

One day Uncle Joe said to her, "If Manuel wants to be a fisherman, how can he keep his mind on addresses and streets and numbers when his thoughts are only of boats and fish? Why not let him take one trip with me?"

Mrs. Madieros said nothing for a long time, and Manuel and his uncle looked glumly at each other. At last she said, "If you go on a trip and find that you are the right sort of boy to take to fishing for the rest of your life, I will not stand in your way. But if the work is not as pleasant as you think it is, will you be a postman when you grow up?"

Manuel promised, but he knew in his heart that he would be a fisherman like his father.

When he went on board the *Philomena* he had a duffle bag, oilskins, all the sweaters he owned, and boots reaching to his hips.

"Why should I take sweaters and warm clothes when it is summer, Uncle Joe?" questioned Manuel.

"Ho, ho!" laughed Uncle Joe. "You'll learn something about cold weather on the open sea, even if it is summer time."

There were twelve men in the crew. The engineer was called the Chief and the cook was called Tony. Manuel went down to the galley to have his duties explained, for Uncle Joe had said, "It is a strong man's work to go dragging, but the cook can use a lively boy in the galley."

The routine of two hours off and two hours on duty was begun, and Manuel stowed his dunnage away in the upper bunk that was his and began his work of peeling potatoes and vegetables and getting the table ready for dinner.

He wondered at the number of steaks he saw being cooked.

"Ha!" bragged Tony. "Best food on earth isn't too good for fishermen. When you see how they work and how little sleep and rest they get, you'll know they need good food."

Going to the Georges Banks was like one long fête day. But the morning Uncle Joe cast out the sounding lead, a very different feeling came upon everyone, and there was an immediate stir of action.

Heavy doors bound with iron weighted the great net at each end. As they went overboard, the net with its glass floats to keep it apart sank rapidly.

"How far down will it go?" cried Manuel, watching the place where it sank.

"Maybe fifteen fathoms—the cod stay within three fathoms of the bottom."

"But how do you know there is cod down there?"

"The sounding lead showed us that. We know from long years of fishing just what fish belongs to certain kinds of sea muck."

Suddenly the net was dragged in, with the winch screeching as it drew close to the schooner.

The doors heaved up and a squirming mass of fish came into view. In no time the fish were dumped into the open hatches and one of the crew shoveled ice between the layers as fast as they came down.

"Heave her out again!" commanded Captain Joe.

Manuel began to wonder why the cook did not give him any kitchen duty. He was hungry, too.

But no one paid any attention to being hungry, it seemed. The net went down over and over again.

Manuel made some sandwiches and brewed coffee, and with a basket of cups he managed to give each man a steaming drink. He went below and cleaned up the galley and sat on his bunk and all at once fell asleep. How long he slept he did not know.

On deck again, he found everything just the same as when he had left hours ago. At last, as the net came up with only a small catch, Captain Joe called, "Guess we cleaned up this ground all right."

The next day was cold, and Manuel, not being as active as the men at work, went below to warm up and listen to the radio. The announcer gave the time. Then came the weather report.

"Storm warning Eastport to Sandy Hook. Storm is moving with marked intensity. Small craft take warning!"

At once he went up to Captain Joe and repeated the announcer's words.

"Go below and listen to the next report. We must get all the fish we can before that storm breaks."

Again the warning came. The storm was moving southeasterly. At the same time, the schooner gave way to a different motion. Manuel dashed up and found the men hauling in a full net, with water pouring over the decks, fish slipping into the hatches and ice being shoveled over them. The holds were full.

"Batten down the hatches!" cried the Captain.

The waves began to lift and spill across the deck, and rain fell.

"Go below and stay there," ordered the Captain with a sharp look at his nephew.

Manuel was thrilled with the tossing of the schooner, but he obeyed the orders like a good seaman and crawled safely down the companionway.

Some of the crew were snoring in deep sleep. In the hot forecastle Manuel found it hard to remember how icy and stormy the winds were.

He listened to the radio for quite a while. At last he said to himself, "Maybe, if I take just one look to see Uncle Joe standing at the wheel like the statue at home, he won't mind."

He put on his sweater, but left the boots and oilskins at the side of his bunk and made his way to the deck. At that moment, no waves were pouring over. There was a lull in the storm. He clung to a rope dangling from a mast and breathed the wild air. Then, before any one of the crew busy on deck knew what was happening, a huge wave thundered over and swept Tony overboard with it. He tossed for an instant on the water. No one rushed to throw him a line.

"It's no use, his clothes are so heavy he will sink," cried Captain Joe with a terrible groan.

Like a flash Manuel dove overboard, remembering his lessons in life-saving on the Gloucester beach. In another flash Captain Joe threw a line after him.

The devout Portuguese crew prayed to Our Lady of the Good Voyage for the safety of the rash boy. Like men watching a miracle, they saw Manuel next to Tony, holding his collar in one hand, reaching for the line with the other.

Someone began to pull in the rope with Tony holding fast. Manuel was keeping his head above water and struggling with the waves.

Another anxious moment. He was gaining toward the schooner, toward a second line that tossed always beyond his reach. In that instant of peril there came to Manuel a vision of the statue of Our Lady between the twin towers at home, looking out to sea; he saw her eyes bent on him and her brave words were whispered in his ears. He kept on struggling, and it seemed as if her arm reached out to give him the line. He clenched it fast in his fist.

Ages passed. He was being hauled on deck. He was carried below and hot milk was given him.

He breathed naturally again and all at once he was asleep.

When Manuel awoke the schooner was rocking

gently. There was Tony grinning at him. "Ho,—so you are awake and hungry, too, eh, Mannie?"

He sat up.

"Did I oversleep? Is it time for me to peel potatoes?"

"Peel potatoes? Ha, ha!" laughed Tony. "A real seaman like you peel potatoes!"

It all came back to him.

"Oh, Tony, I did not obey the Captain's orders."

"Well, this time I guess he will let it go."

Later on, Manuel thought of his promise to his mother.

"Will my mother mind very much because I am going to be a fisherman?" he asked his uncle.

"Not when I tell her that you are strong and fearless and have the salt sea in your veins. I think she will be proud and glad to have you like your father was."

As the *Philomena* drew in to harbor once more, they could see Our Lady of the Good Voyage off in the distance above the roofs of Gloucester town.

"Your mother will be happy when she sees you crowned," said Uncle Joe.

It was the Sunday in June when all the fishing boats were in and the captains and crews gathered in the Square before the church for the ancient crowning ceremony brought over from Portugal by the forefathers of the fishermen of Gloucester. Hundreds of children were there also. The girls were dressed in white, like Palmagra, with broad red ribbons across their breasts. The boys were dressed like Manuel in their best clothes, with red ribbons across their chests and red ribbon bows on the right arms.

There were two bands, three drill teams of young women and an escort of Coast Guards and policemen.

Palmagra and three other girls formed a square with red staffs, and an older girl carried a beautiful banner with the words Divinia Espirito Santo embroidered on it. A silver dove tipped the staff of the banner. Suddenly the parade began as the children were shoved into place. The smallest ones, dressed in white, led it. The fishermen in their Sunday clothes joined it and the band played, and they all marched in and out the streets of Gloucester under American and Portuguese flags until they came to a little house all decorated with banners where Captain Joe Madieros lived.

Uncle Joe looked so handsome and solemn that Manuel hardly knew him. His heart nearly burst with pride as the Captain came down the porch steps carrying a crown covered with a piece of silk and walked into the square made by the girls with red staffs.

Captain Madieros led the parade back into the church square, and the tiniest girls threw paper rose petals at his feet and the band played a slow hymn.

Overhead the famous carillon began to ring. The bell tunes floated over the town and scattered across the sea like far heavenly music. The sun was bright and warm and Manuel could see the statue of Our Lady between the twin bell towers holding the little fishing boat in her arm.

Soon the church was filled and the ancient ceremony began. The priest told how, in the thirteenth century, Queen Isabel of Portugal, against the King's will, took baskets of bread to her poor people.

One day he stopped her and angrily asked what was in the basket.

"Roses," she said.

The King looked and saw the basket was filled with roses, and at the same time a dove from the sky flew down on the Queen's head.

Though Manuel knew the story by heart, he never tired of hearing how the Portuguese made a Saint of Isabel and how, whenever they were in trouble, they prayed to her and pledged themselves to the ceremony of the Crowning if they were rescued.

Now the choir was singing softly and the priest was placing the shining crown for a minute on Uncle Joe's head as he knelt. He had been a good man all the year, as everyone knew, and that was why he had been chosen for the honor. Then the crown was placed on the heads of those who had been delivered from some danger during the past year and, of course, Manuel and Tony were among them.

When the ceremony was over, everybody marched across the Square to the hall for dinner.

Many of the fishermen's wives had been baking bread for days and had even stayed up all night to see that it rose properly. The fishermen and their friends ate upstairs, and the children were downstairs where they could make as much noise as they wanted. Manuel ate his *sopas,* a fine-flavored meat broth with sprigs of spearmint and spongy chunks of bread swimming in it, until he could eat no more.

But somehow he had room for the delicate sweetbread called *resquillas.* The loaves were round and made with a hole in the center so that many could be carried on the arm to give to the poor.

The older people listened to speeches and the children played in the Square after they had taken the leftover food to the sick and those who were kept at home. There was an auction of donated lobsters, fruit, wine, and bread tied with red ribbons and decorated with flowers.

When evening came Uncle Joe said, "Well, Manuel, you earned a share in the profits of the trip. Shall I put it in the bank for you?"

Manuel nodded his head.

"What are you thinking of?" asked the Captain.

"I will save it to buy a schooner some day," Manuel said in a choked and happy voice.

"You are a chip off the old block. A real Gloucester boy," said Captain Joe.

By Ruth Langland Holberg

VASIL DISCOVERS AMERICA

"I come in peace today because I am no more Albanian except in my love for my fatherland."

FROM THE FIRST day Vasil liked grade 4B. There were red and silver fish in a bowl near the window, flowers on the window-sills, gay crayon pictures on the blackboards, and pinned around the walls were silhouettes made by a former class. Miss Hester wasn't young and goldy like Miss Maribell in 3A. She was fat and her face screwed into wrinkles when she laughed, which was often; but somehow Vasil knew she loved boys and girls.

Vasil liked the boy in the seat opposite his. His name was Nikola Novan, but everyone called him Nicky. Nicky had come from Albania. He had lived in America three years, and had an all-American baby sister born in Ohio. Vasil had an all-American baby brother, Peter, but it was only two years since his family had left Albania. Vasil was glad that Nicky was his marching partner.

At noon Vasil rushed home to tell his mother about the new room, Miss Hester, and, most of all, about Nikola, who had come from a village across the mountain from Pogdanoc. To his dismay he found her sitting in the kitchen, her head on the table—crying! In all his ten years Vasil had never before seen his mother cry. Always she was quiet, strong, working for father, little Peter or Vasil, and always there was a smile in her eyes and near the corners of her mouth. And now she was crying!

"Mamma," he cried, "are you sick? What hurts you? Is it Peter?" But rosy Peter was sleeping in the crib.

Vasil caught her arm. "Shall I run for my father?" He pressed close to her. "Oh, Mamma, don't cry."

"Vasil," she said brokenly, "what can we do? Ljuba Novan has moved into this street."

"Ljuba Novan?" He stared at her wonderingly.

Tears slid down her cheeks again. "It is the feud, Vasil, the feud of Pogdanoc!"

"Feud?"

"Yes. Have you forgotten? You father's uncle killed Ljuba's uncle, and the uncle's brother killed your father's cousin, and your father is the only man on his side of the family. You know we do not remember the feud in our country when women are present, and for a year Ljuba Novan stirred nowhere without his wife; then they all came to America. Oh, I hoped we had lost them forever. Why did they have to come to this city and this very street?"

"But, Mamma, has Ljuba Novan a boy like me—Nicky?"

His mother did not know. Neighbors, formerly Albanians, had been in to tell her that the Novan family had just moved into the street, three houses down, two flights up.

When the noon hour was over, Vasil put his arms around his mother. "We will talk to my father," he said. "We will beg him not to carry on the feud."

She held him close. "My son, never once has your father spoken to any of us except in kindness. Every day he works hard, and now every little while he gets more money in the pay envelope. But here in America they do not understand Albanian customs. A brave man lives according to the ways of his country."

Back at school that afternoon, Vasil did not seem to see Nicky, who came over to him in the yard at recess.

"We are going back to Ohio," he said. "My father came home this noon and said we must move back. Some one in our street has a feud with us. But we have to stay here a month because the rent is paid."

Vasil's heart fell. So much could happen in a month.

Next day Nicky kept aloof from Vasil. But two or three days later they met at the drinking fountain, and Nicky said, "It's your father has a feud with mine."

"I know it," responded Vasil unhappily.

Nicky took a long drink. "That makes a feud between us, too, doesn't it?"

Vasil nodded thoughtfully. "I suppose it does," he said. After that, he and Nicky met only at marching time.

The month was almost over. Vasil's mother showed strain and anxiety. Peter was sick, and his father moody and stern. Vasil carried a weight of dread.

One morning Miss Hester began to talk of a program for Columbus Day. She told her forty-eight bright-eyed immigrant pupils the old, old story of the brave adventurer who would not turn back even when his sailors mutinied. As soon as she had finished, forty-eight waving hands shot up.

"Oh, please, Miss Hester, can I speak a piece?" "My mother wants always I should sing alone." "My father likes I should play the violin." "Oh, Miss Hester, Antonio you just gave the piece to, he don't speak no good English. I'm American. I could speak it better." "So could I, Miss Hester. I was born in New York." "Oh, Miss Hester, I'm American. I was born in the Loop." "You was not!" "I was so!" "I'm American, Miss Hester; my father's got his first papers." "My father's got his second ones, teacher. I want a piece!"

Voices ceased when Miss Hester called Vasil and Nikola. On Columbus Day Vasil was to stand in the front of the room and lead the singing, so he must know very well indeed the words of "The Star Spangled Banner" and "America, the Beautiful." Nikola had a wonderful piece to speak that began,

> "Breathes there the man, with soul so dead,
> Who never to himself hath said,
> This is my own, my native land!"

Then, from the back of the room came a question that struck 4B speechless. "What is papers?" asked Carlo

Depella, who had come from Porto Rico five months before. Everyone wanted to tell him, but Miss Hester hushed them all and explained. Carlo from Porto Rico was already an American, so he would never need naturalization papers. But people from other countries who wanted to become citizens wrote their names in an office and received papers.

Milan Neditch jumped to his feet. "You take papers. You forget your country. You say, 'Bah, my country dirty, dumb place. I 'shamed to be born there.' But I say and my father say, 'Never! Never! America, rich, clean land, but I always Montenegrin. I always love my Montenegro!'"

Miss Hester understood. "That is right, Milan. You must always love your country. She is like your mother. You would never forget or stop loving your mother."

"Miss Hester, please," said Little Wu Long, "we floget only hard days in old country. Days, no rice, baby sick, much hunglee. But lotus flower on water, we not floget, temple we not floget, and honored ancestors we never floget."

"Yes, Wu Long," agreed Miss Hester. "All the good we are proud and glad to remember."

Patrick Mulligan, eldest son of a city policeman, spoke. "My father says we come to this country because it's the land of the brave and the rich and the free, and we got good schools and public baths and a police force to look after us, and it ain't good to be taking everything and giving nothing back, not even a thank-you, and he's been American ever since he was twenty-one, and all us seven kids is American."

Vasil besought Miss Hester's attention. "But dead cousins, Miss Hester, cousins that was shot, do we say, 'Oiya—let it go!' Is it like that?"

Miss Hester was puzzled. Nikola eagerly explained. "He means feuds, Miss Hester. Do we forget feuds?"

A glimmer of understanding came to Miss Hester. "Yes, Nikola, you do not bring your feuds to America. They are left behind with the kind of clothes you used to wear and the kind of lessons you used to learn."

A great hope made Vasil's heart beat quickly, and when they all settled again to their lessons he found it hard to keep his mind on his work. Perhaps that is why he did not look carefully before he crossed the street on his way home that night. Suddenly he looked up. A huge truck was bearing down upon him with terrible speed. Fright paralyzed Vasil. His schoolmates on the sidewalk screamed, but before a policeman could reach the spot, there sounded high above the children's shrieks and the clang of traffic a wild, shrill, ringing call that Vasil recognized. It was the call of the Albanian mountaineer to his friends, the greeting he had often heard echoing from peak to peak in the land of his birth. He turned. Nikola was standing on the sidewalk, his hands over his ears as Albanians hold theirs to keep the ear-drums from bursting when they call in the thin atmosphere of the mountains. Vasil darted back out of danger just as the great truck swept on.

"Nikola made you turn around; Nikola saved you!" the children said, crowding about Vasil.

"I know it," responded Vasil, still pale from the

vision of the great truck wheels steering directly for him. "Tonight I shall tell my father."

"When you get papers," explained Vasil that evening to his father, "we forget the feud, we remember only that Nikola gave the Albanian call and it made me run."

Vasil's mother spoke, "Marosh, must our sons grow up with this feud hanging over their heads?"

Marosh Tsilta was a man of few words, and he made no reply to his wife or to Vasil. Then one evening he spoke. "Elena, call Vasil. We will take Peter and go to the house of Ljuba Novan."

Vasil's mother turned white, but she put on Peter's things, and Vasil silently found his cap. The news ran quickly from door to door. Neighbors watched them cross the street. Some even followed them up two flights of stairs and waited while Marosh knocked at Ljuba's apartment.

There was no response until one of the followers called shrilly, "Have no fear, Ljuba. Elena, his wife, is here, too." A bolt slid back; the door opened a crack.

Marosh Tsilta touched his heart and his forehead. "Peace to this house," he said.

The door space widened. They went in, and the bolt was shoved back again to keep out the inquisitive neighbors.

"Ljuba Novan," said Marosh, "I come in peace today because I am no more Albanian except in love for my fatherland. Today I have first papers! Soon I shall have second and last. I have said in writing that America is my country. And now, as my Vasil's teacher said, I leave in Pogdanoc the feud between your family and mine."

Joy overran the rugged face of Ljuba Novan. "And I, my friend and brother—only yesterday took my first papers and as soon as may be will come the second, then we will all be Americans." Ljuba's wife tried to speak, but suddenly she and Elena were in each other's arms crying together.

Nicky and Vasil edged toward each other.

"I never knew the uncle who carried on feud in your family," said Ljuba.

"It was my father's cousin's son who was killed, and never had I set eyes on him," explained Marosh.

So they drank cups of thick syrupy Turkish coffee, crying to each other the Albanian greeting, *Pacim sa malit!* (We have seen you as the mountains.) And Marosh thanked Nikola for sounding the mountain call that had saved Vasil.

On Columbus Day the parents of Vasil and Nikola sat side by side listening to the program of 4B. Marosh Tsilta nodded appreciatively when Vasil's clear voice soared above the others:

> "America, America, God mend thine every flaw,
>   Confirm thy soul in self-control,
>   Thy liberty in law."

By Leslie G Cameron

A BOY NAMED JOHN

It was with a feeling of great satisfaction that he returned to his seat, murmuring: "I am John Grimm . . . John Grimm." . . . He sang the name to himself, and now it sounded like music to him, because the Grimms had written such beautiful fairy-tales and they had given him such pleasure. "John Grimm . . . John Grimm." . . .

Already he pictured himself coming home, and saying to the astonished family, "Do you know what my name is? . . . I give you three guesses!" He felt important, carrying this great secret. He was becoming an American, he thought proudly.

ON THE DAY school began, Vanya presented himself at the nearest school, together with Katya. Because Katya was quick to learn and had already mastered a little English, she was put in the third grade. Vanya, slower to learn, was put in the second.

Even there, after taking a seat with another boy, he could scarcely understand a single word the teacher said. She was a pretty young Irish woman by the name of McGettigan.

Miss McGettigan, smiling, called him to her desk and asked a boy who knew Russian to do the interpreting.

"What is your name?" she asked, softly, looking at the timid boy with tousled black hair and wistful face.

The question was repeated by the boy who knew Russian.

"Ivan Gregorievitch Grimsky," pronounced Vanya, as though the name were not a name but a chant. He was proud of his name. He liked its organ-like sound. He intoned the GEE-ARRS with a kind of determination that made the name ring fiercely indeed.

Keeping a straight face, the teacher said:

"Ask him to repeat it!"

"Iv-an Gre-go-rie-vitch Grim-sky," Vanya repeated, rather pleased that he had been asked to do so. The teacher must have liked his name, too, he thought.

To his surprise and chagrin, she burst out laughing. Vanya suddenly felt hurt. What was there so funny about his name?

"It's a fine-sounding name, right enough," she said, at last, smiling. "But it's rather a mouthful, don't you think?"

The boy explained as best he could the teacher's words.

Vanya was argumentative. "By no means," he said. "I know Russians with much longer names. Why, my own mother—that's before she married, of course—was called Euphrosinniya Constantinovna Rojdestvenskaya. . . ."

"My, my," said Miss McGettigan, "I should say that was three mouthfuls—at the very least. Again she wanted to laugh, but Vanya looked so serious, she hadn't the heart. "Aren't you wonderful to be able to pronounce it," she went on. "I'd have to practice, and then I should slip up. . . . By the way, Ivan means John, doesn't it?"

"Yes," answered the boy, speaking for Vanya.

"Ask him if he minds being called 'John Grim,' " she said. "That would be short and to the point." She was looking at Vanya's earnest and unsmiling face, at this moment troubled by the problem of his too-long too-alien name.

"John Grim? . . . " he repeated, obviously disappointed by this major amputation of his sonorous name.

Miss McGettigan laughed. "I'll tell you what we'll do," she said. "We'll spell it G-R-I-M-M. Have you heard of the brothers Grimm, who wrote fairy-tales?"

"Of course," John replied, as his face lighted up. "I've read their tales in the Russian!"

"Then it's settled, Johnny," said Miss McGettigan.

The addition of that little letter "M" quite reconciled Ivan Gregorievitch Grimsky to becoming a mere John Grimm, no longer Vanya for short, but Johnny.

It was with a feeling of great satisfaction that he returned to his seat, murmuring: "I am John Grimm . . .

John Grimm. . . ." He sang the name to himself, and now it sounded like music to him, because the Grimms had written such beautiful fairy-tales and they had given him such pleasure. "John Grimm . . . John Grimm. . . ."

Already he pictured himself coming home, and saying to the astonished family, "Do you know what my name is? . . . I give you three guesses!" And, if he gave them a hundred, they'd never guess. He felt important, carrying this great secret. He was becoming An American, he thought proudly.

So rapt was he in the dream of his new name that he failed to hear when the teacher called:

"John Grimm!"

She had to repeat before he became aware that she was calling him. Even then, it startled him, and for a few moments he failed to respond. It was as if with the loss of several syllables of his name he also lost his legs and his tongue.

Confused, he rose and walked over to the blackboard, where Miss McGettigan was standing with a pointer in her hand. Picking up a piece of chalk, she drew a straight line.

"A line," she said, and asked him to repeat.

She drew a circle.

"A circle," she said, and again he repeated after her.

She drew a triangle.

"A triangle," he repeated after her.

Then she drew a square, an oval, an oblong, a semi-circle, and each time he repeated after her the name of the shape.

She gave the pointer to John and asked him to tell the class what each object represented.

He was not prepared for that. So abashed he felt at facing the whole class, and he a mere Greenhorn at that, that he suddenly began to tremble and everything turned faint before him.

He raised helpless eyes to the blackboard, and the line and the circle and the triangle and the square and the oval and the oblong seemed to be doing strange things. To his blurred gaze, they appeared to be trying to get near each other and to dance a kind of crazy dance, the like of which he had never seen. And his tongue refused to move altogether.

The class could see only his lips stirring but could hear no words coming from them, and as they were not deaf mutes accustomed to reading lips they were naturally in the dark as to what Vanya—I mean John—John Grimm—was trying to tell them.

When at last he found his tongue he called the line a circle, the circle a triangle, the triangle an oblong; for some of the others he had no name at all. When the teacher corrected him, he forgot all over again . . . the words simply vanished somewhere, though but a little while ago they had been all in his head.

Just then the class tittered, and he heartily wished that they'd vanish too!

His anger served a good purpose. It cleared his head, made him determined. When he looked at the blackboard again, the chalked shapes no longer performed crazy antics. They remained, as originally, fixed on one spot. They seemed to be definitely staring at him, as much as to say, "Well, go on! We dare you to call us names!"

And he did. This time they were the right ones. He called a circle a circle, a triangle a triangle, a square a square. . . . And all these shapes seemed to be smiling now, even as the teacher was smiling, even as the sun out of doors was smiling. . . . And John suddenly felt like a hero, who, he didn't know.

Later, Miss McGettigan was to congratulate him. She was to pat him on the shoulder and to tell him that the worst thing of all in this world was to be afraid. For, if you were afraid, you were not yourself. Something went out of you, and your memory, too, however good, went out of you also, together with your courage and with what the grown-ups called "presence of mind." She was to congratulate him for having conquered himself, as she was to put it.

John liked Miss McGettigan, and he thought she liked him. It so often happens: we like those who like us.

The bell rang, calling an end to recess. John filed in with the rest of the boys and took his seat in his class.

The teacher began the second half by going to the blackboard, and writing out three words there: BOUGH—THROUGH—ENOUGH.

Here were three words that rhymed, thought John, who came to this conclusion because of their similar endings. Imagine, then, his surprise when Miss McGettigan, with a deliberate, clear enunciation, pronounced the words as though they were BOW—THROO—ENUF.

John simply could not understand it. What a strange language, and how difficult it would be to learn it!

The teacher rubbed out the words and wrote again, placing them in a different order: ENOUGH—BOUGH—THROUGH.

"John Grimm!" she called, directing a pointer at the board. "Read," she said.

And, despite the earlier experience of the morning, John again became confused. Looking at the words, he blurted out: "ENOW! BOO! THRUFF!"

The class roared with delight, and Miss McGettigan could not resist laughing with them. Though John did not understand what she said, she tried to ease his position with the class by saying:

"John Grimm is a humorist. He knows better than that. . . . Try again, John Grimm, and stop laughing!" John Grimm, in fact, was laughing with the rest of the class.

This time he pronounced the words perfectly, and this made the class think that he had really done it all on purpose. Though, of course, he hadn't. He indeed felt like crying over his stupidity.

After his morning, John ran home to tell the news. When he arrived at the door of the house, he suddenly remembered that Katya couldn't be home yet from school, and he wanted every one there when he told of all the happenings. He wanted to watch their faces. And so he stopped on the outdoor steps and waited.

Presently Katya came jauntily along. Before John could open his mouth, she laughed and said:

"Well, Vanya, what do you suppose my name is?"

"How should I know," he said sulkily, suddenly feeling unhappy because it looked as if she were going to rob him of the surprise he was planning to spring on the family.

"Well, if you'd like to know, it's Catherine Grimsky —Kate for short!" she blurted out.

"Is that all?" John let out a derisive laugh. "Now maybe you'll guess what my name is." And he puffed out his chest.

"What is it?" Kate was terribly curious now, and looked it.

John was in no hurry to tell her. He enjoyed watching her face, with its eyes so eager to know.

"Well, tell me," she urged.

Even then he lingered a little before he spoke. "My name is—" he paused teasingly.

"Go on, silly!" she pleaded.

He suddenly burst out, "I am John Grimm. . . ."

He watched her, then added: "Not Grim with a single M, mind you, but Grimm with a double M. Grim with a single M is nothing, but with a double M. . . ." He smacked his lips. "It's spelt exactly like the Grimm who wrote the fairy-tales!" And he looked at his sister in triumph.

"You don't say!" said Kate, almost in awe. "I'll get my teacher to knock off the 'sky.' And then I'll also be a Grimm—with the double M!"

"Let's get everybody in our family to change their names to Grimm," suggested John, with enthusiasm.

"Yes, let's!" Kate agreed, and they rushed up the stairs, feeling very important, for they had a secret between them, and what a secret! All their life the family had borne the name of Grimsky, and presently, in a single instant, the Grimskys would be no more, and, instead, they'll all become the Grimms—not the ordinary Grim with a single M, but Grimm with the double M!"

On the landing they exchanged a few whispers; then, like conspirators, they entered the apartment.

Mother Grimsky was cooking dinner on the coal range, and the bare kitchen table was set with plates and spoons, and knives and forks.

They approached their mother, as if they were visitors, curtsying.

"Allow me to introduce to you Miss Kate Grimm," said John.

"Allow me to introduce to you Mr. John Grimm," said Kate.

"I have no time for jokes," said Mother Grimsky. "Don't you see, I'm busy."

Disappointed in their mother's lack of interest, John said, "It's no joke, Mother. I am really John Grimm, and Katya is—or will be—Kate Grimm." And he proceeded to explain the happenings of the morning, while the rest of the family listened open-mouthed.

"But, Vanya—" Mother Grimsky began.

"John, you mean," insisted John.

"John, then," his mother yielded, "what will Papa say when he comes? And he's coming soon. Don't you know, he's a proud man, and he is proud of the name of Grimsky. That is his name, and it has always been his name. His father before him was a Grimsky also, and, for aught I know, there were Grimskys way back to the time of Ivan the Terrible. . . ."

"Don't you think we've had that name long enough?

And, anyhow," said John with sudden inspiration, "we came here to forget Ivan the Terrible and all the rest of the Tsars. . . ."

"Yes, Mother," chimed in Kate, "the teacher told us today about George Washington, and what a wonderful man he was—not at all like Ivan the Terrible. She told us we must be good Americans. . . ."

"And it's easier to be an American with a name like John Grimm than with a name like Ivan Gregorievitch Grimsky," John added, with conviction.

"There may be something in that," conceded Mother Grimsky, smiling at the fervor of her two eldest children. "All the same, I don't know what your Papa will say."

"Let us all call ourselves Grimm," said John, pressing his advantage.

"Or else we'll get kind of mixed," added Kate.

Thus, the Grimskys became the Grimms, and, with the change in their name, they felt they had become less Russian and more American.

The Grimms wondered what Papa would say when he heard that they were Grimsky no longer, but Grimm. They feared he wouldn't like it. To their delight, he only laughed and said:

" 'What's in a name?' as Shakespeare said. 'A rose by any other name would smell as sweet.' "

He said this in Russian, for Russians loved Shakespeare almost as much as the English did. "No," he added, "I don't mind at all shaving the 'sky' off my name. But I'd object strongly if any one insisted on my shaving off my beard."

"Beards are not so popular in this country as they are in Russia," said John.

"That's silly of them," said Papa Grimm with a laugh. He was in a happy mood, and again he quoted Shakespeare: "'He that hath a beard is more than a youth, and he that hath no beard is less than a man.'"

There was a reason for this talk of beards. Indeed, the very first time Papa Grimm went out into the street, a group of boys ran after him and shouted:

"Bz-z-z-z . . . Bz-z-z-z . . ."

"What are they saying?" he asked.

"They are laughing at your beard," explained John.

"What's funny about it? It's like any other beard, isn't it?"

Just as John was about to reply, a youngster bolder than the rest ran forward and made a gesture that clearly showed the intention of pulling at Papa Grimm's beard.

Quick as a flash, Papa Grimm lunged an arm, and almost caught the boy. But he would not be defeated. As if he were a youngster himself, he dashed in pursuit.

It made a funny sight—thought John later—to see this bearded man, his father, run like one of them, after the rude boys. People stopped to look, with broad grins on their faces. "Catch 'im! Catch 'im!" some of them shouted.

Papa Grimm, his streamlined whiskers parted in the middle, the two halves of them flowing over his shoulders, needed no encouragement. Speedier than the culprit, he caught up with him and, with a quick, deft movement, planted a hand on his shoulder, causing the boy to stop.

Without much ado, poising himself on a single leg, he raised the knee of the other and put the boy across it, giving him a wallop or two on the part of the anatomy reserved for the purpose.

Then he released him. The boy scampered off as fast as his legs could carry him, Papa Grimm gazing after him with a broad grin. At a distance, the boy rallied his fellows who in a single voice shouted:

"Bz-z-z-z . . . Bz-z-z-z-z . . ."

By now, John, who witnessed the whole performance with astonishment, thought it high time he took a hand, all the more as he realized he had a real protector in his father. So, putting his hands to his mouth to allow his words to carry, he shouted at the boys:

"Sticks and stones may break my bones,
But names can never hurt me!"

What a strange country in which little boys tell their elders whether they may wear beards or not, thought Papa Grimm.

All the same, a few days later, Papa Grimm took a walk, and when he returned his own family scarcely recognized him.

In place of the luxuriant beard which covered his chest so that you didn't know if he wore a necktie, he now had a tiny Vandyk which hid nothing but the point of his chin. For one whole day it created no little excitement in the Grimm household.

"In Rome, do as Romans do," was all Papa Grimm would say when Mama Grimm twitted him.

Secretly all the Grimms were mightily pleased: they wanted so much to be taken for Americans. And **Papa's** beard was like the flag of another country.

By John Cournos

THE DOZIER BROTHERS BAND

Little Willie finally thought of a wise thing. While they stood there, looking sorrowfully down into the park, he touched Rags on the back and said, "Listen, big shorty, I know what."

"What you know, little half pint?" his brother said, smiling.

"Let's us go play some music and forget about what we has and what we hasn't got."

Slumber snapped his fingers, mocking his Uncle Jasper Tappin.

"Dog my cats," he said. "That's just the ticket."

THE DAYS grew hotter and hotter after the parade. A great many men came out on the streets of Harlem with little white wagons and sold water ices to the children. And it was not long before Slumber and Rags and Willie had spent all the nickels that Uncle Jasper Tappin could afford to give them. Then when the nickels were all gone, they found themselves still thirsty for water ices, and the days were still hot. Where would they get more nickels for water ices?

Slumber worried a great deal during the long afternoons. Harlem was surely no place to be without money. Harlem made you want things you never wanted before —like water ices and Eskimo pies and popsickles—but it didn't help you to get the money to buy these things. Slumber began to wish again that he were at home with his mama.

"If I were back home," he told Willie and Rags as they stood against the iron fence, looking down into the park, "I wouldn't be wanting no water ices or nothing like that. I wouldn't be studying about nothing such like. I'd just be chewing on a stalk of sorghum and feeling good."

"No, you wouldn't be feeling good," Rags said. "You going to always be wanting what you seen up here in Harlem. Even when you get back home again, you'll be wishing you had some popsickles. Once you start in wanting things, you can't never get over it. You shouldn't of come to Harlem."

"I reckon I shouldn't, but I want to go home just the same," Slumber said softly.

He did not fully agree with Rags about how he would keep on wanting the things he had seen in Harlem, even when he was home again. No, Slumber felt quite sure

that when he reached home again, stretched himself out
on the shady side of the house, scratched his bare feet in
the cool ground and started chewing his stalk of sorghum
cane, he would forget all about Eskimo pies and water
ices and popsickles. But, of course, they were now a long
way from home, and Uncle Jasper Tappin didn't seem
to be in any special hurry to carry them back.

Slumber tried crossing his fingers and making wishes,
but he found that nothing like that would work in Harlem. Those good luck tricks worked very well when he
was at home in Alabama and in the country, but they
didn't do a bit of good in New York. He found that in
the big city to which he and his brothers had come even a
rusty bent horseshoe or a rabbit's left hind foot wouldn't
help you to get a cool water ice when you didn't have
the nickel.

Little Willie finally thought of a wise thing. While
they stood there, looking sorrowfully down into the park,
he touched Rags on the back and said, "Listen, big
shorty. I know what."

"What you know, little half-pint?" his brother said,
smiling.

"Let's us go play some music and forget about what
we has and what we hasn't got."

Slumber snapped his fingers, mocking his Uncle Jasper Tappin.

"Dog my cats," he said. "That's just the ticket."

So they went across the street and down into the furnace room where they did most of their playing nowadays. And there was no question about it—playing music
did help a great deal.

That night when they were in bed, Slumber opened his eyes suddenly with a bright thought.

"Let's us start a band and call it the *Dozier Brothers Band,*" he said.

"Start a band with what?" Rags asked. "Just your harmonica and a tin can and a washboard?"

"Sure," Slumber said. "We can start with that and then look around and see what else we can find. Maybe Uncle Jasper Tappin will let you use that old guitar he got hanging on the wall."

Rags did not answer. The next afternoon, however, when their cleaning was done, he began to look around. Slumber kept his eyes open, too, and his thoughts were busy all morning.

"I seen some folks come in the air shaft with a old no-account band and play till people commenced throwing money at them from out the windows," he told Rags once. "We might could get us some nickels like how they did."

Rags was interested, but he was a little uncertain about the instruments. He wouldn't be satisfied with just a washboard to play on, and he was almost afraid to ask Uncle Jasper Tappin to let him take the guitar from off the wall. Yet, when the work was done, he made up his mind to try his luck.

In the meantime Willie found a broken drum in an ash can. Slumber repaired the old thing and painted the name of the band in big letters, *Dozier Brothers.* He struck the instrument a few strong booms, then handed it to his little brother.

"There now," he said. "You and me is fixed. If Rags

will go ask Uncle Jasper Tappin for his guitar, we'll be ready for business."

Rags left the others in the furnace room and went to see about the instrument. While he was gone, Slumber and Willie went over a song or two, Slumber playing the tune on his harmonica and Willie beating the heavy part on the drum.

"How it sound?" Willie asked.

"Not so bad," Slumber said. "Not so bad."

About that time Rags came running through the door.

"Here it is, bubbers. Here it is," he cried. "Now we's *ready.*"

"I told you so, big shorty," Slumber said, trembling with joy. "I told you he might would let you use it."

"He say it wasn't doing nobody no good up on the wall, 'cause he never yet seen a guitar what was made to be looked at. This old box was made for music, and here it comes. You listen."

Rags turned the strings. Then, when Slumber began another song on his harmonica, he began to chime in with chords that sounded mighty fine indeed. Little Willie kept the drum booming just right. And the more they played, the sweeter the music sounded. The old furnace room had never heard anything like it.

No, sir, not since the building was built had there ever been music such as that in the furnace room. Slumber got warmed up and commenced to bear down on his harmonica. And when Slumber was warmed up, mind you, he could play a harmonica like very few people can play one. Why the little old furnace room windows started quivering and rattling to the tune. Uncle Jasper

Tappin's old coal shovel caught one of the notes and began humming it almost as if it had been struck by Willie's drum stick. Slumber was bearing down, and his brothers were keeping right with him.

"This coming Sunday we can get out and let folks hear us," Slumber decided. "Soon in the morning, just about time they's getting out of bed good, they'll hear us down in the air shaft. Maybe they'll throw some money at us."

"Sometimes you think up some powerful smart things, Slumber," Willie said.

"He sure do," Rags said. "I don't see how he can do it and still be so dumb."

A smile came over Slumber's sad face.

"Sunday," he reminded the other two as they left the furnace room. "Sunday—soon in the morning."

Daisy Bee was sitting by the window reading a funny paper when she heard music down in the air shaft, far below. She stopped reading to listen, but at first she did not look out because it was nothing new to hear poor musicians playing down in the air shaft on Sunday morning. So many of them came that sometimes, when she was busy doing something else, Daisy Bee didn't even bother to open the window and look down, much less toss the players a penny. But today the music was not the same. It reminded her of something she had heard before, and she turned her ear to hear it better.

Yes, she thought, that was sweet playing down there in the air shaft. But that tune—where had she heard it before? Suddenly she remembered a tall country boy dancing lazily, another one beating on a tin can drum, and still another—a sad-faced boy, this third one—playing a harmonica. Then she knew. It was the tune the boys had been playing on the roof the day she saw them first, and she remembered that Slumber had called it something about three country boys in a big city. It was just a kind of tune he made up in his head. But it was a very good tune, even if it was rather sad, and today it sounded much better than usual.

Daisy Bee opened a window and looked down. And there they were: little Willie beating the big drum they had found in an ash can, Rags whipping out chords on Uncle Jasper Tappin's box (or guitar, as some folks call it), and Slumber, the sad-faced boy, patting his foot and making the tune on that harmonica of his. They were a great set of boys, especially that Slumber, and Daisy Bee was glad to see that other windows were coming open and a few folks were tossing down coins wrapped in little scraps of newspaper.

The boys played two or three pieces, picked up their coins and then left to try their music on the people of some other building. So it was afternoon when Daisy Bee saw them again, and by that time they were hungry and pretty well tired out.

"I heard you playing this morning," she said, as the little troop reached the basement entrance with their large instruments.

"Was you listening, Daisy Bee?" Slumber said eagerly.

"Indeed I was," she told him again. "It sounded right good, too."

That pleased the three more than even the pennies and nickels in their pockets, because Daisy Bee was not one to praise what you did very readily. In fact, the boys were quite certain that she had told the band master in the parade just what was wrong with his band, and Rags and Willie remembered that at one time she had criticized them rather sharply for the way they played and danced. Daisy Bee was hard to please, and this was the first time the boys had ever received such a compliment from her.

"That's a mighty nice thing to hear you say," Slumber murmured timidly. "We aim to practice up this week so we can play some more good songs next Sunday."

The boys carried their instruments down to the basement apartment. After dinner they came up and sat on one of the benches looking down into the park. That afternoon they had money enough for all the Eskimo pies and popsickles and water ices and snowballs they wanted.

Daisy Bee, whose father and mother had a car, came downstairs wearing a very pretty new dress and drove away with her parents. But Slumber and his brothers did not forget what she had said to encourage them, and they began to think that playing in a band of your own like theirs was just about the best fun yet.

"Tomorrow we got to practice up good," Slumber said, licking his strawberry flavored snowball.

"You took the words out of my mouth," Rags said. "I was just fixing to say the same thing." He threw away the stick of his third popsickle.

Little Willie had just started on another cup of water

ice, so he didn't say anything. But his brothers knew how he loved to beat that big drum, especially since they had painted the words *Dozier Brothers* on it.

The week passed slowly, but when next Sunday morning came, the band was even more successful than it had been the first time. They got more coins, and more people praised them.

This time it was Uncle Jasper Tappin who said, "Too bad Sunday don't come but once a week. You boys is doing pretty well with that band of yours."

"Yes," Slumber answered sadly, "too bad Sunday just come around now and then. I wish it was every day."

"Seems like you ought to could find somewheres to play on week days," Uncle Jasper Tappin said.

The boys wished it were true, but they had no idea where to go. That afternoon, however, they told Daisy Bee what Uncle Jasper Tappin had said and asked her what she thought about it.

"Sure, I know," she said. "Downtown is the place. I can't go because it'll be night, but mind where I tell you to go and you'll find the place all right. You'll make a lot of nickels, too."

Daisy Bee gave them the directions carefully. Rags wrote some of the words on a scrap of paper and put it in his pocket.

"That sound good, what you say, Daisy Bee," Slumber said.

They hurried downstairs and began getting their instruments in shape. Then, just as twilight was coming to the park, they caught an elevated train at the 155th Street station.

"I don't know where we going," little Willie said, struggling to keep his drum out of the aisle, "but I know we on our way."

"Just don't let anybody step on that drum," Rags said. "We'll get there if the train keeps on running."

In the heart of New York there is the street of bright lights. Down there in that part of the city you walk between the rows of skyscraper buildings as the Indians used to walk between the walls of narrow canyons. You pass beneath the shadows overhead as the black men of the jungle used to pass beneath the trees of Africa. And you feel afraid sometimes when you walk there at night, just as the brave red men were sometimes afraid when they stood in the tall rocky canyons—just as the beautiful jungle men sometimes trembled in the shadows of their trees. But at night, when all those lights are burning, you almost forget the tallness of the buildings and the other things that make you afaid. You even forget sometimes how empty and dark the buildings are and what frightful black shadows they make.

The reason for the lights is that at that hour people are all going to theaters and concerts and places of amusement. Daisy Bee had explained this to the boys, and they were not disappointed. They walked to a place on the side street to which she had directed them. At first they wouldn't find anyone there, she had said, but they were to wait. By and by their time would come. The only trouble was that there was so much to look at as they went along and that people hurrying to be on time to their theaters nearly walked over the three youngsters.

The boys found their place in an alley behind a theater, and sat down to wait, and in less than an hour their time came. The side doors of the theater were flung open, and out came great crowds of people in evening clothes. It was the time of the intermission, and all the people were eager for a breath of fresh air and a chance to smoke a cigarette.

"Here we be," Slumber whispered to his brothers. "This is the time. Let's strike it up, big shorty."

Slumber drew the harmonica across his mouth. Rags whipped out the chords. Little Willie caught the time and began beating the drum.

The theater people seemed delighted. They drew around the boys, forming a half circle. Slumber pulled his cap around sidewise, patted his foot and bore down on that lonesome railroad track tune of his: "Oh, Blow Your Whistle on the Dixie Line."

There was time for just two songs. Then a buzzer rang, and the people had to return for the rest of their program inside. But before they went away, they sprinkled the ground around the boys' feet with nickels and dimes and a few quarters.

Slumber was so excited he could not speak, but he helped his brothers to search well and make sure they had not overlooked a single coin. Then he said, "Well, I reckon we got them all."

"Yes, I reckon so," Rags agreed. "Now we going over to another theater in time for the next intermission. That's how Daisy Bee said to do."

At the second theater they succeeded just as well. A happy, surprised look came over the people's face as they discovered the poorly dressed boys in the alley. Hearing the music, one man said, "This is a better show than the one inside," and he threw down a dollar bill.

"Now," Slumber said, still scarcely able to talk, "we got something to talk *about.*"

"Yes," Rags said, "but you is so tickled and glad you can't keep from stuttering, and nobody won't *know* what you talking about."

"Let's hurry and get on the car before the theaters turn out," Willie suggested. "It's hard to carry this big old drum in a crowd."

"What a city," Slumber thought as they neared the subway entrance. "What a world!"

By Arna Bontemps

INGA OF PORCUPINE MINE

The thought that her [Finnish] mother counted more importantly in the community—even excelling the Cornish women in the making of their national dish—made Inga feel warm and kindly inside and friendly and gracious out."

ONE BRIGHT MARCH day, as Inga joined the other children going home from school at noon time, she realized that the back of the winter was broken at last. Snow was running away in little rivers, and icicles dripped rapidly under the eaves.

She bounded into the kitchen in a jolly, carefree mood, but stopped suddenly as she saw her father sitting with his stockinged feet on the stove fender, his eyes closed.

Her mother was just putting the big soup tureen filled with steaming hot cabbage soup on the table. She looked worried, and quickly pressed a warning finger to her lips. "Sh-h, Pa sleeps. Eyes hurt unt head aches."

Inga ate her soup in silence, and noticed that her mother hardly touched hers. Ma wouldn't act like this just for tired eyes. It was something more. Carrying the dishes from the table and stacking them quietly in the sink, she beckoned to her mother to come out to the woodshed.

After softly closing the door, she whispered, "Ma, what's the matter with Pa? Please tell me."

"Oh, Kultain, Doctor say to Pa this morning ven he makes round unt looks on miners, 'Vithers, you go to office. I vant to look better on your eyes." He shust say like that, so poor Pa lay down vork unt go. Vell . . ." and Mrs. Withers paused.

"Yes, go on, Ma," Inga said impatiently.

"Vell, Doctor look hard on Pa's eyes unt he say, 'Only von ting now left to do, Vithers; you have to have operation.' Oh," cried Mrs. Withers, wringing her hands desperately, "Pa must needs operation! Doctor say vright vay must go hospital at Ann Arbor."

"What's the matter with his eyes?" persisted Inga.

"In-fec-tion, Doctor say. Dust from ore makes sore and infect."

"But, Ma," interrupted Inga, "Pa wears those shat-

terproof goggles when he has to work in drifts where
there's silica. How could he get an infection?"

"Ve-ll," hesitated her mother, "Pa say he vear goggs
only leetle, only ven eyes get sore. He say he can't see
good vit those goggs over his glasses—three eyes—see
notings. Pa say that nose ting vit sieve 'nuf to vear."

"That's a respirator, Ma. They're good things. If
Swan had worn one, the silica wouldn't have gotten in
his lungs."

"I know, Pigeon. But Pa not like not see good. He
can't vork right vit goggs on."

Then she added, "Doctor phone Aunt Evie; she come
this afternoon unt ve talk all tings over."

Inga knew what they would talk about: the money
it was going to cost. Operations always cost lots of money.
She'd heard folks talk and, besides that, Pa would have
to go on a train to the hospital. That cost money, too.

As she went back to school, her thoughts kept coming
back to her father. How he would hate to be away from
work right now, with three shifts running at the mine
to keep up with the war orders. She pictured the big steel
mills at Gary and Pittsburgh as big ugly monsters with
great gaping mouths like caverns that cried incessantly
for ore, ore, and more ore. They were never filled and
never satisfied. She wondered if they starved when navi-
gation stopped and there was no shipping over Lake
Superior during the long winter. . . . Pa got too tired,
but he wouldn't admit it. He said it made him feel good
to think he was doing his part to help win the war.

Everything went wrong at school; she missed in her

spelling and had two problems in algebra wrong. Miss Connor had to speak to her twice about paying attention.

She hurried home as fast as she could and peeked in the window. Around the big table sat her mother, Aunt Evie and her father, in family council. Aunt Evie was talking, saying she thought she had better go down with Will, since Ma did not understand things quickly and did not like to talk to strangers in English.

"I'll get someone to tend store. Maybe Ben'll be able to do it and make up the work at school later. We'll see. It can be managed . . ."

Then Pa spoke up, his voice very grave. "The Company will make some advance against my expenses even though I have to go out of town for this kind of operation. They take $1.25 a month out of our pay for Hospital and Clinical Services, you know. Of course, Dr. McCombs will give me all the care I need free when I get home, but it's the cost of the operation I'm worryin' about."

Aunt Evie replied, "Well, Will, we'll have to work it out somehow. Besides keeping myself down in Ann Arbor, I think I can squeeze out twenty-five dollars toward the operation. Of course, if you have to stay in the hospital a third week, that won't be so easy."

When Inga went into the house, there was such a forced cheerfulness about everyone that she was glad when it came time to go to bed. But she couldn't sleep. She could hear her parents talking through the thin partition, after they thought she was asleep. She heard her mother sigh heavily and turn over several times. Then

Pa whispered, "Dr. McCombs said he thought the operation'd cost fifty or seventy-five dollars. If I only have to stay in the hospital two weeks, what Evie can spare could be used toward the operation. But any way you figure it, we'll have to raise twenty-five dollars somehow. Maybe I can get it from the bank."

Inga heard her mother sigh deeply. "Why," she thought, suddenly getting hot all over and throwing off the blanket, *"I've* got fifty dollars, my art school money!" Then she grew even hotter. That might be just enough for the operation if it cost only fifty dollars. Even if it cost seventy-five and Aunt Evie gave the twenty-five, her fifty would fix things about right.

But this money was her tuition for art school! She had worked hard for it last summer and had had hardly any fun all vacation. Now it was her turn to fidget and turn in the bed. Her mind was divided and she did not know which part wanted to give the money and which part wanted to keep it.

Maybe Ben could help. No, he hadn't any money. He had spent all he made for things he needed for business school. Then she seemed to hear a strange voice saying, "Well, Inga Withers, what if your father goes blind because he hasn't the money for the operation? How would you feel then?" It was a voice she had never heard before, a cold, hard, matter-of-fact voice. It came from somewhere inside.

The voice went on, "Could you go off to be a teacher and leave a poor blind father behind you?" Of course, she didn't want her father to go blind. Did that horrible voice think that she did? But maybe some way could be found so she wouldn't have to give up her precious money. "What way?" the voice asked. If her father went blind, Ben wouldn't be able to finish his business course Pa had so set his heart on. Inga knew Pa wanted something better for him than the hard life of an iron-ore miner. But if Pa couldn't work any more Ben would have to be a miner all the rest of his life to support the family.

Inga heard her parents talking again. They hadn't been asleep, any more than she had. It must be awfully late, too. But her mind was made up at last. Something ached way down deep inside of her, but the voice had stopped.

As soon as it was daylight, she tiptoed down the stairs and went into the parlor. She shut her eyes tight as she stood on the chair and pulled out the mug from its hiding place. She had changed all the money into one dollar bills at the mine bank—even the five dollar bill. Here they were, but they looked strange as she held them in her hand. They felt different too. They were no longer her tuition to art school. They were Pa's eyes. She crushed them in her hand as she slipped quietly into the kitchen and took a small paper bag from behind the woodbox.

When she reached the top of the stairs she listened for a moment for sounds in her parents' room. She could hear nothing and decided that they must have fallen asleep at last. Slipping quietly back into her room, she tucked the bills into the little bag and placed it under her pillow. Then she crawled back into bed and settled herself comfortably to wait for time to get up. In a moment she was fast asleep.

Her father was sitting in his usual place by the stove warming his feet on the fender when she came down to breakfast with the bag in one hand behind her back. She sat down hastily, tucking the bag under her, and tried to choke down her oatmeal and milk. She usually took a long time eating her breakfast on Saturday mornings to celebrate the fact that she didn't have to hurry to school, but this morning she ate rapidly and rose the moment she had finished.

Calling to Juka and snatching up her mackinaw and chuke, she thrust the bag into her father's lap and rushed out of the door and down the lane, never stopping for breath until she reached the woods.

The sun was high in the sky before Inga started back for home. As she came in, her mother smiled at her tenderly and went briskly about the serving of the noonday meal so that Inga could not see the tears in her eyes.

"Come, Pa, dinner ready," she said, and as they sat down at the table, she turned to Inga and said quietly, "Pa, he going vit Aunt Evie to Ann Arbor on evening train."

Her father looked across the table at her from under his heavy brows. His dark glasses kept her from seeing the expression in his eyes, but his voice shook a little as he said, "I didn't know paper bags could hold so much love, Daughter."

In a few days good news came from Ann Arbor, when

Aunt Evie sent the first telegram Inga or her mother had ever seen. It said, "Everything fine and Will doing well." Inga read and reread it to her mother, and showed it to everyone who came in or passed by to inquire.

"Wonder when he'll be home again, Ma?" she remarked one day after a particularly cheerful letter had been received. Her father was now out of danger and would have his sight completely restored.

"Anyway, Ma, now we can plan again for Easter and May Day. Pa'll be home for Easter and you'll have to make him lots of Cornish cream and pasties. And, you know how Ben and I love your Easter *mammi* with all the good things you make to go with it. If Ben doesn't get home for Easter, I'll go to the woods and get birchbark to make the little baskets you bake *mammi* in. Will you let me help make it? Seems to me all you do is sour the meal and water over a stone and flavor it with almonds before you bake it."

"That's vright, but you forget cream. I teach you this year."

"And I'll boil and color the eggs, and paint them as I did last year. We want everything nice for Pa this Easter."

"Yes, unt I make unt make tings Pa likes." Her mother began to feel her old self as she planned for the festival days ahead with her husband at home and well again. "Pigeon, ven you go to voods for bark, you get pussyvillow, too. Ve trim house so nice. No forget."

One afternoon some days later Inga found Aunt Evie sitting with her mother when she came in from school. Both were elated.

"Your Pa's wonderful, Inga," said Aunt Evie as she kissed her. "And he talks of you all the time. They took the bandages off for a few minutes the day I left and he said, 'Tell Inga her Pa can see'."

A big, hard lump stuck in Inga's throat as she tried to swallow, and tears came into her eyes.

Aunt Evie went on happily, "And the operation, in spite of being such a serious and delicate one, cost only fifty dollars, Helia. They knew our circumstances and the operating doctor was real considerate."

"Fifty dollars," repeated Inga, smiling.

Inga sat close beside her father, her hand held tightly in his, and watched the miners from all parts of the County stream in and out of the house to congratulate him on his recovery. They were all eager to pay their respects to the man who was their friend, interpreter, and adviser. Miners were there from the Angeline and the Cambria, from North Lake, and even from mines clear up in Copper County. It was a real celebration.

Fortunately Mrs. Withers had done a big baking. She went hurrying about serving hot coffee and Helmie followed with big plates filled with hearty sandwiches and cakes.

It was good to have Pa home again, thought Inga. She was glad they had had that walk up to Grandma's the day before, because he'd be starting work in a few days and then there would be no time for walks. They had seen the lilacs beginning to bud, too, and if there was no frost they'd be out for her birthday. It didn't seem possible that nearly a year had passed since she had painted Grandma's lilacs. So much had happened since then.

A few days later her mother called from the foot of the stairs, "Come, Inga, ve must get house all clean. Tomorrow is *Vapun Aatto*. Hurry, ve have lots to clean."

Tomorrow *was* May Day, and then Inga's birthday right after that. She sprang out of bed and rushed into her clothes.

Half tumbling down the stairs, she called out, "Ma, why didn't you get me up earlier? It's past eight and I'll bet anything you've been working your head off since Pa left."

"Now I sit vit you unt drink leetle coffee," answered her mother, easing down on a chair close to the kitchen table. "I make *sima* already. Good this year, too," she added proudly.

Inga puckered up her lips at the thought of *sima,* the malt and ale drink which the Finns make for May Day. She didn't like the taste of it one bit.

"Yes," continued Mrs. Withers, "unt yesterday night ven you vas at Library I make *struvaja,* to go vit *sima.*

"Umm, I *do* like *struvaja,* Ma. They're so much better than the crullers Cousin Jennie makes. Now you sit with me while I finish my breakfast, Ma. You work too hard."

As the two worked away, cleaning, scouring, and burnishing everything in the house, Mrs. Withers told Inga that this *Vapun Aatto* there would be no new dresses.

"Pa he miss so much vork vit eyes."

"Goodness, Ma, I don't care," Inga asserted. "Besides, this is war time and I don't think many girls will

have new clothes this year. At school they tell us everyone has to make sacrifices so we can win the war."

"You good girl, Inga. Anyway, I fix up dresses you
vear last summer. They all ready now."

"Oh, thank you, Ma. Do you think it will be nice and
warm outdoors tomorrow so that we can sing and dance?
I love the old country songs and funny dances. Guess it's
the Finn in me," and she laughed.

"I dance tomorrow, maybe," her mother replied
shyly. "If nice out, I vear my old country shawl unt
apron. I love dance, too."

The festival of May Day, with its traditional cere-
monies, ushered in the "Season of Returning Light," and
turned Inga's thoughts toward her fast-approaching
birthday.

"Just think, I'll be fourteen," she told Juka as he sat
watching her washing up the supper dishes. "I'm going
to be a year older and a year bigger than I was last spring,
so I ought to be able to work longer and harder, and
earn more money this summer than I did last. Now I've
got to begin all over to earn my tuition back. But I don't
mind, and I can do it all right," she added determinedly.

When she awoke on the morning of her birthday, she
thought she smelled flowers. As she came downstairs, the
smell seemed to grow stronger.

"Ma," she called, "I smell lilacs!" And there, right
straight in front of her on the table, was a big bowl full
of them. "L-i-l-a-c-s," she breathed and buried her face
in their fragrant depths.

"Look in front room, too, Pigeon, more in there," her

mother said, pointing, as she put the breakfast on the table.

"Why," she said joyously, "there are lilacs every-where in the house. Bet Grandma sent them for my birth-day. But when did she?" She picked out a little fat, curly purple cluster that looked exactly like a feather tip, and stuck it in the yellow braid at the side of her head.

"I find big bunches on doorstep ven I come down. Maybe Helmie bring, maybe somevun going to vork," speculated her mother. "Unt this leetle paper come vit. Here 'tis." Mrs. Withers reached up on the shelf for a small white envelope.

Inga was so excited she could hardly get it open. When she took out the card, something fluttered to the floor. "Happy Birthday," said the card, written in Grand-ma's own writing. "To Inga Withers from Grandma and her lilacs."

She stooped down and picked up a crisp new bill. "Ma, oh, Ma," she screamed in delight. "It's a ten dollar bill. Ten whole dollars from Grandma for my birthday to start my savings fund going again. Isn't that won-derful?"

She caught hold of Juka and made him stand on his hind legs and dance around the kitchen with her.

It was the happiest birthday she had ever had. Her father was well again. He said himself that his sight was better than it had been in years, and he never had a head-ache any more. Her mother had baked her a beautiful birthday cake, and she had invited Angie and Senia to share it. They'd had some of her mother's good raspberry shrub, too. And the house was filled with lilacs! For once in her life she had all the lilacs she wanted. Yes, it **had** been a perfect birthday.

By Caroline R. Stone

STORM ON THE MOUNTAIN

Dan's fourteen-year-old nephew Klee-tso, Randy's closest friend, had first shown Randy the trail. It was so dangerous that only the more daring Navajo horsemen ever used it. . . .

"Some day," Klee-tso had added quietly, "I will ride down this trail on Nuflo, and maybe I will take you with me if you like. Nuflo is so sure-footed he can go anywhere."

RANDY'S FATHER APPEARED with the mail sack and tossed it under the truck seat. After Mr. Bartlett came

Dan, the lean Navajo who had charge of the livestock about the post. He was carrying a bundle of sheepskins which he laid in the truck, covering them carefully with the old tarpaulin.

"Afraid of rain?" Randy's father asked jokingly. Randy looked quickly at the sky. All week he had been counting on the trip down the mountain with his father to the big Indian trading post of Tonalea, one hundred miles away. If it rained his mother wouldn't want him to go!

But there was not a cloud to be seen except that tiny rosy cap on the topmost peak of Sacred Mountain. It couldn't well be a finer day, Randy thought joyously.

Dan too looked at the sky, and presently he said: "It may storm, yes."

"Oh, John, must you go today?" Mrs. Bartlett asked with quick anxiety."

"Unless we can live on stewed squirrel and pine nuts, my dear. The shelves are absolutely bare. Would you rather I didn't take Randy?"

"No," Randy's mother answered. "You're more careful when Randy is with you. But do start home early enough to cross the Snake's Back before dark."

Mr. Bartlett promised, and with a shout of relief Randy gave his mother a hasty kiss and climbed up into the high seat of the truck.

He understood his mother's anxiety for he always felt a little excitement about driving over the Snake's Back. It was a slippery backbone of pink rock connecting two broad mountain shoulders with a sheer drop of the shadowy canyon far below. Cars were guided along the slick surface by great splashes of white paint that Randy's father had set at intervals to guide the few strangers who ventured up to Sacred Mountain. Travellers complained bitterly about the Snake's Back, but the Navajos set their faces against any improvements. They did not want tourists overrunning their country.

In spite of Dan's prophecy the trip down the mountains was mild and bright. Even the Snake's Back looked friendly this morning, and as they crawled along its narrow ridge Randy looked ahead to watch for the spot that always gave him a special thrill. From the piñon clearing at the lower end were wagon tracks made by Dan when he hauled out firewood and beyond the wagon tracks a trail went off down the sheer red cliffs, zigzagging by thread-like twists that seemed to hang over space until it reached a narrow green valley some two thousand feet below.

Dan's fourteen-year-old nephew Klee-tso, Randy's closest friend, had first shown Randy the trail. It was so dangerous that only the more daring Navajo horsemen ever used it, the others going into the canyon by a much longer but safer trail from below. The valley was called Skeleton Valley.

"Some day," Klee-tso had added quietly, "I will ride down this trail on Nuflo, and maybe I will take you with me if you like. Nuflo is so sure-footed he can go anywhere."

Randy, who thought Klee-tso's handsome buckskin pony Nuflo the most wonderful horse in the world, agreed; but as he thought this morning of what it would be like to ride down the hanging thread, even on Nuflo, he turned giddy, and turned his eyes toward the road.

There was a big, shaggy looking man waiting beside the road a mile or so further on. It was Matt Ingersoll who kept a hunter's lodge a few yards back among the piñons. He greeted them eagerly.

"Rang up your wife and she told me you were on the road," he said jovially. "My truck's busted, and I need supplies. I made the list as small as I could." He handed a paper to Randy's father and seemed anxious to chat, but Randy's father cut him off.

"We promised to be back before dark," he explained. "Nora is always nervous about the road."

"Sure," said Matt. He squinted his eyes and looked toward the peak. "That cloud means a storm, I guess."

Randy glanced back, startled. The tiny fluff had swollen and darkened until it hid the whole peak. The rest of the world was in brilliant sunshine.

The day at Tonalea was all Randy had hoped. Cars came and went from distant highway towns; silent Navajos stalked around picking out supplies to take back in their creaking wagons to lonely hogans; and Randy had his fill of gazing into showcases full of gay cottons and belts and knives and all sorts of inviting trinkets. Mrs. Riggs, the postmaster's wife, helped Randy choose a box of pretty handkerchiefs for his mother and a pair of moccasins for baby Sue. Mr. Bartlett added a flashlight for Randy and a stout hunting knife for Klee-tso.

"And now, son, you can be packing the breakables

into the locker while we load the truck," his father said. "We'll be starting soon."

It was fun sorting out and packing the neat packages of medical supplies into the long zinc locker back of the truck seat. When the last package was tucked in Randy climbed down to the platform again and sat on the edge to watch the men packing up the big cartons.

"My, but these clouds are thickening," Mrs. Riggs said as she joined Randy.

Randy looked to the north. The dark cloud masses had grown alarmingly in the last hour, blotting out all of Sacred Mountain and reaching out threatening fingers over the wide pink mesa that stretched from Tonalea right to the mountain's foot.

When the last carton was stowed away Randy's father turned with a smile.

"We can start now, son," he said.

Randy bade I.rs. Riggs a hasty goodbye and scrambled up to his seat. A glance at the post-office clock told him that it was not quite three—there was time to be over the Snake's Back before dark.

"Hi!" called Mr. Riggs. "Wait a minute. Cameron hospital sent over a brace for that Navajo boy with the dislocated back up at Matt's. Told me to get it up there pronto. I'll fetch it."

He hurried inside and came back with a square package in his hand; but before he reached the truck a horn sounded from the bluff and Randy looked around to see a car coming down to the store.

This was no local car, but a sleek blue and gray monster that looked as if it had never before been off a paved highway. The driver, a fair-haired young man with a round, boyish face and thick glasses, skidded to a stop and jumped out as if he were glad to have made a safe landing.

"I'm Larry Hemingway, of Hemingway Saddle Company," he said, including them all in a shy, friendly grin. "Which is Mr. Riggs?"

The postmaster stepped forward and held out his hand. "I've bought many a saddle from your firm," Mr. Riggs said cordially. "Just delivered one a month ago to an old chap in Monument Valley. Been in my storeroom more than a year. I—"

"Fine," said the young man quickly. "This time I'm on a buying trip. Our firm needs sheepskins for a war order. My dad heard that good ones were to be had here in the Navajo country. We want the best we can get—for the Army Air Force."

He touched his own well-made jacket and added with a flush, "I—I hoped I'd be wearing this in the Army, but they turned me down because of my eyes. So Dad sent me West and told me to make myself useful to the firm."

Mr. Riggs nodded understandingly. "You're just in time," he said. "Mr. Bartlett brought down a sample of fine sheepskins today, and he tells me there's a storeroom full up at his post. Bartlett, meet Mr. Hemingway."

Randy's father climbed down from the truck, and he too shook hands with the newcomer. They went over to the bundle of hides on the platform, prodded, poked, talked and prodded again. Randy sighed and looked in at the post-office clock. It said one minute past three.

But Randy's father was wasting no time. He came back to the truck, drawing on his thick gloves.

"If you won't ride with us, you'd better leave your car at Matt Ingersoll's," he called back to the stranger. "The road's fair to that point."

Hemingway waved his hand in assent and grinned at Randy.

"I like him," Randy murmured.

"So do I," said Randy's father. "But his motor's missing, and he's near-sighted. He's got to leave his car at Matt's. I'll insist."

Hemingway's car pulled ahead of the truck and shot down across the red lake bottom in a cloud of rosy dust.

"We'll catch up with him when he begins to climb," Randy's father said confidently.

On the level the other car made good time, but Randy's father was pushing the truck along too, his eyes now and again on the cloud mass ahead of them. The last streak of sunlight was gone from the mesa, and as they neared the mountains the smell of sage and wet piñons came fresh on the wind. Randy sniffed the exciting fragrances like an eager puppy.

As his father had prophesied, Larry's car slowed down at the first steep grade. First they heard the uneven throb of its motor, then it came into view on a curve ahead, disappearing the next moment into the curtain of cloud beyond.

The truck too soon nosed its way into the storm. Rain pelted against the wind-shield and rattled on the roof of the cab. Randy settled back against his father's shoulder and peered through the clear little area the wind-shield wipers made on the blurred glass, and as they swung around each curve he was relieved by the sight of Hemingway's car now not more than half a mile ahead of them.

A sudden rain-squall swept down on them, blotting out sight of everything but the few yards of road ahead. "I must put on the chains when we get to Matt's," Randy's father said. He was driving slowly now, but with all his caution the big truck had to be eased back from an occasional skid. At last they caught sight of the rough sign board marking the turn-off to Matt Ingersoll's lodge.

There was no sign of Larry's car under the big oak in front of the door; but Randy saw a familiar buckskin among the group of ponies stamping about under the tree and gave a shout of joy.

"Nuflo!" he exclaimed. "Klee-tso's back from Kanab!"

"That's fine, son," said Randy's father, "but you can't stop to visit. Tell Klee-tso to ride on up with us. I must catch Hemingway before he gets into trouble."

He pulled out the cartons and mail sack marked "Ingersoll" and reached the door just as Matt Ingersoll flung it wide. The warmth from the big pot-bellied stove in the middle of the room rushed out to meet them. Randy looked about for Klee-tso but at first could see only a necklace of middle-aged Navajos around the stove, their thin faces wrinkling into dignified smiles at sight of Randy and his father.

Then Klee-tso stepped from the shadows. He raised

his hand in greeting and said "Hi," in his pleasant, quiet voice.

Klee-tso, who was three years older than Randy, had watched over him like an affectionate older brother, teaching him the lessons a Navajo boy learns almost from his cradle: how to ride and care for his pony, how to use a reata, what clouds mean rain or snow or wind, and how to meet all sorts of dangers.

All summer Klee-tso had been away with his grandfather in the North Rim country and the two friends had much to talk about; but Randy had only time to fish the hunting knife from his pocket and give it to Klee-tso when he heard his father's anxious voice.

"You mean he went right by?" Randy's father was saying.

"Never saw hide nor hair of him, only heard his car and noticed the motor was missing," said Matt. " 'Bout three minutes before you came along. It was raining hard. He may not have seen the sign."

"Who is it?" Klee-tso asked quickly.

"His name is Larry Hemingway," Randy explained. "He came up to buy sheepskins for his father's factory. They make jackets for the Air Force. He's strange to this country, and he was to leave his car here and ride on up with us. He had heard there were good skins here."

"There are none better," Klee-tso agreed with quiet pride.

"Can't you come up with us and see Dan?" Randy asked as Klee-tso reached for his fringed deerskin jacket and slipped his arms into it.

"I'd like to," Klee-tso agreed simply. "But first we must find this—Larry. It will be snowing and slippery on the Snake's Back."

Randy's father evidently felt the need for haste too. He greeted Klee-tso with a quick, friendly smile and reached for his gloves.

"Coming up with us, Klee-tso?" he said. "That's fine."

Klee-tso murmured a word to his uncle in Navajo. Randy thought he mentioned Nuflo's name, as the three moved toward the door. Suddenly Matt's roar stopped them.

"Bartlett, the brace isn't here!"

"But Riggs went back for it, and I saw it in his hand!" said Randy's father. "It must be there."

Matt shook his head. "I've combed through every package," he said, "Could it be in the truck?"

And then Randy remembered. "It was when Mr. Hemingway came," Randy said. "Mr. Riggs laid the package on the platform when he shook hands."

"Good Heavens!" exclaimed Randy's father. "And I didn't check up on it!"

"That's Riggs for you," Matt commented disgustedly. "Can't even lick a postage stamp without help. And that boy Tsini hell-bent on going back to his folks tomorrow and his back just half healed. Well!"

The two men looked at each other and then Randy's father said in a quiet voice, "I must go back after it. Get Riggs on the wire if you can and have him come to meet me. And get Nora too and tell her not to worry if we're late."

"That's sure too bad," said Matt remorsefully. "There's hot coffee on the stove. Just wait and I'll bring you a cup. But what about this tenderfoot wandering about in the storm?"

"Someone's got to ride after him at once," Randy's father said grimly.

He looked at the older men about the stove, but Klee-tso, at his elbow, spoke up quietly.

"I'll go, sir," he said. "Nuflo is quick, and he will not have gone far."

Bartlett hesitated, but only for a moment. "Good lad," he murmured, laying a hand on Klee-tso's shoulder. "And bring him back here even if you have to rope him."

"I'll go too," Randy chimed in eagerly. "Please, father. Nuflo's used to carrying us both, and Mr. Hemingway knows me."

Randy's father looked troubled but Klee-tso spoke again.

"It will be better, sir. The stranger might not trust me alone."

"Nonsense!" Randy's father said gruffly. "But Randy may be of use. Only be careful, Klee-tso. And if he's gone on across the Snake's Back, don't try to follow. Promise?"

Klee-tso nodded. Bartlett gulped down the steaming coffee and the three went out together, Matt coming with them to help put the chains on the truck.

The rain had turned to snow, and the wind swept down on them from the higher slopes, stinging their cheeks. Randy was glad of his warm woolen mittens and fleece-lined windbreaker. Even hardy Klee-tso pulled his deerskin jacket tight about him.

Nuflo too felt the cold and was in a mood to buck, but Klee-tso was on his back in a bound and pulled Randy up behind him. Nuflo snorted and pranced as Klee-tso turned him up the mountain road, away from the trail that led to food and shelter, but soon he settled into a quick walk, understanding that there was work ahead of him before he could eat.

The sleet turned to snow, and under the white veil the tracks of the big car showed black and clear. On a sharp curve Randy saw how Hemingway had put on his brakes too suddenly and had taken a sharp skid.

"He is brave," Klee-tso said, "but very silly, though his reason for coming is a good one."

They came into a belt of scattered piñons, and through the trees they could see the dim outline of the Snake's Back rising above them. No sound, no light came from that dark ridge, though if Larry Hemingway had gone on he would surely have turned on his lights by now.

Klee-tso pulled up, slipped to the road and bent to look at the tracks. Here was the wagon trail leading into Dan's wood-lot. Klee-tso made a sound between his teeth.

"He has been out of the car here," he said. "He has looked ahead and seen no road, so he has followed the track of my uncle's wagon. We must find him before he goes down the trail beyond the clearing."

Randy's heart sank. Beyond them in the deepening dusk the wagon road ended and there was only the narrow trail, level for a little way, then threading down the canyon wall with terrible hairpin turns. He remembered how he had dreamed that morning of riding down that path with Klee-tso some day. What if Hemingway, near-sighted and confused, had driven his car to the edge of the chasm?

Klee-tso had pushed Nuflo into a trot, and presently they came to a great stack of firewood Dan had left for seasoning. Nuflo shied violently away from the pile. A few yards further on the wagon tracks ended and Nuflo stopped and turned his head in protest. Klee-tso leaned over to peer at the ground, but the snow was falling more thickly, and even when he dismounted his sharp eyes could make out nothing clearly.

"We should have a light," he said.

"We have!" Randy exclaimed suddenly and, fumbling in his windbreaker, brought out his new flashlight. Klee-tso took it with a grunt of satisfaction and began swinging the bright arc this way and that.

"He has gone on," he said grimly and, slipping into the saddle again, turned Nuflo along the narrowing trail.

Suddenly Nuflo shied so violently that only his hold on Klee-tso's belt saved Randy from going off. Klee-tso swung the torch ahead.

A great mass that looked like a giant bowlder, yet one knew was not a bowlder, lay at a tilt a few rods ahead of them. Beyond it was only darkness. The flash-light glinted on metal and glass, but there were no lights on the car. Klee-tso's shout brought no reply.

"Stay here," Klee-tso commanded in a tightened voice. "I will see if he is there."

Randy obeyed and he peered through the falling snow, watching the flashlight move back and forth over the car. The nose slanted sickeningly over the cliff, but the rear wheels were evidently anchored by a tough clump of chaparral. Randy heard Klee-tso speak quietly at first, then sharply, but there was no answer. The light went out, and he was startled by Klee-tso's voice quite near.

"He is lying over the wheel," Klee-tso reported. "His head is hurt. We must get him out before the bushes give way. They already make a sound."

"But—but what if we shake the car? Won't it slide on over?" Randy shuddered. "When Father comes—"

"We can't wait for that," Klee-tso said firmly. "I have the reata that my grandfather made me this summer. There is nothing stronger, and it is long too. Nuflo must hold the car while we get him out."

He handed the torch to Randy and swiftly untied the thongs that held the coiled reata to the saddle. Once, as Nuflo turned his head and snuffled inquiringly, Klee-tso paused to give him a quick caress. Nuflo seemed to understand then that there was a hard job ahead for him, and stood very still.

"Now, Randy," Klee-tso commanded, "stay here with Nuflo."

"No," said Randy stubbornly, "I'll help."

Klee-tso said softly: "O-o-o-keh. Only you must do quickly whatever I say." And, stepping lightly as a cat, he gave the reata several quick turns about the saddle horn, jerked the twist tight, and led the way back to the car.

He stopped within a few yards of the car. "Hold the light on the radiator," he said. "There!"

He lifted the coiled reata, swung it in widening arcs over his head, and suddenly a shining coil glinted in the snowfall, slithered over the top of the car, tightened, then slipped off. Randy let out his breath with a sigh of disappointment. Klee-tso said nothing. He gathered in the slack, swung another graceful arc into the air, Randy directing the flashlight with unsteady fingers.

This time the reata settled around the radiator and rear wheels. Klee-tso tested it once, then again.

"Keep further back," he commanded Randy, and ran toward Nuflo. Randy could hear him speaking in low, clipped Navajo to Nuflo, and gradually the reata rose from the ground, tightened until it sang a little in the icy air. The car creaked under the strain.

"Nuflo's feet are braced against chaparral roots," Klee-tso said a little breathlessly as he came into the circle of light again. "Now, Randy, keep the light on the man, and don't move until I tell you."

It seemed to Randy as if Klee-tso would never get the tilted door open. But then the door was swinging back and Randy saw Klee-tso bend forward in the light and slip a strong young arm about the figure sprawled against the wheel. The next instant Larry Hemingway was lying in the snow.

"Quick, Randy, we must pull him back!" Klee-tso panted.

Randy sprang forward before he had time to be afraid. Hemingway was a heavy man, and half conscious though he was, he groaned at every movement as they half rolled, half dragged him over the thin layer of snow to a fairly level spot some twenty feet from the car.

"The knife," said Klee-tso. He took it from its sheath, spoke a clear command to Nuflo, and as the pony stepped toward them, his breath whistling with the strain he had been under, Klee-tso's knife flashed through the slackened reata once, and then again. The cut ends leaped in the air, then dropped to the snow.

For a second there was silence, then a tearing of roots. The car groaned, tilted and went plunging into darkness, carrying earth and rocks and uprooted bushes with it. Another pause, and a muffled crash far below told that it had reached the bottom. At that sound a great wave of sickness swept over Randy, and his knees crumpled under him.

"Never mind," Klee-tso's voice said soothingly. "We have him safe."

"It's just that—that I was afraid," Randy quavered.

"I too was afraid," Klee-tso told him with a chuckle. "And Nuflo, he had his fears." He reached up and caressed Nuflo's soft nose. He went on briskly, "I will get the blankets from under the saddle. We must wrap the man well, or he will freeze. Then we will see how much he is hurt."

Randy held the light while Klee-tso loosened the girths and pulled out the heavy blankets. He spread them on the snow and with Randy's help eased Larry Hemingway slowly over. The injured man opened his eyes and looked up at them.

"My head hurts," he murmured. His eyes closed

again and his voice trailed away in a whisper, "Must get those sheepskins."

There was a new gentleness in Klee-tso's face as he bent to catch the whispered words.

"Hold the blankets while I tie them," Klee-tso said. He reached for the reata, cut a length and wrapped it loosely about the blankets. Hemingway lapsed into unconsciousness again.

"Listen, Randy," Klee-tso said. "We must have help for him soon. Can you ride Nuflo bareback?"

"Of course!" Randy said.

"Then take the flashlight and ride to the road. They will be hunting for us, maybe with horses, maybe with your father's truck. Much snow has fallen, and they might miss our tracks and go on up the Snake's Back. Save your light till you get near the road, then flash it back and forth often. Here, I will hold Nuflo while you mount."

It was one thing to ride bareback on a dry and sunny day, another to grip shaggy withers slippery with snow. But Randy didn't want Klee-tso to know that he was afraid. He picked up the single rein and clucked to Nuflo. The wise pony looked at his master inquiringly, then stepped forward.

"If you feel sleepy," Randy heard Klee-tso's voice thin through the darkness, "lie along his back—keep your hands in his mane—"

Randy tried to shout a reply, but the wind blew the words back in his teeth. Nuflo bent his head to the storm and in a moment they were alone in the swirling snow.

After a time Nuflo snorted and gave a little dancing step, and so near that Randy could almost touch it, was the snowy bulk of Dan's piñon logs.

"We're halfway to the road," he thought. It was strange, but his cheeks and hands didn't ache any more, they only felt is if they were asleep. And he felt sleepy too. He thought of Klee-tso's last words coming on the wind, "Lie along his back—keep your hands in his mane—"

He pulled up his knees and slipped forward, burying his hands and face in the coarse wet hair. And all at once his sleepiness left him, and he did not feel so lost and alone. He could feel Nuflo's muscles moving steadily as he plodded on through the snowstorm.

Suddenly Nuflo lifted his head and gave a low whinny. Randy sat up stiffly. Nuflo had heard something!

The shrill wind had died away and Randy, wide awake now, heard the sound too. It was the steady chug and grind of his father's big truck!

He fumbled for the flashlight and began swinging it back and forth in his stiff hands. Nuflo had broken into a gently swinging trot.

And then, quiet suddenly, they were bathed in light, and through the snowfall Randy saw the giant form of the truck come into view around the curve just ahead of them.

Matt Ingersoll and Bill, one of the Navajo men, were with his father in the truck. In a queer half dream Randy felt himself lifted from Nuflo's back and managed to stammer: "Klee-tso—Mr. Hemingway—the wagon road—"

"Don't try to talk till you've had this, son," Matt was saying, and something bitter and hot was held for him to drink.

As the truck bumped its way through the piñon clearing, Randy, revived by the hot coffee, told them how they had found Larry Hemingway.

"If we hadn't seen the gleam of your flashlight, we'd have gone on up the Snake's Back," his father said. "Look, I thought I saw a light ahead just there."

"Klee-tso was going to make a piñon torch," Randy said.

Then the truck stopped with a jerk, and there was Klee-tso beside the muffled figure on the ground. Randy's father and Matt were down in an instant, and behind them was Bill and Nuflo.

"Badly hurt?" Randy's father asked Klee-tso.

Klee-tso nodded gravely. "But he begins to talk," he said, "about the sheepskins and how he must not fail. He will get well, I think. You have come in time."

Klee-tso's voice sounded hoarse and tired, and Matt, kneeling beside him in the snow, exclaimed almost angrily, "You fool! You've given him your jacket!"

Klee-tso's mouth curved in a faint smile. "He came to trade with our people. His head must not lie in the snow."

Randy's father put a hand on Klee-tso's shoulder. "Get into the truck at once, son, and wrap that rug around you. There's coffee in the thermos. No, you're *not* going to help. You've done a man's job already to-night."

Klee-tso looked at Mr. Bartlett, and Randy felt that his father's eyes said something to Klee-tso that was better than many words.

By Adelaide Wilson Arnold

OUR LADY OF MERCY

*"Father Thomas," Dave asked, "is this a Christmas
present, is this a present for Christmas, is it?" . . .*

*We just stood there and the cold crept up from the
snow and ice into our feet and legs, up into our hearts.
We weren't allowed to take presents for Christmas! . . .*

*"No, children," he said . . . "this is a gift—a gift
but not for Christmas."*

IT CERTAINLY LOOKED odd to see the old priest sitting on
top of the wagon, clucking to Marcus' big, brown mare.
Father Thomas wore his black coat, a huge pair of teamster's mittens and a cap with fur earlaps. From the loins
down he was wrapped in one of Marcus' red and yellow
blankets.

The mare, too, had a blanket around her. It was
thrown over her back and, as she tromped forward, it

flapped about her round belly. The team went ahead
slowly so many people waved to Father Thomas and he
had to wave and smile back to each one. Indeed, half
the neighborhood was out to see him drive off. For he
was bound for the railroad freight yards to get the tree
that his nephew Joseph, who worked somewhere in the
Canadian forests, sent him each year for the Christmas
holiday. Father Thomas' cheeks were red from the
frost.

It was several hours before he was back. His face
was like a big, ripe apple and his eyes glowed. And the
mare trotted as though she was proud of the load she was
dragging. Now the whole neighborhood lined the street
to watch Father Thomas on the wagon and we too, my
brothers and I, ran after the team to see the tree. It was
so big the wagon looked overladen with firs but it held
just that one.

Down the street the fir tree rode, little spears of frost
peeping from the green branches. Before the parochial
school playground, the team halted. "Whoa, Teresa!"
Father Thomas said softly. Theresa bobbed her head,
for she had already stopped. Then all the young priests
came out of the refectory to help.

We watched how they danced around in the cold
and slapped their hands from the frost and offered young
men's advice. Finally the old man got himself out of the
blankets about his feet, gave a few orders and the tree
was laid in the corner of the playground.

After that Father Thomas drove to the livery stable
and we hitched on the backdrop of the wagon and went
back with him. When he rode in, the teamsters were all

sitting around the stove in Nehemiah Marcus' office. We heard them teasing the father about his driving. But Father Thomas listened good-naturedly. The cold on the long ride must have gnawed into his old bones and he took a glass of brandy that Marcus offered him and drank to the men.

Then he shook hands with the stablekeeper—Good fellow, Marcus!—and thanked him for the loan of the horse and wagon. Marcus smiled and brushed that aside —it was nothing, Father!—and then he offered to teach the old man the teamster business. But Father Thomas only put both hands on his stomach and laughed. A bargain, he said, a bargain, if he could make a priest out of Nehemiah. The teamsters laughed and slapped Marcus' back and Marcus laughed, too. Everyone liked Father Thomas.

Until the week before Christmas the tree lay in the playground. Then one day the old father came out with pieces of fresh pine wood and a kit of carpenter's tools and built a wooden base for it. Then the tree, which was about sixteen feet high, was set up and placed in the paved square in front of the church.

It was hung with red and green and blue and gold ornaments with a white sparkling decoration here and there. On many of the branches little colored light bulbs hung. And on the top of the tree, just at the very peak, a single star shone. But for only a few hours each night was the tree lighted, for the batteries that fed these lights were expensive.

Every evening, then, when he turned the lights on, the old priest came out into the square and stood there, watching the tree with his hands behind his back and a pleased smile warming his lips. We also came out to see the Christmas tree.

Now at our house they did not know where we went, because there were many places my father and mother would rather have seen us go than to the Church of Our Lady of Mercy to look at the Christmas tree. But Father Thomas had always been kind to us and we could not see how there could be any harm in going to see his tree.

The first summer we had lived in the neighborhood the priest had let us go roller-skating on the big stretch of sidewalk around the church and the parochial school buildings—when everyone else was for driving us away. And that was the finest skating sidewalk for blocks around. The paving was smooth, there were no large pebbles in the concrete and for roller-skating it could hardly be beat. There was a half block of it one way in front of the church and a full block around the corner the other way. Father Thomas had refused to listen to the druggist and to the undertaker on the corner who had said we didn't belong there and should get out and stay away.

Also in the early winter had Father Thomas been good to us. One night they ran a pond of water in the parochial playground and in a few days the ice was frozen enough for skating. We watched the parochial children skating but stayed outside the gates. However, when Father Thomas saw us, he walked over, puffing as he always did, and asked why we weren't skating. All three of us got very red and finally my brother Harry said we had no skates. The old priest put his hands behind his back and looked serious.

"Father Dorset!" he called to the young priest who was skating back and forth on the ice to keep order. "Is there no one who would share his skates with these children?"

The young priest said he would ask some of the older boys. So we waited a few minutes, but when we saw Father Dorset returning with two big kids on skates we got scared and beat it. We knew we shouldn't go into that playground. Still we didn't know how to refuse the kind old father.

But the next time we saw Father Thomas he never said a word about our having run away. So we didn't feel at all strange about going to see his tree.

We came with the rickety sled the three of us had made out of old box-wood and stood around the square before Our Lady of Mercy. The church was of brick painted over, but now the old paint had scaled in spots and the gray seams between the bricks showed. Some of the narrow boards of the wooden belfry that rose above the gabled roof were missing, and from the square below we could see the great iron bell rocking to and fro when it was rung.

The old father watched us and then he came over and looked at the sled.

"It is a good sled," he said and picked it up. "It is too bad it has no runners."

I explained that we could not get any iron for the runners but had done the best we could with wood alone. Father Thomas smiled and shook his head and said it was really too bad. But we were all very proud he thought it was a good sled because he was a handy man himself and did all sorts of things in the workshed behind the priests' house.

Father Thomas was short and stout and all bald except for a little skirt of hair below his crown, and always real cheerful about things. The parochial kids said they liked him best of all the fathers in the school.

But they weren't the only ones who enjoyed the tree. Even we enjoyed it. In the middle of the square with the Church of Our Lady of Mercy all snowed up behind it and frost on some of its branches, it certainly looked good. The tree swayed in the cold wind and the ornaments tinkled like little bells ringing.

The parochial kids talked about the stockings they were going to hang up and the presents they were going to get, and so did the other kids. Neither Harry or Dave or I said anything.

Christmas Eve we went to the square again but we returned home early. It was very cold outside, the street lights were dim, the sidewalks were white and nearly all the stores were closed.

At midnight the bells tolled. All three of us slept in one big bed, so we awoke, listened and went back to sleep again. Early in the morning the bells rang again but the ringing meant nothing to us. We never got any presents anyway.

So it was nearly noon of the day after Christmas before we went out again with the sled. The snow was packed hard and the sled rode on pretty good for a sled without runners.

But we had not gone more than a block or so when a parochial fellow came up and said that Father Thomas was looking for us, had been looking for us for two days now. Father Thomas looking for us? We wondered what the old priest could want. And then we remembered that we had bumped into the iron fence on the church sidewalk one day and perhaps someone had told.

Finally we decided that probably the old undertaker or the druggist had snitched again and made Father Thomas order us away. But we went down to Our Lady of Mercy. We were pretty sure the old priest would listen to us, at least. It was swell sledding ground, and would be hard to give up without saying a word. . . .

It wasn't long before Father Thomas came slowly down the high stoop of the priests' house.

"A fine day, boys," he said and we said a fine day, too.

Then he thought a moment.

"I'd like to have your sled for a while, boys," he began. He looked as though he planned to say much more but had changed his mind. Then he added, "You can wait out here or come with me, as you like."

We looked at each other. But we were relieved it was nothing about bumping into the church fence and so we waited outside.

With the sled under his arm, Father Thomas walked slowly down the path at the edge of the priests' house up to the workshed that stood behind it. We edged up close to see what he would do.

We saw him put on a long leather apron over his coat and stoke up a fire in the little forge standing there in the yard. Then he worked a bellows with both hands and a fire blazed up under the hood. We saw the yellow flames coming out lazy and then blowing fierce and hard with a hissing sound.

Then he turned his back on us and we heard a banging on the anvil. We looked at each other again. Harry said he hoped the priest would not break the sled hammering. Dave thought we should go into the yard and take the sled back. But finally it grew quiet and we waited.

We waited and waited and waited and then all three of us began to worry. After all, we didn't know the old priest so very well. He was a good old man but, after all, perhaps he did mean to break it up. . . .

But there he came down the path, carrying our sled in his arms.

"There," he said and set it down, "and I haven't hurt it any at all."

It was queer how he knew what we were thinking of but he only smiled.

"Try it," he said, "you'll see it is as sound as can be."

So Harry took the sled and ran a couple of feet—and then took a bellywop. The sled rode and rode—at least a dozen yards. That was better than it had ever done before. Had the priest tightened the sled up somehow? But just then Harry turned around, swooped down again and rode all the way back.

"We got runners!" he hollered. "We got runners!"

Runners!

He lifted the sled and showed us. The bottoms of the wooden sides of the sled had thick, iron strips fastened on the counter-sunk screws. Dave ran his mittened hand over them and I put my glove on them. Runners! And

the runners were curved to fit the sled just like the runners on bought sleds are. We just stood there and stared
at them.

"A merry holiday, boys!" the priest said and smiled.

I said a merry holiday to him, too, and so did Harry
and so did Dave, but we didn't know just what else to say.
It was all right to say a merry holiday just so we didn't
mention Christmas. It was not right for us to say Christmas or anything like that.

Then the old father turned to walk away. But Dave
spoke up quickly and called him back.

"Father Thomas!" he said. "Father Thomas!"

And I called him, too.

"Father Thomas!" I said. "Father Thomas!"

The old man turned around and looked at us kindly.
That was the first time either of us had called him Father
Thomas.

"Father Thomas," Dave asked, "is this a Christmas
present, is this a present for Christmas, is it?"

"Yah, Father Thomas," I asked, too, "is this a present for Christmas?"

We just stood there and the cold crept up from the
snow and ice into our feet and legs, up into our hearts.
We weren't allowed to take presents for Christmas! It
was almost as bad as crossing yourself or eating pig.

Father Thomas looked away and wrinkles showed in
his forehead. He squinted his eyes as though the light
from the snow hurt him.

"No, children," he said and his lips were round and
red, "this is a gift—a gift but not for Christmas."

He mumbled something to himself.

"No, not for Christmas."

"You can say," he went on slowly, "a man named McKenna gave them to you. Yes, a man named McKenna. Thomas McKenna."

"Thomas McKenna," Dave said and Harry and I repeated it after him. "Thomas McKenna." For we were very glad that the gift was not for Christmas and that the old priest had nothing to do with it.

By Louis Zara

MERRY CHRISTMAS IN DAKOTA

They had never loved America so fiercely and so proudly; they had never cherished Norway with such deep affection.

FROM THE STOVE came the spicy odor of Christmas cakes as Guri peered into the oven.

At the window her mother looked across the snowy fields. "It is good that Ole Moen built such a big house. There will be many people for this Christmas celebration."

"Yes," Peder nodded, "our prairie is filling up. Already it is less lonesome. It takes many men's hands to fight your trolls, Karen, who are always trying to sneak through the grass, and steal our farms from us. It is not grasshoppers and deep snows we have to fight."

There was truth in that. On their isolated claims the first settlers found loneliness as well as opportunity. The wild prairie grew back around their corner stakes so that it became difficult for a man to find the borders of his own land. About that vague island of possession the wild earth was a presence, visible and strange; and the wilderness enclosed not only a settler's landmarks, it also bordered the mind. Sometimes the emptiness of the new country rose up like a wall and the four sides of it drew together. It could crush people easily, and it could keep them locked apart from all the world. Even people who remained in the familiar valleys of Norway seemed to understand that experience; something told them what it must be. An old woman in the hill town of Stjordal explained that she had eleven children—"five living, five dead, and one in America."

So the holidays were hailed with joy, as a time when people could come together with happiness, sharing their common memories and their common hope. One such day was the Norwegian national holiday, May seventeenth, when they met in the school house, or in a prairie farmyard, to hear the story of Norway's constitution and to sing part songs and join in the movements of the old peasant dances. Another eager celebration came with July Fourth, the day for a huge picnic in some creek bottom beneath a fringe of trees; then there was a reading of the Declaration of Independence, and a grand feast, and an afternoon of music and dancing and games beneath the trees. In these ways began the song festivals and choral societies for which the Scandinavians in America became famous.

But all other holiday festivities paled in the brightness and color of Christmas. At Christmas it was easier to think of the past, to remember things almost forgotten, to sing an old song and say an old prayer. (This is the reason why even now in all the prairie towns barrels of *lutefisk* are in the stores before Christmas, and why on Christmas Eve the families eat the flaky white fish by candlelight, according to tradition, and their thoughts turn with gentleness to other years.) And at Christmas it was natural to think how a man who had reached the land of his dreams, how he had a fine farm every acre his own, and a house, built with his own hands, for his loved ones. As if that wasn't enough, past and present together, it was easy at Christmas to know that the future was bright—oh, brighter than anyone could foretell! Wasn't the wilderness settled, the land occupied, civilization coming now as inevitably as the next season? Wasn't the future ready to burst on them like daybreak? All these thoughts to have and the food besides—the *lutefisk,* the rich brown fowl swimming in its juices, the cheese and clotted cream, the *flatbrod* and pasty! Christmas was something to remember.

Yes, it was a good thing that Ole Moen's house was larger than most, Karen said again as they drove up in the snowy twilight and found their place in the line of bobsleds, with blanketed horses and oxen, along the fence. They were almost the last to arrive. The house was filled when they entered.

"Ah, Ole! How fine it looks!" Peder cried.

Fine, indeed! With branches of dried grass woven in knots for holly and no less than six candles gleaming in burnished pots that hung beside the stove, pouring their radiance over the whole noisy room. Knud Aanund and old Ivor Skeervold were playing dominoes; some of the other elders were absorbed in old-fashioned Norse euchre. Elsa and Nils and Guri lost no time in joining the young people who were romping in the jolly old country games.

"Wait and see! You will learn what a wonderful place Dakota is!" Peder boasted to a knot of newcomers.

Presently old Ivor got out the fiddle he had played many times in fishing vessels off the Lofoten Isles. He struck up a polka. In a few minutes Eben Weborg went outside to his bobsled and when he came back he had a feed sack under his arm.

"What is that you are carrying with you?" they asked him. "More food, I'll be bound. Didn't you get filled up yet, Eben?"

Eben only smiled. When he opened the sack out came a violin, brown as a saddle, its curved sides giving back the candlelight from the wall. He had never played it in America. He hadn't had time or been happy enough, perhaps; and nobody remembered that he had brought a fiddle with him. Now he tuned up the strings and ran the bow across them and fell right in with the polka. The people laughed and clapped their hands and shouted with pleasure.

Eben's shoulders began to rock with the tune.

"Hi there, Nils!" someone shouted. "You dance the Halling!"

Syver Lasson got out his mouth organ and caught up with the fiddles. Now the shouts were louder.

"Nils! Nils! Get back to the walls, people. Give him lots of room. Go to it, Nils! Now you will see how a young man who hardly remembers Norway can do the Hallingdans."

Nils stepped into the center of the crowded room, looking flushed and happy and a little shy at being the center of so many eyes. But when the music set up a lilting tune he began the dance. A few quick steps and he was in the midst of it, his arms flying, his feet faster than drumsticks on the floor, his blond hair jumping up and down on his head. He leaped with feet outspread, he twisted and whirled like a tumbleweed, he put a hand on the floor and turned a circle in the air, landing on one foot which sent him back in the air for another circle; he stood on his hands, he cartwheeled back and forth, he leaped to his feet and whirled in a dizzy circle over and over. Then for a tense moment, while the music went frantic with suspense, he stood on his head, rigid as a tree, his arms outstretched, legs straight in the air, every muscle taut and still. The music entered a new measure and with one heave of his hands he threw himself upward; his feet came down on the floor. Now he began to jump higher and higher. The music worked up a note at a time and the people were shouting so excitedly they almost drowned the fiddles. But Nils was with the music, his feet kicking higher and higher; now up to his head, now above it, till his toe hit the ceiling, once faintly, then louder, then *Thump! Thump!! Thump!!!*

The young folk crowded around him as he stood still,

brushing the hair back from his face, his eyes ashine, his shoulders swelling with deep breaths. The elders nodded their heads and clapped loudly.

"Good! Fine! We never saw it done better in Norway."

The women brought out more food. This time it was "poorman's cakes" and mugs of fragrant coffee floating with boiled cream. At last Ole Moen's wife, Kjersti, appeared with the big frosted Christmas cake.

"It's a real Christmas cake," she said, "with the lucky almond in it. Who gets the lucky almond will have his wish."

Guri and Elsa took their pieces and sat against the wall, eating it slowly. Guri broke each bite carefully, on her plate, and put it, bit by bit, into her mouth. Suddenly her fingers were still.

"Elsa," she whispered. "Look!" The last corner of cake broke open and there lay the lucky almond.

"Oh!" cried Elsa. "Guri has the lucky almond!"

"Then she can make a wish," said Kjersti Moen.

"She has to tell it," declared big Gunder Skeervold with his eyes on Guri.

"No, she doesn't have to tell it. She only has to say it to herself."

Guri stared at the almond on her plate. It was wrinkled and brown, as though it had traveled many miles and been kept for many seasons until there was time and happiness enough for the baking of a Christmas cake. It was as dry and hard as a seed, but to Guri it seemed so precious and beautiful that her breath caught in her throat.

Soon the violins struck up again and people began to sing. Guri went to the door and stepped outside. The music faded behind her as she walked over the snow under the cold white Christmas moon. The lucky almond was held tightly in her fingers. Her eyes turned to the west, over the far cold country that lay immense and silent under the stars.

There were tears in her eyes when she was ready to make her wish. "Jeb—" she whispered. "May he be safe in the forests or the mountains. May he come safely back again."

When she returned to the house, Ole Moen was proposing a favorite game. "Who wants to go to Norway?" he asked. "Who wants—"

His voice was lost in their shouting.

Ole clapped his hands. "Then get your partners, all. Hi! there, get a move on, you violins! We're off for Norway!"

Now the fiddles twanged and the young people were crowding into line, each one clutching the one in front

"Nils! You and Guri lead!"

Behind the leaders the rest fell in, not only the young people but some of the middle-aged ones as well. Otto and Mari took their place in the restless group, and with the flush of happiness on their faces they looked as young as any couple in the room. Behind them Elsa guided Robert Brown into the line. The game was new and strange to him but his feet quickly caught the beat of the music and his eyes exchanged a happy excitement with Elsa.

"Now we're off!"

The violins swept into an old dance tune, lilting and lively. The marchers began to circle the room.

"Sing, everyone! Sing!"

Old and young joined in together, dancers and lookers-on raising their voices:

> "Now weave we some homespun!
> Now strike we together!
> Lift the heddle!
> Drop the heddle!
> Let the shuttle fly through!"

The line moved faster, making the circle with a lively step, heads high, voices lifted, eyes on the leader. Nils circled nearer the center. As he sang he began to use his hands in the motions of weaving. The rest followed, weaving in unison.

"Now strike we together!"

The circle pressed more closely toward the center.

"Lift the heddle!"

All the shoulders were lifted high.

"Drop the heddle!"

Down went the circle of shoulders, wilting, drooping.

"Let the shuttle fly through!"

On the signal every elbow shot out, first to right, then to left, then to right again.

All this time the circle was closing and revolving. Now the movement became more difficult, the line grew tighter and tighter. With shuffling step, heads, arms,

feet all kept time to the music; eyes were fastened on the
one in front.

"Watch your partner!" Ole cried.

"Look out!"

"Don't fall, now!"

With gleaming eyes the musicians sawed their strings
and stamped with the rhythm. All around the room the
old folk pounded the floor and moved their arms in time.

Within the circle the coil was complete; everybody
was squeezed so tight there was not another step to take.
Then came a new note in the music, and Nils, at the very
core of the circle, began to work his way out.

"Follow your noses!"

"Hang onto your partners, front and behind!"

The coiled line wavered but it did not break as Nils
began to set it free.

> "Now weave we some homespun!
> Now strike we together!
> Lift the heddle!
> Drop the heddle!
> Let the shuttle fly through!"

Now the leaders had won through to the outside, and
they marched in pairs about the room.

The song ran on:

> "Now weave we some homespun!"

The last pair was out and the marching circle was
completed.

> "Let the shuttle fly through!"

The music stopped and a chorus of voices broke out. "At last we've reached Norway!"

"A rough trip this time!"

"The old North Sea is always rough!"

"But Norway, old Norway, pays for all the roughness!"

Still humming the tune, they found their coats and caps and mittens, bundling themselves up till there was only a glimpse of ruddy face and laughing eyes to tell each other good night and cry one more Christmas cheer.

But such a Christmas could not pass like any other into memory and the wide unrecording air above the blank prairie. Ole Moen wanted more than that, he was so grateful and so full of happiness. And so, knowing no other way, he did a simple thing. He took his knife and, standing out in the snowy moonlight and the cold, he carved the numerals of that date over his doorway.

Years later, when he had a fine new house overlooking the low sod building, those weathered numbers had a curious hold on him. They made him loath to see the sod house go. "We'll keep it standing here," he said, not knowing for just what reason.

But the others agreed with him. "That's right," they said. "It must never be torn down."

Now, putting his knife back into his pocket, Ole frowned over what was difficult to say. "It will be a link with the past," he declared slowly, and they all knew they would never forget the Christmas night he carved those numbers above the door.

Around them the cold moonlight lay over the vast

American plain. All the people went home filled with a great longing and a great joy. It made them quiet as they drove across the snowy waste. They had never loved America so fiercely and so proudly; they had never cherished Norway with such deep affection.

By Walter and Marion Havighurst

TOLD UNDER THE STARS AND STRIPES

Stories selected by the Literature Committee

of the

ASSOCIATION FOR CHILDHOOD EDUCATION *

MAY HILL ARBUTHNOT, *Associate Professor, Western Reserve University, Cleveland, Ohio*

DOROTHY W. BARUCH, *Author, Los Angeles, California*

ROSEMARY EARNSHAW LIVSEY, *Los Angeles Public Library, Los Angeles, California*

KATHERINE M. REEVES, *Head, Nursery School; New York State College of Home Economics, Ithaca, New York*

MARTHA SEELING, *Co-ordinator, Butte County Schools, California*

JENNIE WAHLERT, *Principal Jackson School, St. Louis, Missouri*

MARY L. MORSE, *Chairman*

* The Association for Childhood Education became The Association for Childhood Education International in 1946.

BY WAY OF EXPLANATION

Told Under the Stars and Stripes is a collection of stories brought together in the hope of helping interpret our America more understandingly to her own boys and girls through stories of each other. It is of the boy next door, the boy or girl in school, perhaps new there, with a different way of speaking, with different clothes or habits and customs, that a story concerns itself. It may deal with the customs and cultures ingrained in one's own family unlike those of other boys and girls. The rich, sturdy life of our America is what it is because of what has been brought to her from all over the world. To understand such is to understand her.

Some people call an understanding of another's differences and accepting them as such, tolerance. Felix Frankfurter has called it "the hospitality of the human spirit." Whatever its source, he speaks of it as essentially American. We, people who have lived and worked with children, know how natural to childhood is this spirit, yet how easily it can be broken down. To maintain and nourish "the hospitality of the human spirit" for boys and girls the stories in *Told Under the Stars and Stripes* have been assembled.

For the last three working years the Literature Committee of the Association for Childhood Education has been giving steady service to *Told Under the Stars and Stripes,* a fifth book in the Umbrella series. Of its forerunners, *Told Under the Green Umbrella,* published in 1930, presented a collection of selected versions of the old folk tales. This was followed in 1933 by a compilation of real and nearly real stories published under the title of *Told Under the Blue Umbrella.* In 1935 *Sung Under the Silver Umbrella,* an anthology of verse for young children took book form, while, in 1939 *Told Under the Magic Umbrella* assembled thirty-two tales of modern fancy. Now, in 1945, the members of the Literature Committee present *Told Under the Stars and Stripes,* a collection of stories concerning American boys and girls with varying national, racial, and religious backgrounds.

Each book in the Umbrella series has offered stories or verse, not always available otherwise to children widely distributed over the United States, every one tested with many boys and girls and proven to be their own in interest, in real or fancied approach, and in story or verse form. Such standards as have been inherent in its predecessors our committee has sought to maintain in *Told Under the Stars and Stripes.*

Early in our committee discussion the decision was unanimous that no barrier be raised against a story of any group living under our stars and stripes. Still further, we determined especially to seek stories in connection with groups living here around whom have been built up barriers and about whom there have existed the strongest tensions. Conflicts between black and white, Jew and Gentile, have been fed into flames for years. More recently the second World War has evoked intense antagonisms even in connection with loyal German and

Japanese Americans. Yet each has made a contribution to our America.

Seeking typical stories of representative groups, our committee delved into story material already published, asked of many selected authors any story they could contribute to our collection, and then surveyed the result. At this point some of the stories we desired most were fugitive. To seek them we widened our scope of inquiry to people in close touch with, or representing, our needed story backgrounds. Among other like responses here, Pearl Buck led us to Carl Glick, the author of our Chinese story, *My Song Yankee Doodle,* and Ethel Benson, of Chicago's Junior Red Cross, suggested asking for a German-American story of Nan Gilbert, who wrote for us *House of the Singing Windows.* Sometimes, to our sorrow, we were led to stories not available for our use and, at other times, to stories too adult for our collection. Centered around the stories in *Told Under the Stars and Stripes* there has been much cooperative interest from people of varied backgrounds and interests, from authors, teachers, and librarians. That our collection is as representative as it is, is due partly to Arna Bontemps, Margaret de Angeli, Elizabeth Orton Jones, Maud Hart Lovelace, and Elizabeth Palmer, who offered, or were willing, to remake out of a longer story of their own the short story we needed. For the original stories written by Adelaide Arnold, Ann Nolan Clark, Nan Gilbert, and Florence Crannell Means we are deeply grateful.

Told Under the Stars and Stripes now carries within its covers twenty-seven stories selected by a majority committee vote, each story representing a typical group living in and contributing to whatever our America is or may become. To be found among them are stories of what the Albanian, Bohemian, Chinese, Dutch, English, Finnish, German, Indian, Italian, Japanese, Mexican, Negro, Norwegian, Polish, Portuguese, Russian, Spanish, Swedish, and Syrian Americans have brought to our children's heritage. Regardless of nationality or race there are two stories of children of itinerant families, with three others built around children of Amish, Quaker, and Orthodox Jewish faith. To other seekers of stories with a purpose like to ours in their seeking, the field is now open for the stories we sought but could not find before our deadline drew near.

Our committee members had thought when we started our present collection that our stories would be largely for children of elementary-school age. They center there and are fairly evenly divided between the children of primary and intermediate ages. Some three or four stories will be appreciated by children who are older still. As a group the stories are placed in a generally approximated age order.

We are sincerely indebted to Nedda Walker, whose background experience has fitted her so admirably to meet the illustrative needs of our collection. To The Macmillan Company, publishers of each book in the Umbrella series, we register our appreciation for seventeen years of cooperative partnership.

As we look back into why we, as a committee, sought to collect the stories published between the covers of *Told Under the Stars and Stripes* and into what we found ourselves thinking as we did so, we know of no one who has put this more clearly than did Franklin P. Lane, Secretary of the Navy, in the *Book of America's Making Exposition*. We are privileged to quote him:

"America is a land of but one people, gathered from many countries. Some came for love of money and some for love of freedom. Whatever the lure that brought us, each made his gift, Irish lad and Scotch, Englishman and Dutch, Italian and French, Spaniard, Slav, Teuton, Norse, Negro—all have come bringing gifts and have laid them on the Altar of America.

"All have brought their music—dirge and dance and wassail song, proud march and religious chant. All brought music and their instruments for the making of music, those many children of the harp and flute.

"All brought art, fancies of the mind, woven in wool or silk, stone or metal—rugs and baskets, gates of fine design and modelled gardens, houses and walls, pillars, roofs, windows, statues and painting—all brought their art and handcraft.

"Then, too, each brought some homely thing, some touch of the familiar field and forest, kitchen or dress— a favorite tree of fruit, an accustomed flower, a style in cookery or in costume—each brought some homelike, familiar thing.

"And all brought hands with which to work.

"And all brought minds that could conceive.

"And all brought minds filled with home—stout hearts to drive live minds; live minds to direct willing hands.

"These were the things they brought.

"Hatred of old neighbors, national prejudices and

ambition, traditional fears, set standards of living, graceless intolerance, class rights and the demands of class—

"These were barred at the gates.

"At the altar of America we have sworn ourselves to a single loyalty. We have bound ourselves to sacrifice and to struggle, to plan and to work for this land. We have given that we may gain, we have surrendered that we may have victory. We have taken an oath that the world shall have a chance to know how much good may be gathered from all countries and how solid in its strength, how wise, how fertile in its yield, how lasting and sure is the life of a people who are one."

And now, that American boys and girls in these United States of ours may have a chance "to know of how much good may be gathered from all countries" and how solid this strength may be—at the Altar of our America, *Told Under the Stars and Stripes,* stories of her boys and girls from varying racial, national, and religious backgrounds, is laid.

MARY LINCOLN MORSE, *Chairman*

1945

ACKNOWLEDGMENTS

THE Literature Committee of the Association for Childhood Education wishes to express its gratitude to those authors who were kind enough to adapt their work for inclusion in this volume.

For special permission to reprint the stories included in *Told Under the Stars and Stripes: An Umbrella Book*, the Literature Committee of the Association for Childhood Education records its appreciation to the following:

American Junior Red Cross News, Washington, D.C., and the authors for "A *Piñata* for Pepita" by Delia Goetz; "Vasil Discovers America" by Leslie G. Cameron; and "Gloucester Boy" by Ruth Langland Holberg.

Brandt and Brandt for a selection from *Renascence* by Edna St. Vincent Millay (Copyright, 1917, by Edna St. Vincent Millay) published by Harper and Brothers.

Council Against Intolerance in America for "Theresa Follows the Crops" by Clara Lambert, and for "Who Built the Bridge?" by Lucy Sprague Mitchell from *We're All Americans*.

Thomas Y. Crowell Company, New York, for "Queen of Summer" adapted from *Over the Big Hill: A Betsy-Tacy Story* by Maud Hart Lovelace.

Doubleday, Doran & Company, Inc., New York, for "Gloucester Boy" adapted from *Gloucester Boy* by Ruth Langland Holberg (Copyright, 1940); "The Costume Party" adapted from *Up the Hill* by Marguerite de Angeli (Copyright, 1942, Doubleday, Doran & Company, Inc.); "The Market" adapted from *Henner's Lydia* by Marguerite de Angeli (Copyright, 1936, Doubleday, Doran & Company, Inc.).

Farrar and Rinehart, Inc., New York, for "Merry Christmas in Dakota" from *High Prairie* by Walter and Marion Havighurst (Copyright, 1944, by the authors).

Harcourt, Brace and Company, Inc., New York, for "Primrose Day" from *Primrose Day* by Carolyn Haywood (Copyright, 1942, by Harcourt, Brace and Company, Inc.).

Holiday House, New York, for "Inga of Porcupine Mine" from *Inga of Porcupine Mine* by Caroline R. Stone, and for "Two Namesakes" from *New Mexican Boy* by Helen Laughlin Marshall.

Houghton Mifflin Company, Boston, for "The Dozier Brothers Band" adapted from *Sad-Faced Boy* by Arna Bontemps.

Alfred A. Knopf, New York, for "The Ice Skates" from *Shoo-Fly Pie* by Mildred Jordan (Copyright, 1944, by the author).

The J. B. Lippincott Company, Philadelphia, for "Benjie's Hat" from *Benjie's Hat* by Mabel Leigh Hunt (Copyright, 1938, by J. B. Lippincott Company).

The Macmillan Company, New York, for "Maminka's Children" adapted from *Maminka's Children* by Elizabeth Orton Jones.

Oxford University Press, New York, for "Macaroni: An American Tune" from *Macaroni: An American Tune* by Myna Lockwood.

G. P. Putnam's Sons, New York, for "Araminta and the Goat" from *Araminta* by Eva Knox Evans.

Charles Scribner's Sons, New York, for "Give Me a River" adapted from *Give Me a River* by Elizabeth Palmer, and for "A Boy Named John" from *A Boy Named John* by John Cournos.

This Week, New York, for "My Song Yankee Doodle" by Carl Glick (Copyright March 13, 1938).

The Viking Press, New York, for "The Contest" from *Blue Willow* by Doris Gates (Copyright, 1940, by the author).

Appreciation to the authors is also expressed for permission to print the following stories:

Adelaide Wilson Arnold for "Storm on the Mountain."

Ann Nolan Clark for "Little Von-Dos-Smai."

Nan Gilbert for "House of the Singing Windows."

Florence Crannell Means for "Hatsuno's Great-Grandmother."

Louis Zara for "Our Lady of Mercy."